"I should let you get to your search, and I'll—"

Kiah reached out his free hand and grasped hers. Sparks shot up his arm. "No. Wait. You offered to hold my hand if I need it."

She hesitated. Her hand trembled in his. Her gaze lowered to his mouth.

Oh, the temptation.

But even without looking, he realized most of the people who'd come out to watch the runaway horse drama still stood there, keeping their eyes on him. And her. Them. Both.

He shifted. "Is there someplace more private we can go? To talk?" Just in case she thought he had more than talking in mind.

Well, okay, he did. But he wouldn't. Shouldn't.

His gaze dropped to her oh-so-kissable lips.

Who was he kidding?

Because, given the opportunity, he would.

PRAISE FOR THE HIDDEN SPRINGS SERIES

The Amish Wedding Promise

"In Laura's signature style, you'll find a swoon-worthy hero battling his own insecurities, a daring heroine longing for the one who fulfills her heart's desire, and an ever-loving God who can calm the raging storms of life. Once you begin reading this author's books, you'll want to read them all."
—Jennifer Spredemann, author of *An Amish Deception*

"When Laura V. Hilton tells a story, expect the unexpected!"
—Charlotte Hubbard, author of
New Beginnings at Promise Lodge

The AMISH SECRET WISH

A Hidden Springs Novel

Laura V. Hilton

FOREVER
New York Boston

Copyright © 2021 by Laura V. Hilton

Cover design by Elizabeth Turner Stokes
Cover photograph by Shirley Green
Cover copyright © 2021 by Hachette Book Group, Inc.

Forever
Hachette Book Group
1290 Avenue of the Americas, New York, NY 10104
read-forever.com
twitter.com/readforeverpub

First Edition: April 2021

Forever is an imprint of Grand Central Publishing. The Forever name and logo are trademarks of Hachette Book Group, Inc.

ISBN: 978-1-5387-0066-2 (mass market), 978-1-5387-0067-9 (ebook)

Printed in the United States of America

CW

10 9 8 7 6 5 4 3 2 1

To the God who loved me enough to die for me because He loved me first

ACKNOWLEDGMENTS

Thanks to Marilyn for information about the Illinois Amish.

Thanks to Jenna, Candee, Lynne, Linda, Heidi, Marie, Christy, Kathy, Julie, and Marilyn for your parts in critiques, advice, and/or brainstorming. Also to my street team for promoting and brainstorming. Candee, this story would not be what it is without you.

Thanks to Jenna for taking on the bulk of the cooking while I'm on deadline.

Thanks to Forever for taking a chance on me, to Tamela Hancock Murray for representing me.

The
AMISH
SECRET
WISH

CHAPTER 1

God, I don't know what to do. I wake every morning hoping the darkness will be less oppressive, but each day is as bleak as the one before.

Hallie Brunstetter bent over the lined white paper on the table in front of her, penning her innermost thoughts by the dim flickering light of the candle. She should write the article due for *The Budget*, and she would, but first she needed to talk to *Gott* in a physical way. Maybe then He would answer. Besides, she used to love keeping a prayer journal and seeing how and when *Gott* answered.

She also wanted to write a letter to her pen pal. She loved writing Kiah and sharing her innermost thoughts and secrets, but lately he'd started talking about wanting to meet. Something she couldn't allow due to district rules.

Besides, it was rather scary. What if she was a big disappointment in person? She'd always felt like she was a disappointment to Toby. He was forever correcting her. She had to discourage her pen pal from coming. Absolutely had to.

The darkness permeated the kitchen, and she squinted. She

didn't dare light the lantern or the gaslight. The brighter beam might wake someone. And she wanted to be alone. Needed to be alone. *Mamm* and *Daed* slept right through the open doorway on a full-size bed that was always kept pushed up against the wall in the living room. A visiting preacher and his wife from someplace in Indiana were staying in their bedroom for the weekend. They arrived late last *nacht*, long after Hallie had gone to bed. She'd heard the low murmur of voices, but rolled over and went back to sleep.

She glanced at the clock, faintly backlit by a battery. Since she'd need to head into work in about an hour, she probably wouldn't meet them until this afternoon.

She should have time to finish her prayer, though. Maybe the letter to her pen pal if she hurried. She turned her attention back to her letter to *Gott* and reread the words she'd written. Would it be selfish of her to pray for a special male friend so her loneliness would ease? A special friendship would help. Maybe one with someone like her secret pen pal…Kiah Esh. Someone she felt an immediate connection with, even through the mail. She was more than halfway in love with him just from their letters. They were best friends now; she told him everything. Mostly. What would their relationship be like in person?

He wanted to meet…The reminder flashed again. But, no. Love equaled hurt and eventual loss. She didn't want to live through that pain again.

Gott, *please comfort us. Me. Toby's family. Send the light.*

Light flickered across the page.

Hallie caught her breath and lifted her head. A thin beam from the rising sun filtered through the sheer lace curtain hanging over the window.

Outside, the darkness of night receded, and soon the world would brighten.

Perhaps the same would be true of her life.

Or not.

But for right now, she would cling to hope.

Because if she didn't, she might not make it through another day.

Creaks came from the bed in the living room as her parents got up, and Hallie quickly slid the paper she'd written on under a few other pages filled with notes for her article, gathered them together, and stashed them in the drawer in the hutch where she kept her writing supplies.

A few minutes later, *Mamm* shuffled into the kitchen wearing fuzzy bunny slippers. The long, fluffy, pink ears wiggled with movement. Those slippers used to make Hallie giggle. Now...when was the last time she'd smiled at something, other than a polite, forced one?

It had to have been before the off-season tornado destroyed everything, slaying her dreams along with her beau. Eighteen long, painful months ago.

Hallie blinked back the sting in her eyes as *Mamm* lit the lantern. *Daed* smiled at her as he went past on the way to the barn, but concern filled his eyes. It always seemed to be there these days. In fact, it had been there every time he looked at her since that horrible day when she got the news.

"Were you writing the post for *The Budget*?" *Mamm* asked as *Daed* shut the door behind him. She extinguished the candle and pushed in the chair Hallie had abandoned.

Hallie grabbed her purple pen and put it away in the mug with the other writing utensils. "Gathering my notes and my thoughts for it." It was a truth-stained lie. Her notes now waited in the stack of papers she'd put away, and she always prayed before she wrote her weekly article. She tried to think of a way to change the subject. The guests would distract *Mamm* from discussing what she thought Hallie should write about. "I thought I heard the visiting preacher arrive late last night?"

"Very late, around midnight. He and his wife brought their son along as well," *Mamm* said as the door off the newly built attached *dawdihaus* opened and Hallie's grandparents came in. They'd lost their home during the tornado and opted to move in with Hallie's family rather than rebuild.

"Aw, how sweet. I guess I'll meet him when I get off work." Hallie glanced from her grandparents to the clock again. "I'll feed the chickens and gather the eggs, then get ready to go. Unless you think the little boy would like to go out with one of our neighbors' younger children to see the chickens."

"I'll hitch up the horse and buggy for you," *Daadi* muttered as he headed out to the barn.

"Our neighbors went to a funeral in Ohio. Remember?" *Mamm* reminded her. "And he's not so lit—"

"Good morning." A strange voice entered the conversation. Male. Must be the preacher. Hallie forced a polite smile and turned to stare at a handsome, beardless man with green eyes and dark blond hair. He held a straw hat in one hand. He most definitely wasn't a preacher. He'd have her undivided attention if he stood behind a pulpit. Something odd and unexpected pinged her heart. And for a moment—a very brief moment—interest flared. Somehow she knew that this man had the power to melt her heart.

Those beautiful green eyes snagged her attention, and she leaned nearer, caught by the lights flickering off what looked like shards of green sea glass lying in the sunlight. Begging to be gazed at and studied.

His breath hitched, and for a moment, he leaned toward her, something flickering in his expression. Before she could identify it, he frowned, pulling back a little. "What?"

"Your eyes…they are like sunlight on glass."

An impish smile appeared and he leaned into her space again. "*Jah?*"

She steeled herself. Despite her crazy unwritten wishes and her prayer, she needed to guard her heart. Especially considering the unexpected flare of attraction.

He looked familiar, as if she'd seen him before. She narrowed her eyes, trying to figure out where. When.

A spark of recognition and something else—interest, maybe—flashed in his baby, uh, greens. So they *had* met. He smiled. "I remember you. Holly, right? But you said you're not a Christmas baby."

"Hallie. Not Holly," she corrected automatically. But oh. There was only one person who'd asked that question...and he'd been standing in a woodshop at the time. That explained where and when. Her forced smile died. Almost a year and a half ago during the most terrible time of her life. Toby's funeral.

His smile widened. He winked. "Holly and Hallie sound the same to me. But I would love to help you collect eggs."

And he was a flirt. *Lovely. Just lovely.* She ignored *Mamm*'s not-so-subtle head tilt toward the door that urged her to take the boy, er, man, er, guest—because this specimen was certainly not a boy—out to the barn and to be polite. She didn't have the patience today. Unfortunately, she'd have to put up with flirts all morning at her waitressing job. Most of them were retired, traveling with their significant other and harmless, but there were always a few she had to watch out for. The ones who reached out to pat, touch, or pinch waitresses in inappropriate places. She shuddered.

The green-eyed man's smile faded.

"I forgot your name." She glanced at *Mamm*, who frowned at her with narrowed eyes while beating batter for pancakes. *Right.* Message received. Be polite. "I mean, nice to meet you. Um, make that welcome to the area."

"*Danki.*" His lips quirked. "Hezekiah Esh, at your service. My friends call me Kiah."

They weren't friends in real life. Not even close. But his name…Her heart lurched as she thought of the stack of letters hidden in her locked hope chest upstairs, forwarded to the community scribe—her—by *The Budget*, all written by Kiah Esh. Letters she'd responded to, using her initials. Maybe they were friends. Secretly. So secret he didn't even know. At least he didn't know her in person. But, oh, she was anxious to talk with him…She just couldn't reveal her identity. That was the first rule in her district regarding the scribe. No one was allowed to know who the scribe was. Unless the bishop revealed it. Because the bishop would take the job away and give it to someone else.

Mammi adjusted her trifocals and tapped nearer with her wheelless walker. She peered into Kiah's face, reached her hands up to touch his cheeks, and studied him; then she pinched his cheeks before she released him and patted his arm. "So you're the one who's going to marry our Hallie."

"*Jah*, I mean, no. I mean…" Kiah spluttered, and coughed, his eyes bugging.

Hallie's face burned. She stared at the floor. At least *Mammi* had good taste in men. But, oh, what Kiah must think. "I need to go to work." No point in trying to correct *Mammi*. She wouldn't understand. "What about the eggs?" Kiah's voice sounded somewhat strangled.

"You can collect them with my sister." Hallie pushed past them.

Her arm brushed against Kiah's as she passed. Weird sparks shot through her. An electrical charge? She shook her head and went upstairs.

Kiah's last letter, the one she hadn't responded to yet, had said he would be coming to Hidden Springs, Illinois, to visit her—the one he was writing to, the one with the initials GHB. Actually, he didn't know she was her. He'd said that while he only knew her initials, he'd be on a mission to find her. He hadn't said when. Or where he'd be staying. If only she'd known so she could have been better prepared. She'd planned to discourage him from coming. But too late now. She'd have to make the best of it and ensure he'd never find his mystery girl. She didn't want to lose her job as scribe.

Because the safest place to hide was in plain sight.

* * *

Kiah turned away from the disconcerting *mammi* and watched Hallie high-tail it for the stairs—the ones he'd just come down.

It was *her*.

The woman of his dreams.

The unknown woman he'd long intended to marry…

At least until the scribe had written her way into his heart, understanding the pain his ex-girlfriend had caused and his destroyed dreams, and encouraging him to heal, to establish new dreams, and to maybe start over. With her. Though she didn't say that.

Hallie was a very intriguing girl—and he'd felt sparks when they'd accidentally touched—but now he wasn't interested. Okay, he was. Actually, he was *very* interested. She *was* the one he'd imagined and dreamed of the whole time he was writing, after all. But he held himself back. He'd fallen in love, sight unseen, with the scribe for *The Budget*. He just had to find out her real name and then convince her she was the one he'd been waiting for. And he was the one she was waiting for.

He'd just wanted her to be Hallie. The woman he'd met and fallen in love with at her boyfriend's funeral. Love at first sight even though they'd barely exchanged five words in person. But in his thoughts, Hallie was the one he wrote…

Please, Lord, let Hallie be her.

He pushed that thought away. Because as much as he wanted her to be, she couldn't be GHB. Hallie didn't start with a *G*.

The scribe's real name—would it be Gabby? Gizelle? Gina? Gail? Whatever the *G* in GHB stood for, he'd find her. And woo her.

Of course, that would be assuming she was young and not married to someone else.

His *mamm* said it was pure craziness, because the scribe was probably eighty if a day. But the handwriting in her return letters didn't look old. *Daed* called it a "wild-goose chase" because if she was available and interested, she would've told him her name. And maybe they were right. But he wanted to find out for himself.

He turned back to the kitchen to face the unsettling *mammi* and the pancake-frying *mamm*. He cleared his throat. "I'm not on the market, but Hallie seems like a really nice girl." *Really nice.* "I'm actually already involved with someone else from this area. Perhaps you know her? She writes for the Amish newspaper, *The Budget*, and her name starts with a *G*. GHB."

Both women stared at him. The *mamm*'s mouth gaped, her eyes wide, startled. A measure of doubt clouded Kiah's vision. Maybe G *was* married.

The troubling and bothersome *mammi* cackled. "Talk to Hallie," the older woman said with a gleam in her eyes.

Right. Because she believed he was going to marry Hallie. Then again, maybe Hallie would know where to find G.

And maybe if he and G didn't hit it off, he would have a chance to explore the sparks he'd noticed between him and Hallie.

A floorboard creaked and Kiah turned to see *Mamm* and *Daed* emerging from the hallway. And Hallie coming downstairs, carrying her purse.

"Hi." Hallie greeted his parents with an overly polite smile. "I don't mean to be rude but I'm running late for work. I'm looking forward to getting to know you this afternoon."

Kiah didn't think she meant it. She'd sounded too sugary sweet. And she didn't quite make eye contact. He caught her *mamm*'s frown.

Hallie's smile faded as she skittered past Kiah, with her head dipped, gaze down, and careful not to brush against him. So she must've felt the sparks, too. *Interesting.* The scent of lavender trailed her.

"My husband's in the barn," the pancake-frying *mamm* said.

Daed nodded. "Come, Kiah. We can make ourselves useful."

Kiah put his straw hat on and followed *Daed* and Hallie out of the *haus.* A small barn stood on the other side of the circular driveway. The air smelled fresh, as if they'd had a heavy dew overnight. There were no noticeable signs of the terrible twisters that'd touched down with destructive damage almost a year and a half ago. A horse and buggy were already waiting, ready to go, in front of the porch. Hallie put her purse on the seat and climbed in.

Kiah stopped beside the buggy, adjusting his hat to better see Hallie. If he wasn't already so heart-connected to the scribe, he definitely would act on the temptation to get to know the beautiful woman. Or at least accept the challenge to break through her odd reserve around him. But he'd been different ever since the tornado, which led him to write to the scribe in the first place.

He gazed up at her. "Can we talk later?"

She paled. Shifted. *Odd response.* "I might be working a double shift."

"Whenever you get home is fine. Your *mammi* suggested I talk to you about some information I need."

Her glance darted toward the door and then back. She opened her mouth, hesitated, then shut it. She shook her head and muttered something he didn't catch. Probably something about her crazy *mammi.* His heart sank to realize the woman might have steered him in the wrong direction, yet he couldn't leave a possible avenue unexplored. Hallie clicked her tongue.

The horse slowly took a step forward.

Kiah stepped back to avoid getting run over. "Your *mammi* thinks you might know someone in this district with the initials GHB."

Hallie frowned, gazing over his head as if she was thinking. When she glanced at him again, her expression could only be called a smirk. "George Harold Beiler." She wiggled the reins and drove off.

A man?

Kiah mentally reviewed the handwriting. It was neat. Beautiful. But some men had pretty writing. Kiah's best friend, Zeke, who'd recently married, had great handwriting. He said it was because he had to read his measurements.

But the writing had looked feminine.

And most of the return letters had used lavender ink. Not a usual male color choice.

Hallie's *daed* stood in the wide-open doorway of the barn watching his daughter drive away. His gaze shifted to Kiah, and his head tilted as if he were sizing him up. He gave a tiny nod as if he had passed some pop quiz. "She works as a waitress in town. I'll give you directions later if you want to go, order a slice of pie and have some conversation."

Did he think Hallie knew who GHB was, too?

Or maybe he'd made his interest in her a little too obvious if her *mammi* and *daed* picked it up.

Or . . . Kiah cringed. What was wrong with the woman that she needed so many obvious matchmakers?

* * *

Sometimes it seemed as if the breakfast crowd never left before the lunch crowd arrived. The Friday morning coffee club had filled every seat in the entire overflow dining section. Hallie refilled coffee mugs innumerable times, dodged the expected and inevitable wandering fingers, and delivered breakfasts, doughnuts, pastries, and pies. Now she was left with messy tables, sticky chairs, and a floor that needed sweeping and scrubbing.

At least the coffee club left good tips.

She filled a gray tub to overflowing with dirty dishes, hoisted it into her arms, and turned to deliver them to the dish room.

And there, in plain sight, was Kiah, legs kicked out under a small table, an infuriating grin on his oh-so-handsome face.

Her heart lurched. Why did he have to be so appealing? Handsome?

His teasing green eyes met hers. "Service, please." Somehow he managed to infuse the words with enough humor that it wasn't an order, but more teasing. Teasing like Toby used to do. Except sometimes Toby's teasing had been mean.

But Kiah didn't resemble Toby at all. He was light-headed with sandy blond hair and green eyes, while Toby was dark-headed with black hair and black eyes. Those eyes always looked angry. Plus, Kiah was tall and slender and Toby was short and stout. Really, Kiah was much more handsome. Did they have the same sense of humor? Would Kiah's teasing become unkind? It appeared they shared the same careless ease, and Kiah's presence rubbed salt on the wounds of her broken heart with the constant reminder of what she'd lost.

However, the man in the letters had revealed an unexpected depth. Was it possible this teasing flirt had actually written those letters? Or was there more than one Kiah Esh in the world? The odds of two men by that name coming to Hidden Springs and asking for GHB were more than slim. Nope. As much as she wanted to deny it, this man was her pen pal.

Her lips quirked before she caught the involuntary movement and stiffened them. She liked his teasing. Liked his boldness. It made a part of her sheltered and barricaded heart come to life, as if his humor had slipped through a crack like that sliver of sun through the curtain. However, she couldn't allow it to gain any more ground. "This section is closed until the other dining room overflows." She tilted her head toward the exit.

"When I asked where you were, your boss, I guess, her name is Helga, and her name tag said manager..." He quirked a brow.

Hallie nodded.

"She told me to come back here. She said it was so nice to meet your new boyfriend."

Boyfriend? She used to have a boyfriend. Not anymore. Had he introduced himself that way or had Helga merely assumed that any young man asking for her must be a boyfriend?

"What's with all these people matching us up?"

"I don't know and I don't like it." Hallie shifted the heavy tub and sighed. If her boss sent Kiah back here, Hallie had no choice but to let him stay. If she were honest, she wanted him to anyway. She also needed to think up more GHB names to "help" him. If he only knew... "I'll be right back to take your order."

"Coffee and a slice of pie for both of us. I don't care what kind. Your boss said to tell you to take a break. I ordered fifteen minutes of conversation, too."

He ordered conversation? That could be done? Hallie frowned at him but she could see how he had charmed her near-retirement-age boss into giving her an unscheduled break. That smile? That dimple? Those good looks?

However, she wasn't in the mood for either coffee or pie. She *was* in the mood to be contrary. She carried the tub to the dish room and returned with a cup of coffee, a slice of caramel apple pie, a glass of cola with ice, and a bowl filled with grapes, apple and orange slices, and strawberries. She set the coffee and pie in front of him, then set her cola and fruit on the opposite side of the table before sitting across from him.

"Oh, it does feel good to sit down." If only she could kick

off her shoes and socks. "I may not get up again." She only half joked, because in her haste to leave him behind, she hadn't been able to find her shoes this morning and had borrowed her younger sister's sneakers. They pinched and she'd definitely have blisters.

Kiah studied her name tag. "Your name really isn't Holly like the Christmas plant." As if he hadn't believed her. "H-a-l-l-i-e. That's an odd spelling. What's your given name?"

"You don't go by your given name. How do you spell Kiah?" No way would she share her real name.

"Touché." But his gaze remained fixed on her name tag. "Hal is short for Henry. Is your name Henrietta?"

"Good guess." But wrong, wrong, wrong. Her name was Hallelujah. She took a sip of her cola and tried not to smirk.

"Henrietta, in the interest of full disclosure, despite our matchmakers, I am here to find the woman I love."

She tried not to react. But... "Hallie, please. Not Henrietta." She'd forget to answer. "And is your girlfriend lost?"

He picked up his fork and toyed with the pie. "I only know her initials. GHB. And that she's a scribe for *The Budget*. Good thing I like puzzles." He chuckled. "Unfortunately, I'm not very good at them. Because I imagined she was you. Can you help me find her?"

CHAPTER 2

Kiah glanced away from his rapidly crumbling pie to look at Hallie. He hadn't taken a single bite of it yet, instead mutilating it with his fork. It was all nerves, of course. Never had he imagined explaining to his love-at-first-sight girl that he also was in love with an unknown scribe.

Sometimes an interest is just an interest.

And sometimes it isn't.

He took a deep breath and studied the pie while he prayed for wisdom. Which was an interest and which was real?

He peeked at Hallie. Exhaled. His interest in her was real. Very real.

The crust was super flaky. Whoever made it was an excellent crust maker. He stabbed a slice of apple.

Hallie's lips pursed as if she were deep in thought. "How do you know it's a woman? I think George Beiler would be a good place to start." She twisted a grape off the stem.

Kiah's face burned. "It'd be rather awkward if she's a he. Besides, most of the letters were written in lavender ink. And they were scented."

"Scented?" Hallie's eyes widened and she scooted her chair farther from the table. She picked up a raw apple slice.

"Like lavender. Like you."

Hallie paled. "Popular scent. It's supposed to be calming." She bit into the apple slice.

Kiah shrugged. "Maybe so. My *mamm* likes it." He nodded at her bowl of fruit. "She likes fruit like you do, too."

"Your *mamm*?" She sounded strangled.

"No. She. GHB." He'd read and reread the letters so many times he almost had them memorized. In fact, he'd brought the precious letters along in a leather pouch to prove his identity if he needed to. "Please, Hallie. Help me find her. That will keep the matchmakers from pairing us together while I'm here with my parents." *Jah*, right. But maybe she'd believe it. He doubted it, though.

Besides, he wanted to be paired with her.

She muttered something that sounded like "If only." Then finished three apple slices and a handful of grapes. But she leaned toward him, a faint twinkle in her blue eyes. "How well do you know her—or him?"

"I know her so well, I could pick her out in a room filled with strangers." Maybe he shouldn't have boasted that, but it almost seemed as if it could be true. He mentally listed a few things. She loved the color lavender, loved fruit, had an aversion to buggy racing... and her sweet spirit filled her letters.

For some strange reason, his comment caused Hallie to brighten. She straightened and leaned a little nearer, mischief lighting her eyes. "I still think you need to talk to George Beiler. There is also Gabe Brenneman and Gideon Brunstetter. I don't know their middle names, though. But George is a deacon and he keeps track of visitors to the community, so he would be the logical one to write for *The Budget*."

Kiah sighed. "Okay. Give me directions and I'll talk to them, but I still think GHB is a young, unmarried woman."

"Why do you think that? Other than the lavender ink and scent, I mean." Hallie's gaze slid to the left and she stood. "My boss just motioned that I need to get back to work. I'll bring your ticket out." She picked up her bowl and glass, both still mostly full, and headed for the kitchen.

Kiah doctored his coffee with a packet of sugar and a little plastic cup of creamer, and finished both the hot beverage and the caramel apple pie by the time Hallie returned with his ticket and written directions to the homes of the three men she'd mentioned. She also carried a rag and a carpet sweeper as if she intended to clean the room.

"The apple pie was great. And it was nice talking to you." Although she was sort of reserved and not overly friendly. Though maybe it was because she was at work. He glanced at the bill. She started to wipe a nearby table. "You didn't charge me for yours."

"It wasn't a date. And I get some things free. Pay at the counter up front." Short. To the point. If only she'd delivered it with a sweet smile like the brief one at her home earlier.

"*Danki* for talking to me." He tried to make her smile again. "See you tonight." He stood.

Her brow quirked in response—whatever that meant. There might have been a flicker of a brief smile, and she gathered his dishes, turned, and walked away.

Okay, then. He now had a second reason for staying. He wanted to win Hallie's friendship. He'd wanted that since the moment they met. And he wanted to make her smile. A real one that reached her eyes and eliminated the lingering depths of sadness filling them. She did have a valid reason, though, and grief knew no timetable.

Kiah picked up the maps she'd drawn to the three men's houses and looked them over. They should be easy enough to find. He pocketed them and headed toward the register with his ticket.

A very round, middle-aged Amish woman wearing a pine-green dress smiled at him. Her name tag read Suzy. "Did you enjoy your meal?"

He handed her the slip of paper. "It was good. *Danki*."

"So you're seeing our Hallie." It wasn't a question. Suzy leaned closer. "Don't hurt her. She's fragile. If you do, you'll have a lot of people to answer to."

Kiah raised his eyebrows.

Suzy glanced around and lowered her voice. "Her previous boyfriend died in a tornado not too long ago. A year now, I think."

Right. He knew that. His best friend had explained it to him when he met Hallie over a year ago and she'd sternly rebuffed his attempt to be friendly. She was pretty. A guy would have to be blind not to notice. But the woman—then and now—was only remotely friendly. At least not as friendly as GHB was in her letters.

Speaking of which...He studied the woman behind the register. She probably knew a lot of people in the area. "Do you know a woman whose initials are GHB?" he asked Suzy. "I'm looking for the scribe for *The Budget*."

"Gracie Bontrager," she answered without hesitation. "Except her middle name is Lynn and she's married."

"To my best friend," Kiah said. His lips twisted at the thought that Zeke's bride could be a pen pal to another man...and what would Zeke have to say about that?

Suzy laughed as if he'd told an outrageously funny joke.

"There's also Ginny Baer, Gabriella Brenneman, Regina Beachy—she goes by Gina, Abigail Byler—she goes by Gail. Oh, and Gloria Brunstetter. Just to name a few."

Oh. He sagged. This search might take longer than the weekend.

Suzy took his meal ticket and rang it up. "Why?"

"I want to find her." He took out his wallet. "Do you mind writing those names down? That'll get me started." Those and the three men Hallie was sending him to visit. Those men would be dead ends, though. He was sure of it. But he'd go anyway, just to eliminate the slight possibility that one of them might be the scribe. And he'd earnestly pray they weren't.

Of course, if they were, it'd be a good excuse to pursue Hallie.

Suzy tore off a sheet of paper from a notepad and wrote down the five names. "I'm off work tomorrow if you want company on your quest."

Kiah eyed her. Surely she wasn't asking him out. She might not be old enough to be his *mamm*, but she was close to it.

Suzy giggled. "I know what you're thinking, you naughty, naughty boy. I'm happily widowed."

Kiah's face heated.

Wait. *What?* Happily widowed?

"I have a son close to your age, I daresay." Suzy winked.

"I can go with him, if he needs his hands held, Suzy." Hallie appeared from somewhere and dumped a plastic bag full of peppermint candies into a wicker basket on the counter. The glance she aimed at Suzy was almost a warning. *Back off. He's mine.* But maybe he imagined that. Or wished it.

Kiah didn't need his hands held. But it might help to break the ice, so to speak, to have a native with him. Plus a bonus—he might be able to tease a real smile from Hallie's lovely face. It'd be worth a try.

For a brief moment, he considered being overly dramatic, throwing himself at her feet and going to the extreme. A year and a half ago, he wouldn't have thought twice about playing the fool. But based on what he'd learned about Hallie, it would probably backfire. So he produced a hopefully benign smile— one that gave no hint of the eventual teasing sure to come. "Appreciate that, Hallie."

She gave a brusque nod and didn't glance at him. Or maybe she did. A brief peek.

A perfectly good smile, wasted. He probably should've thrown himself at her feet.

She crumpled the bag the candies had been in, turned, and started to walk away. Hips swaying. He could watch that all day.

He forced his attention back to Suzy.

Suzy looked at him with expectation. As if he was supposed to...what?

Behind her, in the gift shop, the manager, Helga, straightened a display of faceless plain-dressed dolls and eyed him, brow raised.

Oh. The waitstaff believed he and Hallie were dating for some weird reason. *You're the one who's going to marry our Hallie.* Her *mammi*'s disconcerting words replayed. They left a funny tickle in his stomach.

Kiah opened his mouth to say something. What, he didn't know. He glanced at Hallie. "See you later, sweetheart."

The words were unintentional. They just emerged without thought. But they felt right on his tongue.

Hallie stumbled. She turned, long enough to glare at him; then she squared her shoulders and strode away.

Her reaction wasn't what he would've hoped for if he'd planned it. If she was GHB, he'd be reeling right now from the rejection...then resolving to change her mind.

But Suzy's mouth gaped.

Never mind heated. Kiah's face burned. Had he told her that he was in love with GHB and not courting Hallie?

Somehow his short-term memory had faltered and he wasn't sure. Of anything.

But making Hallie smile raised a good ten points on his mental must-accomplish list. Even if GHB was in some way unsuitable, his trip would be a roaring success if Hallie laughed.

When Kiah had come to this area eighteen months ago as a volunteer after the off-season tornadoes, the Mennonite missionary in charge had said, "God sent each one of you here for a reason. Find it."

Kiah glanced away from Suzy to the woman scurrying down the long hallway back to the small room where he'd had his pie.

This might be why he was so attracted to Hallie.

After all this time, he'd found his reason.

* * *

Hallie speed walked down the hallway to the overflow dining room and the stack of napkins and the still-warm silverware from the dishwasher waiting to be wrapped up in them.

The man was insufferable. That's all. And so hugely appealing there should be a law against it. It probably was against the *Ordnung* in some way.

The twinkle in his green eyes. His impish, mischievous smile. His full, very kissable lips. His dark blond hair that just begged for her fingers to run through it.

He was hot.

Sizzling hot.

He made more than her blood boil.

He was also off-limits. In love with a woman who didn't exist. But also a woman so hurt…

What man would want a woman with her wounds?

Not only that, but the fun-loving flare of mischief in his eyes screamed that he was the type who'd risk his life just for the thrill of racing buggies in a tornado. And would come to the same bad end as her former beau.

Gone. But not forgotten.

She just couldn't—wouldn't—walk that road again.

"Hallie. Wait up." Someone called her name behind her.

Hallie turned. Her friend Elsie's younger sister, Mandy, rushed up to her. Somehow, Mandy wore someone's cup of coffee on her apron along with what looked like syrup splatters. She was a recent new hire and so far just did not have the fast-paced, coordinated skill of the waitressing staff. The boss was already muttering about transferring Mandy to the kitchen crew.

The cooks didn't want her.

Hallie couldn't help but feel sorry for Mandy. "Suzy told me to help you roll silverware up into napkins." Mandy continued past her.

Hallie fell into step beside her. "*Danki.*"

"So, who was that man who asked to order a fifteen-minute conversation with you? That really set tongues to wagging. Everyone is saying he's your new beau." Mandy raised her eyebrows as they reached the overflow dining room.

Hallie sat in the chair that was pulled out. The same one Kiah had sat in. "He's nobody." A nobody she desperately wanted to become somebody...

Mandy snorted as she pulled out the chair Hallie had so recently vacated and sat. "Some nobody. I'd like to have nobody like that in my life."

"Honestly. Today is only the second time I've ever seen him. The first was eighteen months ago. At Toby's funeral." Hallie's voice broke. And not because of Toby, but because what Kiah wanted would never be. Because she was forbidden to tell.

Mandy reached across the table and grasped Hallie's hand. "Are you okay?"

Hallie forced a smile and nodded. But truthfully, she might never be okay. Memories never faded.

"But..." Mandy frowned. "You remember him from one brief meeting eighteen months ago? Really? He is good-looking, but that's a long time to remember a random stranger."

And there was the issue. Why and how, in the midst of her grief, had he stepped into her thoughts and stayed for eighteen months? They hadn't even exchanged more than a handful of words. Was it because of their letters? Except, she hadn't caught his name eighteen months ago, and she never used hers in her letters. Just her initials.

Hallie had rolled a small stack of silverware in napkins before she noticed Mandy's attempts. Silverware crumpled in the napkin. Crumpled. Not rolled. Hadn't anyone ever taught her? She stood and walked around the table. "Here, let me show you." She laid out a napkin and rolled it up, starting at the corner closest to her, explaining each step. "Now you try."

"So that's how it's done," Mandy muttered. She copied what Hallie had showed her, albeit a lot slower.

Maybe Mandy would survive as a waitress if someone took the time to teach her. Hallie would talk to her boss and see if she'd allow Mandy to follow her around to get a little more instruction beyond what was normally provided.

"So, that man. What's his name and what'd he want?" Mandy asked.

Hallie grimaced as she returned to the other side of the table. Mandy wasn't easily distracted. At least not with this topic. And if Hallie refused to talk, Mandy would tell her still-newlywed sister Elsie—one of Hallie's best friends—and Elsie would drag everything from her. Not a little. A lot.

"His name is Hezekiah Esh and he's from Shipshewana. He came with the missionaries after the tornadoes, and now he's here with his parents. His *daed* is the visiting preacher this weekend. He's trying to find the scribe for *The Budget*." Hallie had never told her friends that she wrote for the Amish newspaper. The bishop had approved it only if she didn't divulge her identity. Only her parents and grandparents knew, because *Daed* had to approve it.

Daed hadn't hesitated. He'd hoped it'd take her mind off her grief.

It hadn't. Wouldn't. How could it when she reported other peoples' happiness and sadness? The only thing it did was force her attention off of herself and on what happened around her in the community.

"Why did he ask you who writes for *The Budget*? Though I guess some districts allow everyone to know who the scribe is. Our bishop thinks it might cause pride issues." Mandy frowned. "I can see that. If I were the scribe, I'd be tempted to shout it from the mountaintops. Something I'm good at." She barked a short laugh.

"You're good at a lot of things. You just need to pay attention." Hallie glanced at the newly mangled silverware packets.

Mandy waved the comment away. "Anyway, why does he think you know?"

Hallie shrugged, but inside her stomach was churning. "I guess because his parents are staying at my *haus* so I'm convenient and maybe because I work in town where I meet people and might have heard something."

Though it wasn't funny that *Gott* put him directly in her path.

"Why does he want to find the scribe?"

Hallie sighed. *Nosy much?* "He said he fell in love with the scribe and wanted to meet her. But he only knows her initials. And he says that he knows her so well he'd recognize her in a roomful of strangers." Which thankfully was not true. Although the things he'd noticed had caught her by surprise. Her lavender scent. Her pen color of choice. A fondness for fruit. She'd need to be very careful.

"So romantic." Mandy sighed.

No. It was frightening.

"But then he called you sweetheart. So maybe he changed his mind and decided he likes you."

"He's a flirt."

Mandy ignored her. "And if you do go with him to find the scribe, maybe he'll fall madly in love with you instead."

A girl could dream.

And for another moment, hope bloomed.

Then she squashed it down.

* * *

Kiah stopped the borrowed horse and buggy in front of a tiny *haus*. One that reminded him of the *haus* he'd stayed in when he came to Hidden Springs as a rescue worker. One bedroom. Elderly couple. Overrun with tiny ants and not so tiny cats. And nothing to eat but bean soup during his entire stay.

In fact…Kiah eyed the cracks in the uneven cement sidewalk, then glanced at the rundown garage situated behind the *haus* and off to the side. It was the same *haus*. So George Beiler was the semiretired buggy maker. He cringed, embarrassed that he hadn't cared enough to learn his host's name when he was here before.

There was no way he was the scribe. The man was also more than half deaf and communicated with shouts. Not to mention he had some mental issues.

And Hallie said he was a deacon?

Kiah sat there, staring at the *haus*. There was no point in asking George if he was the scribe or even if he knew who it was. This was a waste of time.

He pulled out the map for the home of the next man and studied it. Gabe—

"Hello there, young fellow!" The shout came from beside Kiah's ear.

He jumped, fumbling the paper, and looked at George Beiler. "Hey, George. Remember m—"

"Hay? You want some hay?" George yelled. He balanced himself with his cane.

"Um, no. *Danki*. How are you doing?"

"Sue's brewing? Brewing what?" George cupped his free hand over his ear. Not that it'd help.

Kiah gulped. Might as well end this eardrum-shattering conversation sooner rather than later. "I'm looking for the scribe—"

"You're looking for a tribe? Speak up, boy!"

"Scribe!" Kiah bellowed. "I'm looking for the scribe!"

"You need a scribe?" George's brow wrinkled. "Can't you write? What do they teach children in school these days?" He hobbled off, muttering at full volume. "Not only that, but they make no sense whatsoever. I need to discuss this matter with the bishop."

Maybe he should. And hopefully the bishop would see the need to use the benevolence fund to purchase hearing aids for George. Or were they not allowed in this district?

On the other hand, the bishop would know where to find the scribe. Kiah glanced back at the map. His home was marked on the map to Gabe's *haus*. Almost directly across the street.

"Come back Monday and I'll teach you your letters!" George hollered in Kiah's ear.

Kiah yelped, dropping the map this time. How did the man get around so quietly?

"A big boy like you needs to know how to write!" George whacked the buggy with his cane.

The horse startled.

Reared.

And came down running.

CHAPTER 3

Hallie wasn't needed for a double shift, but she didn't want to go home and risk seeing Kiah. She wanted to avoid him, avoid the questions, and avoid the very real chance of exposing her identity. He was sure to want to talk to her about the list of women Suzy had given him with the initials GB. Not all of them had the middle initial H. In fact, Hallie wasn't entirely sure what most of their middle names were.

She'd drive by the addresses she'd given Kiah just to see if she could find him so she could avoid him. If he was at any of those places, she'd head home to a Kiah-free zone, hide in the bedroom she shared with her older sister, Hosanna, and write the article for *The Budget*.

She hitched Licorice to the buggy. The horse was named after *Daed*'s favorite candy, even though the mare was a caramel color. But *Daed* didn't like caramels. Unless it was baked into apple pie.

Apple pie made her think of Kiah. He'd shared in a letter that caramel apple pie was his favorite. Would he be impressed if he knew she'd made that pie? It was the foolish reason she'd chosen it. But he'd only picked at it until after she left, so she hadn't been there to hear any moans of pleasure. Probably a good thing. It was hard enough to be humble when her pies won first place at the county fair. Pies entered under her initials so no one knew who truly won. Their bishop frowned at his people trying to appear better than anyone else, so if they competed, they had to do it in a way that kept their identity secret.

Hallie drove down George's street but didn't see any sign of Kiah. George was out in his yard, batting at something hanging from the eaves and yelling for his wife to come out there to see the baby spiders. Hallie shuddered and drove on.

She turned down the dead-end road that Gideon lived on and glanced at the cloud of dust rising up ahead. What on earth? Probably boys playing kickball in the dirt road.

She drove around the curve and gaped. There, in the cul-de-sac, a horse raced around and around, the open buggy careening wildly behind it. A group of spectators huddled on the front lawns. A man stood in the buggy, holding the reins. What kind of off-in-*den-kopf* fool drove his horse like that?

The type who would try to outrun tornadoes. In a buggy.

Rage filled her, but she knew better than to get too close. She pulled on the reins. "Halt!" Once Licorice stopped, she climbed out and secured Licorice to a white-washed fence and slowly walked toward the racing animal.

As she neared, she recognized her sister's horse, Jellybean, pulling their old buggy around and around the circle. The buggy creaked and groaned. She squinted to see who was driving it. The man standing in it yanked on the reins, and the horse went another round.

It might've been her imagination, but maybe this round was slower.

The man's mouth moved as he passed by, but she only caught the accompanying wink he aimed her direction.

The wink...*Kiah*.

Of course it was. Who else would it be?

Why couldn't he be more like the man in the letters? Except at least this "real" Kiah made it easier to keep her heart protected.

Was the horse safe? And their buggy. The man could get what he deserved.

She huffed, her hands went to her hips, and she glared. The same posture and expression that she'd earned when she told *Mamm* she didn't want to apprentice to be a midwife. How could she celebrate new life and hope when her life was stalled in the darkness of the valley of the shadow of...

The night Toby died, she'd been assisting *Mamm* with a difficult birth. Both the new *mamm* and the baby had almost died. They'd fought to save them, but *Gott* had punished her by taking Toby. He hated the idea of her being a midwife.

She shook her head, repositioned her feet slightly farther apart, and concentrated on sending angry vibes at the man in the buggy.

Not that it bothered him any.

No. It just earned her another wink.

Despite her irritation, that wink did strange things to her midsection.

He took the horse on another, more sedate, turn around the circle, the horse finally slowing to a walk. One more round and Jellybean stopped on the far side of the circle. But her eyes were wide, fear-filled, and her sides heaved.

For a moment, time stilled. Hallie dared to take a breath.

Across the circle, Kiah slowly loosened his grip on the reins, then climbed out of the buggy. His hands quivered. But a wide smile spread across his face. And with a cocky swagger, he headed her direction. He whooped. "That was some ride!"

The world turned red. Bloodred. Hallie marched across the

expanse to meet the stupid but good-looking man, and shoved her finger against his chest. "You idiot! If you want to get yourself killed, do it in your own city, with your own horse and buggy, and honestly, you should've known better racing my sister's horse. What if you've injured her? Don't you have any common sense? What is it with men and horses and trying to outrace tornadoes…" The words spilled out, uncensored, morphing into a dull roar that filled her ears, but she couldn't tell where one sentence ended and another began. She might've forgotten to breathe.

Kiah's mouth opened and shut a few times. His eyes darted to the clear blue sky without a single dark cloud in sight, then off to the side where residents of the neighborhood gathered to watch her make a spectacle of herself, an Amish woman daring to yell at a man. Perhaps one of them would chime in and restate Kiah's candidacy for the idiot-of-the-year award.

Seriously.

"Oh, honey. You care." His quiet words barely managed to register in the continuing verbal vomit, but without hesitation he closed the distance between them. He stood so close she could admire his thick eyelashes and the specks of mischief glittering in his green eyes.

That should've warned her.

His calloused fingers slid from her jaw to cup her cheeks. Sparks ignited into flames at his gentle touch. The next second his lips touched hers, killing the rest of her lecture. A mere brush of his mouth against hers, but she gasped, breathing in a manly, piney scent.

He pulled back, gazed into her eyes for a second, and then his lips returned, claiming hers with an unknown intensity. He tasted of the peppermint candy she'd dumped into the bowl beside the cash register. Her hands flattened against his chest, gripping his suspenders, reveling in the assault on her senses.

Her lips moved, a tentative response.

And then it was over.

He backed away, out of slapping range, if she was so inclined.

She wasn't. She was too busy trying to find air. Wishing for a repeat performance. What was wrong with her? He was in love with GHB, not her. Well, her but he didn't know that...so kissing her truly did make him a flirt and a cheater and oh how she wished her lips weren't still tingling from his touch.

"I wasn't racing." Kiah's voice shook a little. From rage? The racing horse? Or dare she hope, their too-brief kiss? "George, he's a bit deaf."

Oh. *Jah.* She should've thought to warn him. And really "a bit deaf" was an understatement.

"He misunderstood me when I tried to talk to him and ended up offering to teach me my letters. 'A big boy like you needs to know how to write.'" He mimicked George's quivery voice.

A giggle, unbidden and unwelcome, with eighteen months' worth of rust and disuse on it, bubbled into Hallie's throat. She swallowed it.

"And then he whacked the buggy really hard with his cane. He might have left a dent. I haven't checked yet. But it scared the horse and he bolted. I was trying to keep him away from traffic and get him under control. I figured a dead-end road would leave him with no choice but to stop. I wasn't expecting it to end in a circle."

"She," Hallie corrected. "The horse is a mare."

Kiah rolled his eyes. "Whatever. The point is—"

"You kissed me." The words emerged in a gasp of wonder.

Kiah startled, staring at her as if she'd grown horns. "I'm sorry. I shouldn't have. It was the only way I could think of to shut you up."

Shut her up? "You kissed me," she said again. She lightly touched her lips with her fingertips. His warm, firm mouth had pressed against hers, a vast difference from Toby's fumbling, clumsy kisses.

"You liked that, did you?" He eyed her. Assessing.

Jah. Jah, she did. Very much so.

She wanted to kiss him again and again.

But no. She wouldn't go there.

"You kissed me." A third repeat. Her gaze slid to the small crowd of gawkers standing on their porches and in their yards. Her face flamed.

He glanced around. "Oh. I suppose this is a bad time to mention to them"—he waved his hand toward the onlookers—"that I'm in love with the scribe and need to find her."

"You think?" What would his reaction be if he knew he'd just kissed the woman he was looking for?

His attention swung back to her. He studied her, his gaze taking in her probably pink face, then dipping to her lips. They tingled. "But that was…nice. Very nice."

Nice? No. It was amazing.

* * *

Kiah couldn't quite comprehend the heart connection he felt with Hallie. It was almost enough to make him want to give up the search for the unknown scribe and focus on the very real, living and breathing woman standing in front of him. Wooing and winning her instead.

But then he remembered the letters, the articles, the way something about them reached into his core, touched his heart and made him care. Made him want to reach out to this mystery woman, meet her and court her…

No. He was in love with GHB. Hallie was lovely, appealing, and…

And.

And wow, she could kiss. He ached to tug her back into his arms and kiss her again and again.

But...

He shouldn't have kissed Hallie. He could help her find her smile, open her heart for friendship or more with some other fortunate man, but he needed to focus on finding GHB.

He stared at Hallie. Wouldn't it be so nice if she was GHB and greeted him with a "I got your letters..." That would make it so easy.

And actually, he was an idiot. He should write GHB and ask her to meet him. Maybe at the restaurant where Hallie worked. He could order coffee and some of that amazing caramel apple pie...

Something shuffled behind him, followed by a creak, then a snort. A horse's head appeared in his peripheral vision. The runaway horse. Kiah turned, grabbed the bridle, and patted her head. "Good horse."

"Her name is Jellybean," Hallie said. "And since you have everything under control now, I should let you get to your search, and I'll—"

He reached out and grasped her hand. Sparks shot up his arm. "No. Wait. You offered to hold my hand if I need it."

She hesitated. Her hand trembled in his. Her gaze lowered to his mouth.

Oh, the temptation.

But even without looking, he realized most of the people who'd come out to watch the runaway horse drama still stood there, keeping their eyes on him. And her. Them. Both.

Would this end up being written about in *The Budget*? Maybe the scribe had watched this whole scene unfold.

If she had, she'd have seen him kiss Hallie. And she wouldn't believe that he loved her—the scribe. She'd think he was unfaithful. And he had been.

His stomach hurt.

He'd known he shouldn't kiss Hallie.

He'd known.

And he'd kissed her anyway.

Too late for a redo. He shifted. "Is there someplace more private we can go? To talk?" Just in case she thought he had more than talking in mind.

Well, okay, he did. But he wouldn't. Shouldn't.

His gaze dropped to her oh-so-kissable lips.

Who was he kidding?

Because, given the opportunity, he would.

* * *

"Follow me." Hallie's hand lingered against his as she pulled away. Or at least she tried to make it linger. Flirting wasn't something she was used to.

Why was she trying anyway? The man was reckless, even though he claimed the horse had bolted. Why hadn't he gotten control of the horse right away? Most likely he hadn't wanted to. He was flirting with danger. An accident in the making. The type who raced buggies during a tornado for the fun of it.

Ugh!

She scowled. And he'd kissed her. What should she make of that? He'd thought it was the only way to shut her up? She could think of plenty of other options.

The problem was, now she was focused on *the kiss*. On Kiah, as a man. On her hopes and dreams and desires. All of which were dead and buried. Murdered by a twister.

And then brought to life again in a written prayer and a sliver of light from the rising sun.

She sagged as she neared her buggy. He imagined himself in

love with another, and she didn't want the heartbreak of another beau leaving her.

She'd have to make him understand that kissing her couldn't—wouldn't—happen again.

Not even if she wanted it to.

CHAPTER 4

The buggy groaned and creaked as Kiah climbed back into it. It seemed to have survived the runaway horse, but when he got back to the Brunstetters' place, he'd check the nuts and bolts and make sure nothing was loose. He wasn't a buggy repairman, but he did know a little about preventive maintenance. He'd also check for a dent from George's cane. Kiah wasn't entirely sure that George hadn't deliberately scared the horse in order to drum up more business for himself. Not that he'd ever say so.

Kiah glanced over to where Hallie plodded down the road toward her buggy. Her head was bent, shoulders slumped. For a second, maybe longer, he fought the urge to run after her, pull her into his arms, and encourage her with advice his *daed* shared multiple times: "It is never too dark to look up and see the stars." But that bit of wisdom didn't seem to apply because it was currently too light to look up and see the stars. Except for the sun. And that was dangerous to look at.

What if he was the cause of Hallie's distress? He'd kissed her, after claiming to be in love with another. It seemed rather conceited, thinking his kiss was all that. Probably closer to the root of the problem was that he'd been driving a runaway horse, reminding her of her beau losing a race against a tornado.

Either way, he owed the woman a serious apology. Both for stealing a kiss and for scaring her. But the spark of anger in her eyes and her hands on her hips were way more life than he'd seen in her all day. It wasn't a smile or a laugh, but at least her emotions weren't hidden behind a polite smile that didn't reach her eyes.

She untied her horse, climbed into the buggy, and reversed before proceeding back the way she'd come. Toward the main road.

He lined his borrowed mare up behind hers and followed her through a confusing maze of turns that ended at a playground with a gazebo. Maybe the gazebo was built with young lovers in mind.

He swallowed. That kiss was affecting his thought processes.

Right now, the gazebo was vacant. A woman in shorts and a tank top jogged the running trail with her black dog while a man pushed an empty stroller around the fenced play area, following a preschooler who ran from one thing to another without settling in long enough to play.

Hallie climbed the gazebo steps and sat on a narrow slab of wood close to the entrance. She nodded at a bench across from her. "Have a seat."

He sat next to her, just for the reaction. His arm deliberately brushed hers.

She shifted away.

Oh, that broke his heart. After that kiss . . . He needed physical contact with his Hallie. Not a shunning.

He folded his fingers around hers. "Hands are meant to be held."

She stilled, her cheeks red, and stared at their clasped hands.

Oh, he was bad. Kiah groaned. He stared at their hands, too, second-guessing everything he'd said or done since that morning. But they'd felt right, as if she was the scribe that he loved.

Or imagined himself to love.

Something inside him knew her. His heart recognized her. She'd been the face of the scribe since he'd started writing her. And it may be wishful thinking, but...

"I think you're her," he said, running his finger across the back of her hand.

She trembled. Jerked her hand as if she wanted to pull away.

He held on. "Or maybe I just want you to be because I like you. But your name starts with *H*, not *G*."

She gulped, still staring at their hands.

And he felt ten times the fool. He released her hand, grabbed his straw hat off his head, and twisted it out of shape. Even if Hallie was GHB, he was coming on way too strong. It was time to cool it down, slow it up, and take it easy. Treat her as he would a skittish horse and win her trust.

"Look, Hallie..." He swallowed, not entirely sure what to say. But women always wanted to talk about relationships. Or so he'd been told by his not-yet-married but thrice-engaged sister. She knew a sight more about it than he did, because he'd been engaged very briefly only once—less than two weeks— to a woman he'd refused to have more than the bare minimum of the relationship talk with. But really, what could they say? She was the one who stepped out with another man when Kiah was here in Illinois for tornado cleanup. It was over and done, and he had nothing to say. No, he didn't want to get back together. He didn't care how much she whined to his parents. Furthermore, he hadn't wanted to hear her excuses.

And even though he hadn't really loved her, it still hurt. And maybe that was why GHB's articles touched him so. She, too, knew the pang of loss. Somehow.

If Hallie wasn't her, she could be GHB's friend. Maybe they could help each other.

"I know," Hallie said quietly. "You shouldn't have kissed me, you're sorry, and it won't happen again."

Huh? He frowned, then remembered his unfinished sentence began with "Look, Hallie."

Something about the resignation in her voice suggested she'd been down this road before. But that hadn't been what he'd intended to say. At all. Trouble was, he didn't know what he should say. He took a deep breath and breathed a prayer. *Lord, help. Give me the words.*

He still didn't have the beginning of an idea. But he needed to be honest. He sighed. "No. Well, *jah.* I shouldn't have kissed you, but I'm not sorry, and I would love for it to happen again. Honestly, Hallie, something inside me screams that you're her. I know you're probably not, but it seems as if you are. I want to date you. But I'm torn because I came here to find and woo GHB, and well, I don't want to look for her and pursue you at the same time. I mean, I love her from her letters. But you intrigue me. And well," he chuckled, "I don't want to lead either one of you on and—"

Hallie gaped at him.

Jah. He sounded like a blathering fool. He grimaced.

"I'm not looking for a relationship. I don't want a boyfriend," Hallie stated firmly.

That was a waste. Kiah frowned. "Why ever not?" And that sounded rather chauvinistic. He shook his head. It was none of his business. "Never mind. I don't need to know." He just wanted to.

"I have no intention of telling you." Her grin was fleeting.

Grin? Wait. He wanted to replay her facial expression. But he was certain one appeared, no matter how briefly.

* * *

Hallie got up and moved to the far side of the gazebo. She stood, her back to Kiah, watching the *Englisch daed* and child in the fenced play yard. "Tell me about GHB. Why did you start writing to her?" Oops. That was a slipup. "Um, him. Or her."

What do you love about her? That was the big unspoken question.

Hallie gripped the narrow wood ledge in front of her, staring out the opening, the father and son fading into a blur of nothingness as she tried to remember Kiah's initial letter introducing himself. He'd written about his trip to Hidden Springs, mentioning the devastation after the severe storms and how he helped with cleanup and a few other odds-and-ends jobs. Talked about how he and his preacher *daed* raised and trained buggy horses.

Hmm. Maybe she should ask him to train Jellybean not to react to whacks from wooden canes. She did startle at loud noises, so maybe the runaway horse story did happen the way he said. After all, George was a very noisy man.

She opened her mouth, then clamped it shut at her almost blunder. Oh, she needed to be very careful around him. She had no way of knowing he trained buggy horses unless she was GHB and read his letters. Deceiving someone was hard work.

"My name was mentioned in her article as one of the relief workers. Hezekiah Esh. And she mentioned a cat scaring another volunteer...uh, a furniture maker, a straw hat flying off a roof, and other humorous events...It caught my attention. I liked her voice. And...wait. You were there for the cat incident." Growing realization colored his voice.

She was there for the hat, too, even if she hadn't actually seen it happen or been able to retrieve the hat when she found it at the tiptop of a tall tree. Panic clogged her throat. He couldn't figure it out. She shrugged and coughed a couple of times. "Amish do like their jokes. I suppose news got around." She left the gazebo and strode toward the walking path.

Kiah followed and fell in step beside her. "I guess." He sounded doubtful. "Maybe." That word was drawn out, loaded down with skepticism.

She could almost feel his gaze on her, could almost hear the dots being connected in his head. Panic stiffened her spine. "And about twenty-five or more people saw you kiss me. Including Gideon Brunstetter." She emphasized the name. Her great-great-uncle Gideon would quickly deny that he was the scribe, though. Especially since his handwriting was illegible due to his failing eyesight. In fact, he probably heard gossip about the kiss, rather than witnessed it even though he was in the crowd.

"True. You certainly wouldn't write about the kiss." A strange sound filled his voice. Relief? Regret?

Oh, that hurt. Why had she gone and brought up that touchy subject? Now she was obligated to write about it just to prove a lie as truth. Or was it to prove truth as a lie? And how could she write about it as an observer when she was a surprised-but-willing participant?

Or at least she would've been a much more willing participant if he'd given her an opportunity. But it was over almost as soon as it began. It was better that way. As it was, she almost made a fool of herself. Of course, it probably would've been best if it hadn't happened at all. But that would've been a shame.

"Would you?" Was that insecurity in his voice?

Wait. What were they talking about again? She twisted around to look at him. Raised an eyebrow in question.

"Would you write about the kiss? Our kiss." His brows rose.

"If I am the scribe, you mean?" Her voice caught. "Nothing to write about."

"Ouch." He looked away, bowed his head, and clasped his hands as if he was praying.

She looked away from him. Probably foolish, considering she didn't trust him.

"Well, I'm sorry. It shouldn't have happened. I'm in love with GHB, you aren't her, and you aren't interested in a relationship anyway. Or so you say." His voice was muffled.

"It would've saved time if you'd agreed with me in the first place."

"What?"

"I said that." She turned to face him again. "You shouldn't have kissed me, you're sorry, and it won't happen again."

"You're right." Kiah peeked up at her and nodded. "You did say that. But I wasn't planning on saying that then."

"Whatever." Hallie mimicked the *Englisch* girls, complete with eye roll, lip curl, and attitude.

"And it will happen again, if I get a chance."

"You won't get a chance." But she wanted it, too. She wanted a relationship with Kiah. Wanted to be loved by the man she'd corresponded with. The man standing in front of her.

But she didn't want the pang of loss. The heartache sure to follow.

She gulped.

For a long minute, they stood there on the path, gazing at each other. Then her eyes darted to his well-formed lips.

They quirked.

Hers tingled in response.

And he chuckled. "We'll see about that." There was a brief hesitation. Then, "Twenty questions." He started walking again. "What's your favorite pizza?"

* * *

Kiah was so bad. He shouldn't tease her. Really, he shouldn't. Especially since the kiss really shouldn't have happened and he needed to be faithful to GHB if she wasn't Hallie. It just seemed so inconceivable that she wasn't, especially as they walked two or three laps, talking, sharing, and getting better acquainted. It was amazing how much they had in common with each other and how much she had in common with the scribe.

But if they truly were different people, the scribe and Hallie undoubtedly knew each other, and well…If word got out that he went around kissing girls, it'd ruin his reputation, destroy his chances with GHB, and might even cause him to be sent home in disgrace. Not only that, but *Daed* would surely curtail any future hopes of finding his bride.

Hezekiah Esh and GHB…

He groaned. Because, because, because…He, well, shoot. Hallie was GHB. She simply had to be. He couldn't believe otherwise. He wanted to spend the rest of the day with her, talking. So he asked if they could.

"I want you along, but it'd probably be best if I go alone," he said. "I'll visit the other two men, then this evening we can talk about what I discovered and how they can't possibly be the scribe, and then you can tell me how to find the women Suzy mentioned."

"And if one of the men is?" Her gaze was wide-eyed innocence.

"Then I'll make an awkward exit, find you, and convince you to give me a chance."

Hallie's cheeks flamed red. She averted her gaze and said nothing.

She knew. More than she pretended. He was certain of that.

Kiah cleared his throat.

She raised her eyes but avoided his.

He stood. "You could save time and frustration and just tell me who it is. I still think you know."

She shook her head. Mute. Still not looking directly at him.

"Either that or it's you."

Her glance slid toward the ground.

Her silence said volumes.

He wouldn't admit to his identity either if some random stranger came to town claiming to be in love with him. He'd make them put in the effort, prove their devotion, and play it safe.

He'd follow by her rules, but he knew.

At least he was pretty sure he knew.

CHAPTER 5

Hallie was a terrible liar. She always had been. Which was a good thing for an Amish girl but a bad thing if she wanted—needed—to keep her identity secret from an entirely too appealing Amish man. Not that she wanted to keep it secret. It was just that she had to if she wanted to continue her work as scribe.

But even though Kiah went his way to visit the two men she'd mentioned, something—she didn't know what—about his expression indicated that he seriously suspected her of being the scribe.

Of course, he'd said as much. Twice. More than twice. Several times.

How had she given herself away? Or did he truly know her so well from her articles and letters?

Her head pounded with the beginning of a tension headache, so she stopped by a restaurant for a cold drink. When she pulled into the driveway at home, *Daadi* came out of the barn and met her in the yard, taking control of the horse while she grabbed her purse and a sweating to-go cup full of soda pop and carried them into the *haus*.

The kitchen was blessedly empty. At the table, chairs were left pulled out at awkward angles, and an abandoned half-full cup of coffee, a half-eaten cinnamon roll, and a note were at *Mamm*'s place. The note was written on a recipe card with Hallie's lavender pen. *Called to a birth. The visiting preacher and his wife (and possibly their son) are eating the noon meal with the bishop. Your* mammi *will feed the noon meal to anyone home in the* dawdihaus. *Start supper if I'm not back. Roast for sandwiches in refrigerator.*

Hallie shoved the chairs in, then dumped the coffee and the dried out pastry into the slop bucket. She glanced around. Homemade bread cooled on the counter. She'd check on early lettuce and radishes in the garden and make deviled eggs to go with the sandwiches, too.

She glanced at the cookie jar. She'd made peanut butter cookies and shortbread cookies the day before the visiting preacher arrived. That sweet should be adequate for dessert tonight, especially considering the big meal following the preaching tomorrow. There'd be plenty of pies, cakes, and other treats then.

Kitchen straightened and supper menu planned, Hallie grabbed her writing supplies from the drawer and her favorite lavender pen from the cup and headed upstairs to her shared bedroom. It was empty; Hosanna had probably attended the birth with *Mamm*. Anna was interested in *Mamm*'s career and helped out all she could. With Anna working as *Mamm*'s apprentice, *Mamm* certainly didn't need another. Especially not one as uninterested in midwifery as Hallie.

Well, it wasn't that she was uninterested. It was just there were too many variables, too many things that could go wrong. Too many things that did go wrong. Like the last birth Hallie assisted. The cord was wrapped around the baby's neck, and he was very blue. *Mamm* had handed Hallie the baby and told her to rub him hard and not stop. Hallie had rubbed the baby with a soft flannel blanket until he was bright red and screaming. *Mamm* said she saved the baby from brain damage or worse. Never mind that *Mamm* also said that Hallie was a natural and stayed calm under pressure. Hallie only knew that she had been absolutely terrified, and she didn't want to do it again anytime soon.

Never would be too soon.

She plopped down on her bed and sifted through her notes. She hesitated when she came across the prayer she'd started that morning. *Send the light.*

And light had come flashing across her white paper in unexpected brightness. As well as the unmentioned, but thought about, portion about *Gott* sending her pen pal to be her boyfriend.

Gott certainly had a sense of humor, dropping Kiah into her life as He had. No warning. Just "Hello" on the first visit. On the second visit, "I love you"—well, technically, that was for GHB, but still. "Won't you tell me your name?" on the third.

Stuff like that didn't happen in real life.

At least not to her.

She wasn't sure she wanted it to. Well, she did, but what if *Gott* ripped Kiah from her? Still, the excitement of romance made her heart pound and her pulse skitter, and disrupted her quiet, passive world.

She shook her head, rearranged the papers, uncapped the lavender pen, and went to work.

There was a formula to these articles. First the date, then the weather. Sunny and warm. It was beautiful, especially after all the rain they had recently. Some of the creeks and rivers were still overflowing their banks. Fields and gardens were still muddy. That was followed by the community news. Who visited Hidden Springs and why. Who traveled, where they went, and why. Who married, who died, and who was born to whom with mentions of maternal and paternal grandparents. There were a lot of names in there. The Amish loved to read their names printed in *The Budget*. Then, of course, there were the retractions if she accidentally reported the news wrong. It routinely happened. The mistakes were reported to Bishop Nathan, who slipped the corrections and other news to Hallie's *daed*.

Then all that was left were the fun little tidbits that apparently had attracted Kiah Esh's attention.

She hesitated, pen poised over the page.

Hallie was obligated to mention the kiss since she assured Kiah she wouldn't, and she wanted to deflect his suspicious attention. And if she deliberately got some of the facts wrong, then that'd prove it wasn't her.

What was the nursery rhyme about someone kissing the girls and making them cry?

She sighed. She might not have cried, but cry she would when her family slept and she was able to sneak out of the *haus* to weep alone in a dark loft in the barn. The hoped-for relationship that would never be hers needed to be mourned.

After she made some vague but funny comments about a stranger racing a horse in broad daylight and then celebrating by kissing a bystander—and making her cry—before he ran away, written in such a way it could be attributed to a random storyteller, Hallie trifolded the letter and placed it in the envelope. She addressed it, added a stamp, and ran it out to the mailbox.

The mail carrier generally ran in the late afternoon, so it'd go out that same day.

What would Kiah think about the misrepresented facts? He wouldn't dare ask the bishop to have the scribe correct them, and it should work to draw his attention away from her.

She kicked at a tall milkweed plant. Guilt ate at her.

What she'd done was lie. In print, which somehow made it worse.

But no one would ever know. Except Kiah and her.

And *Gott*.

She turned to look back at the mailbox.

None of them would tell.

The ends justified the means.

Tears blurred her vision as she turned her back on the mailbox. It didn't matter that something about Kiah touched her broken heart. Toby was her one and only chance at love.

The tears flowed, a steady stream. She stumbled into a lurching run. Hopefully, neither *Daed* nor *Daadi* would come out of the barn and witness this breakdown.

* * *

Kiah double-checked the address on the mailbox, then parked the buggy next to a curbside tree. There was plenty of shade and grass for Jellybean.

The crowd had dissipated since Kiah's runaway horse incident. Most people had retired to their homes or outbuildings. A few boys played a rowdy game of street basketball. Kiah nabbed the ball when it bounced his way and dribbled it across the road to the basketball hoop. The ball circled the rim twice before dropping through. He waved off offers to join the game, instead jogging across the street and up to Gideon Brunstetter's front door. He lifted the heavy knocker and let it fall against the wood. It made a satisfying thump.

From somewhere inside, there was a muffled grunt, followed by tapping. A moment later, the door opened to reveal an elderly man with a yellow-stained beard, dark sunglasses, and a white-tipped cane.

This was definitely a false lead. Gideon was blind.

"*Jah?*" Gideon squinted at him. "Whatever it is you're selling, I'm not buying." He started to shut the door. Then he stopped. "State your piece, boy."

Kiah wasn't sure what to say. Except the truth. "Someone suggested that you were the scribe for *The Budget*."

Gideon stared at him a moment. "Ha! Do I look like a scribe?"

Kiah grimaced. How could he answer that?

"Probably that fool Gloria who married my twin brother. She likely is the scribe and is just trying to annoy me. You go talk to Gloria Brunstetter." And then the door slammed shut. At least Kiah had gotten confirmation on a name to check on.

He knocked again to say thank you.

No answer.

A third knock.

"Go away, boy!"

That seemed rather awkward to say thanks in response, so Kiah turned away.

On the plus side, Gideon hadn't mentioned *the kiss*, so if he'd heard about it, he didn't associate it with Kiah.

Fifteen minutes later, he found the other man, Gabe Brenneman, mucking the cow barn at his property. A small boy pushed a toy tractor through the dust on the floor.

This man was married with children. But Kiah would ask anyway. He couldn't think of a good excuse for his visit otherwise. He cleared his throat to get Gabe's attention. "Gabe Brenneman?"

Gabe looked up, removed his hat, and wiped the sweat from his brow. He was maybe in his mid- to late thirties. "That's me."

"I'm Hezekiah Esh. My friends call me Kiah. I need to talk to you."

"Sure. That's my boy, Benny." Gabe glanced back at Kiah. "Get to work. I've several more stalls to clean. I'll listen."

Get to work? Kiah hesitated. Talking and working might earn him more information. He grabbed a pitchfork and pitched in to help.

He cleaned half the stall while explaining his relationship—both real and hoped-for—with the unknown scribe and how he wanted to find her. Tons more than he'd intended to say.

Gabe listened politely. The small boy made rumbly tractor noises. A cat meowed.

Kiah finished the other half while Gabe made "hmmm" sounds.

Then Gabe handed him ten dollars. "My middle name's Stephen. I'm sure you'll be glad to know I'm not your one true love." He laughed. "I don't know who the scribe is, but ask the bishop. He lives across the street. Then write the scribe a letter and ask her out."

Jah. Good advice. Too bad he hadn't thought to do that from the beginning.

"*Danki.*" Kiah tried to return the money. "You don't need to pay me. I didn't do much."

Gabe waved it away. "Appreciate the help. I wish you the best with your one true love. Use it to buy her a malted milkshake. Go on now."

A malted milkshake sounded good. Real good.

A couple minutes later, Kiah parked behind a horse and buggy across the street. *Daed* and another man were heading in from the barn. Right. Bishop Nathan. Where his parents were eating the noon meal. Him, too, since he was invited and had arrived in time. At least he'd have sustenance, but asking who the scribe was, and explaining why he wanted to know, in front of his parents? Even though they knew his reason for coming?

Awkward.

But maybe the bishop would admit what Kiah strongly suspected. Hallie was the scribe. He truly hoped she was, though why hadn't she admitted to it? Then again, caution could be understood.

Both men turned toward him as he exited the buggy. "Glad

you could join us, Kiah," *Daed* said. "This is Bishop Nathan. Bishop, this is my son, Hezekiah."

The bishop nodded. "I remember you. You came with the group from Shipshewana after the tornadoes. You worked with George, disassembling the buggy and removing it from my living room."

Kiah grinned as he remembered that task. And the headache he'd suffered from because everyone shouted at George so he'd understand them. "*Jah*, I did."

"We appreciated your help."

"Glad to be of service."

"I should warn you, before we go in. My Martha, she has some medical problem that causes her to be freezing all the time. She's going to specialists to try and figure out why. But in the meantime, it's very hot inside." Bishop Nathan opened the door. "Come on in. Wash up and we'll eat."

Kiah followed the bishop and *Daed* into the over-warm kitchen. Sweat beaded on his forehead. Despite the temperature, the older woman bringing over serving dishes wore a black sweater over her dark gray dress. *Mamm* carried glasses filled with ice water. Her face was flushed and she looked miserable.

After washing, Kiah sat where Bishop Nathan indicated and glanced at the table laden with sausages, sauerkraut, mashed potatoes, and green beans. A heavy meal on a warm day in a hot *haus*. But it'd be worth it for answers.

"Let's pray." Bishop Nathan bowed his head.

Kiah dutifully bowed his head, then after his silent recitation of a memorized portion of scripture—*our father who art in heaven*—tried to plan the best way to bring up the topic of the scribe.

The bishop cleared his throat. "Amen." He reached for the mashed potatoes. "So, Kiah. I didn't expect you to come with your parents to Hidden Springs. What made you decide to join them?"

Mamm gasped and gulped ice water, then lunged to her feet to refill the glass.

Daed dipped his head and focused on lining the silverware up in straight lines.

Kiah's face burned. "I came to find the scribe," he mumbled. Why did his parents have to act so embarrassing? And why did this have to be so awkward?

Bishop Nathan startled and gave Kiah a second look. "The scribe, you say? And did you find her?"

So it was a her.

"The boy fancies himself in love with her." *Daed* abandoned his eating utensils and accepted the mashed potatoes from Bishop Nathan.

"In love? So you did find her? And she admitted to being the scribe?" Bishop Nathan pinned him with a stare.

Kiah pulled in a shaky breath. *Honesty is the best policy.* "I think I found her, but she has admitted nothing. So I'm not sure enough to mention any names." Especially in front of his parents, who might mention something to their hosts, and that would only make things *really* awkward. Especially since *Daed* gave him the weekend only. The clock was ticking. "My...my heart recognizes her."

Daed harrumphed. And took a sausage and a spoonful of sauerkraut when it was passed.

"Hmmmm." The bishop didn't look away from Kiah. "Explain yourself."

"Something in her articles for *The Budget* spoke to me, so I wrote her, in care of the paper, and we started a pen pal relationship. She always signed her letters GHB. I fell in love with her through the mail."

"I warned him that she's probably eighty," *Mamm* said.

Bishop Nathan's eyes shifted to her, then back to Kiah. "But you don't know her."

"I *feel* I know her. I imagine I love her."

The bishop frowned. "Love is not a feeling. Love is a commitment to listen, care, and serve. The feelings are found therein."

And with that, the bishop was off and running with a five-point sermon filled with rabbit trails on what love meant and how Kiah couldn't possibly love the scribe without knowing who she was and her unique issues.

Daed gave Kiah his *you'd best be listening to this* look. Steely eyes, firm lips, and drawn brows. He also probably planned his own five-point sermon about why Kiah should forgive Molly and marry her regardless of her unfaithfulness.

Kiah listened. And ate. And sweated. And inwardly argued. He *knew* the scribe. He did. And he loved her. He hadn't told her, though. It wasn't time. She would be totally freaked out. Understandably.

Though the bishop did have some good points. What if she was married? Engaged? Much, much older than him? Or too young for him? So many questions Kiah had no answers to.

Thirty minutes later, grateful to be outside in the still warm—but much cooler than the bishop's *haus*—air, Kiah gripped the reins with white-knuckled fingers as he drove away. Even after the conclusion of the bishop's sermon, he still didn't have the coveted information.

Stubborn and stupid.

Jah, that totally described him.

It seemed like a thin line between the two adjectives.

Stupid and stubborn.

He exhaled loudly, and the horse indicated her agreement with his negative self-assessment by snorting, flipping her tail, and making a hefty deposit on the road.

It was a total waste of the late morning and noon hour.

He'd go back to the Brunstetters' *haus*, ask to borrow paper, and write a letter to the scribe asking her to meet him at the restaurant.

How long would it take for a letter to get from Hidden Springs to *The Budget*, and for it to be forwarded to the scribe?

His heart rate increased. Would Hallie be the one who showed up? And would she show up? Because if it was her, then she knew it was him and she'd already gone on record as not being ready for a relationship. Would his request make a difference?

A better question: How long would *Daed* allow him to pursue this foolish quest? Would he give him longer than the weekend?

And if he failed, then what?

* * *

Alone in the silent *haus*, Hallie retreated upstairs and flung herself across the bed. She was long overdue for a full-fledged pity party. Her pen clattered to the floor. The papers containing her community notes crumpled beneath her and she sat up long enough to shove them out of the way before letting the tears fall.

By the time quiet voices intruded, her nose ran, her throat hurt, and her pillow was soaked. She caught a gasping breath and listened. She couldn't understand what they were saying, but they were somewhere downstairs. Probably the kitchen since that was the hub of the home. One of the voices was male. Her breath caught. Kiah. Somehow, the timbre of his voice reached deep inside her. The volume increased. Was he coming upstairs?

Hallie pushed herself off the bed. His borrowed room—that belonged to her brother Aaron—was right across the hall from hers and her door was wide open. She hurried toward the entrance to her room and went to push the door shut, but she peeked out first. No one was in sight.

She dashed toward the bathroom and stepped inside, right as the noisy bottom step creaked. Safe. She quietly shut the door.

She started to wash her face, then glanced at the shower. A warm, slow shower would be nicer. Much nicer.

Hallie stayed in the water until it ran cold; then she hurried into her dress. She opened the door and listened but didn't hear any noises. Maybe Kiah went back downstairs. Leaving her hair loose, she scurried down the hallway to her bedroom.

The door across the hall was ajar. She ducked into her room and shut the door, flipping the lock, then turned.

Kiah stood beside her bed, her favorite lavender pen in one hand. Her community notes were in his other.

She stumbled to a stop and slapped her hand over her mouth. *Busted.*

His green eyes widened. A brow rose. And his gaze slowly slid over her wet, tangled hair, down to her bare toes.

"You violated my privacy." Her voice emerged in a wimpy-sounding squeak. And then she hated that was all she could think to say.

He waved the community notes toward a small pile of folded clothes on the edge of the bed. "Your *mammi*—"

"You're in my room." That came out a bit breathier than she liked.

He dropped the papers on her quilt. "*Jah*, your *mammi*—"

"Get out!" She turned and jerked at the door.

It didn't open.

She yanked again, fresh tears burning her eyes. Nothing. She pushed and pulled and would've kicked, but she was barefoot. And, oh, why did he have to see her like this? Find out this way?

His empty hand closed over hers. Tingles shot up her arm. "It's locked."

Hallie caught her breath and stared up at him.

He laid the lavender pen down on the dresser beside the door. His hand rose and caught a strand of her tangled hair. He gave it a gentle tug. "I'll be glad to comb it for you sometime."

She sucked in a noisy breath.

Kiah winked.

He flipped the lock with his thumb and opened the door.

"We'll talk later . . ." The fingers holding her hair slid down the length, then brushed her cheek as he pulled away. "Scribe."

CHAPTER 6

Kiah grinned as he walked across the hallway to his room. Behind him, the door clicked shut and the lock kicked into place. Finding GHB was way easier than he'd thought it would be. And she was who he'd hoped she'd be. What did the *G* stand for anyway? He mentally ran through a list of all the women's names he could think of that started with *G*, but none of them made sense with Hallie. Or Henrietta.

Of course, maybe the *G* was added just to throw people off, because for some reason she wanted to conceal her identity.

Whatever it was, it would all be revealed eventually. Because now was the time to start seriously wooing the woman. Prepping her for their maybe eventual courtship, if she was willing. Despite the interest in her eyes, she'd already stated that she wasn't interested in a relationship—or something to that effect.

Though, of course, he needed to be cautious, too. His former relationship had ended badly. Although maybe not as badly as Hallie's. His ex-girlfriend—very brief ex-fiancée—was still alive…and very apologetic. She was wrong, but…then she blamed him for something as her gaze followed another man. No. It didn't matter how many times Molly asked him to take her back. He couldn't trust her.

Enough. Molly was his history. Hallie was his future.

Hallie was *hopefully* his future. Right now chances were real good he'd crash and burn.

Kiah blew out a puff of air and twisted the knob to open his temporary bedroom door. Downstairs, two men conversed in low tones.

He needed to win Hallie's friendship. For real. And her trust. Which he'd seriously violated by invading her personal space and picking up the papers filled with her familiar handwriting and community notes. Especially when her *mammi* said to leave the clothes on the floor outside the door and he'd deliberately chosen to disobey and snoop when he saw that telltale lavender pen on the floor.

She'd also said—multiple times in her letters—that she had lost someone she loved. Whoever that was. Was she referring to Toby's death? Or a different failed relationship?

He walked over to the bedroom window and stared out at the barn. The sliding wood doors were open, revealing bits of the dim interior.

He stared at the dusky darkness. Were his feelings coming across too strong and she wanted to let him down easy?

Or worse, maybe she already had fallen in love with someone else? Oh no. No. No. Wait. Kiah's blood chilled. It had been over a year since Toby died. Was he too late? She could have found another man who lived somewhere in another Amish community.

That meant she'd be gone.

Gone!

He hadn't put that together until now. He turned away from the window and started pacing the room.

He was determined to try to win her love and woo her away from some other man. But wait. That meant encouraging her to step out on her boyfriend. To make her do what Molly had done to him.

His stomach roiled. He stopped in his tracks and turned toward the hallway and eyed Hallie's door. What should he say? Do? Should he apologize? He crossed the hall and raised his hand to knock. Then he paused, fist still posed in a knocking position. Of course, he could—and would—pray, but it didn't seem to be enough.

It had to be, though. Because other than winning her friendship and her trust, what other option did he have? If there was one, he couldn't think what it might be.

No wonder the bishop had said something about caring for her unique issues. He'd been giving Kiah a clear-cut warning to proceed with caution. To slow down. Maybe to treat her like a skittish horse. With a lot of patience.

He lowered his hand and backed up until he leaned against the wall opposite her closed door.

But what about the shadows in her eyes? The pain of loss in her letters? Since Toby died, had another boyfriend broken up with her?

His brain hurt. The beginnings of a migraine threatened. That'd be bad if he came down with one on this visit. The prescription pills—and the headache both—made it extremely hard to focus.

The noisy step creaked at the bottom of the staircase, and he turned his head. A young woman, with hair the color of honey and wearing a lavender dress, came into view. She was attractive, but not beautiful. She had a lavender pen tucked in her prayer *kapp*, just over her ear. A brow arched as she neared Kiah.

He sought a grin, but his lips hurt. His eyes zeroed in on that pen and his stomach sank. He might have jumped to too quick of a conclusion. "Hezekiah Esh. My friends call me Kiah."

Her smile reached her eyes. "Kiah Esh. I've seen that name before." She stuck out her hand. "Genesis Hosanna Brunstetter. My friends call me Hosanna, or usually Anna."

Kiah's stomach tickled. He reached out and gripped her fingers.

Genesis Hosanna Brunstetter. GHB.

He should've known Hallie wasn't her. It'd been too easy. And, of course, she wouldn't give away her sister's secrets. He'd dreamed of and kissed the wrong sister. Flirted with...

The stomach tickle faded as the contents went on a roller-coaster ride.

Anna's smile grew. "I'd stay and talk, but I need my notes. I'm assisting at a birth." She gently tugged her fingers free with the tiniest of winks. "Perhaps we could talk later?"

"I'd like that." His stomach lurched again. He'd definitely need to apologize—again—to Hallie and beg her to keep the kiss secret.

Anna turned away and twisted the knob. The door didn't open. She knocked. Pounded, really. "Hallie, let me in. I need my notes."

Rustling came from the room for a moment; then the door opened just wide enough for a familiar-looking stack of papers to slide through.

Kiah's head hurt worse. He needed to get away somewhere and think. He started downstairs to get a glass of cold water. Perhaps that'd stop the headache before it got worse. He was seriously dehydrated from the bishop's hot *haus*.

Hallie's door slammed shut.

Slammed.

Wood probably splintered.

Kiah twisted around, stumbled on the edge of the step, and

slipped. He skated all the way down and somehow landed on his feet. But his back hurt.

Along with his head.

And his lips.

Had he somehow made Hallie mad?

But then again, he'd been snooping in her room.

And jumping to wrong conclusions.

* * *

Hallie probably shouldn't have slammed the door in her sister's face, but then again, she shouldn't have been eavesdropping on her perfect older sister flirting with the sizzling-hot Kiah Esh. Letting him believe she was the scribe, though to be fair they hadn't mentioned it. But something filled his voice after Anna told Kiah her full name.

Realization. Horror. Something.

She should be grateful to Anna but—

Loud thumps and thuds came from outside her door.

"Are you all right?" Anna sounded alarmed.

"Fi—" Hallie began.

"That looked like a nasty tumble. Did you hurt yourself?"

What? Hallie fumbled the lock and jerked the door open. She plowed out into the hallway, knocking Anna sideways. Kiah stood at the bottom of the stairs, gingerly stretching his back from side to side.

"I might need a medical professional to look me over." He aimed a quick grin up the steps.

"Of course. I can't have a handsome guy getting killed on my watch." Anna elbowed Hallie. "Dibs," she whispered. "I saw him first."

Untrue, but with Anna now running down the stairs to reach him, not to mention the mutual flirting…Hallie blew out a frustrated breath. She didn't want a relationship anyway. Really. Love hurt.

But then again, missing out on love hurt, too. Was that a sign that her broken heart was coming back to life and the light was seeping into the cracks and chasing away the darkness? No. Couldn't be.

"Where do you hurt?" Anna sounded suitably professional.

My heart. Hallie thought the words as Kiah said them.

Anna giggled.

Hallie tried not to snort. But she might not have succeeded, because Kiah's eyes rose and locked on hers.

They stood there, staring at each other until Anna apparently noticed something was off and Kiah's attention wasn't on her. She turned. And glared at Hallie.

The spell broken, Hallie retreated to her room. Then realized too late that her hair was still loose, tangled, and uncovered. *Mamm* would scold her for that.

Anna said something and giggled. Kiah chuckled.

Hallie locked the door, moved her notes out of the way, and flopped onto the bed.

A fresh round of tears burned her eyes. She fisted her hands and rubbed at the moisture. She'd cried enough. At least for now she had. She'd had a chance with Kiah, and she'd chosen to push him away. Had chosen not to admit that, despite there being numerous GHBs in the district, she really was the scribe. She told him flat out that she wasn't interested. But she was.

Very interested.

And missing out on this chance of love hurt, too.

Though, really, she'd thought he'd figured out the truth. She was the scribe. She was interested. Please, woo her…

Woo her.

Win her.

Love her.

Too late now.

More laughter came from outside. A horse whinnied.

Hallie sat up enough to peek out the window. Kiah held Anna's hand as he helped her into the buggy. As if Anna was unable to get in by herself. Why hadn't Kiah helped Hallie? It wasn't like she needed assistance, though.

She sighed and flopped back on the bed.

An annoying *rat-a-tat* tapping came from somewhere above her head. Clip-clops came from outside. At least with Kiah ogling Anna as she was taking her leave, Hallie needn't have foolish thoughts about him tossing a handful of pebbles at her window.

More *rat-a-tat*s followed the first. Hallie glared at the ceiling. It sounded as if a woodpecker had taken a remodeling job in the attic. This had happened a couple years ago and *Mamm* had caught the bird with a fishnet, releasing it miles down the road.

If *Mamm* could do it, Hallie could.

She firmed her jaw, rolled off the bed, grabbed her notes and slid them under her pillow, then marched to the doorway. After unlocking the door, she peeked out to make sure Kiah hadn't returned and taken sentry right outside her bedroom.

All clear.

She dashed to the square in the ceiling that concealed the ladder leading up into the attic, yanked the rope tied to the metal ring, and pulled the ladder down. Dim light came in through the grimy window at the far side of the attic. Not enough.

Hallie found the lantern-style flashlight *Mamm* kept up there, not necessarily for bird-induced emergencies. She flicked it on to make sure it worked, then pulled the steps up, closing the escape route so the bird wouldn't head south into other areas of the *haus*.

Daed's fishing gear was near the exit. Hallie grabbed the fishing net and the flashlight and waded deep into the shadowy attic jungle. She found Woody renovating the area behind where *Mamm* had stacked all the old children's games.

She swung the net.

Missed.

Woody raised his red head, looked at her with a quizzical eye, then apparently decided they were playing a game of tag. He fluttered to the rafters.

Hallie made a makeshift staircase out of old chairs, left the flashlight on one of them, and started the climb.

Woody waited until she reached the summit, then dived straight toward her eyes.

She screeched, flinging an arm over her face, barely keeping her balance. Moments later, she watched the bird perch on the other side of the attic. She could've sworn he wrinkled his long beak at her. Maybe he even smirked.

"Okay, this is war, Woody." Obviously she read too many adventure novels.

Woody made *churring* sounds that may or may not have been taunting.

She chose to believe they were.

Once safely descended from Mt. Wobbly Chairs, Hallie found a child's swimming mask that belonged to her brother Aaron and yanked it over her head to shield her eyes. *Daed*'s old straw hat covered her loose hair to protect it from whatever damage a woodpecker would do to it.

Armed with the net and the flashlight, she eyed her prey and stalked across the cobweb-filled expanse.

Woody waited until she was in swinging distance, then did a flyby, buzzing past her face.

She screeched and dove for the floor. "Man the battle stations! Incoming!"

* * *

Kiah watched the buggy carrying GHB until it turned out of sight; then, strangely disquieted, he trudged inside. He still needed a glass of cold water. Maybe an icy drink would help cure the headache that threatened. He'd also take half a headache pill. Maybe that'd be enough to hold the stress-induced migraine at bay.

Then he needed to find Hallie and have a heart-to-heart with her. That made his head hurt worse.

He needed to figure out why he had this strange instant, very strong connection with Hallie that seemed to be lacking with Anna. He wanted to give up on Anna and pursue Hallie. But maybe it was because he'd dreamed of Hallie for so long. He needed to give the relationship with Anna time. If the bishop was right, the love-feelings would come if he set his mind on loving Anna. It just seemed, though, that something was off.

In the kitchen, he gulped multiple glasses of ice water as he read the note—written in lavender—that the Brunstetter *mamm* left for Hallie. Cold roast beef sandwiches sounded good for supper. Lavender ink, on the other hand, was entirely too prominent in this *haus*.

He refilled the glass with more cold water and climbed the stairs to take that half pill and have a chat with Hallie. Hopefully she'd fixed her hair by now. Hallie with just-tumbled-out-of-the-shower messy hair was entirely too... enticing.

The bedroom door was open. Hallie was gone. So were the notes, because Anna had come to get them. The lavender pen was still on the dresser where he'd laid it.

Kiah went into his room, bit a headache pill in half, swallowed part, and returned the other partial piece to the container. He took another gulp of water, then set the glass on the floor in the hallway and was starting to lower himself beside it to wait for Hallie's reappearance when a loud thump came from right above his head.

"Man the battle stations! Incoming!"

What on earth? Kiah straightened and looked around. "Hallie?" he shouted.

"I'm in the attic! Proceed with caution! This is war." She screeched again.

"War?" He pulled the ladder down and climbed up. "Who are you fighting? An itsy-bitsy spider?"

She scowled at him. "Woody the woodpecker." She wore an oversize man's straw hat and royal blue swim goggles.

He snickered. Then laughed outright. She stared at him, still scowling.

"Woody the—" A red and gray blur flew at his face. "Whoa. What'd you do to get on his bad side?" Kiah flung his arm up to ward off the bird and purposely collapsed on the floor, face-first.

Hallie reached over his legs to close the hatch. He thought maybe her softness brushed against his legs, but wasn't sure. But he certainly hadn't felt this instant chemistry with Anna when he'd helped her into the buggy.

"We don't want him to escape."

"I'm pretty sure he wants to stay." He wanted to stay, too.

Hallie's fingers brushed his hand as she pressed something into his grip. Tingles shot up his arm. "Man up, Kiah. I'm going to try to get him to fly this way. You catch him."

"Man up?" Kiah sat and pretended to glower. "You're the one screaming like a girl."

She swatted at him. "I am a girl. In case you haven't noticed."

His gaze slipped from her tangled, straw hat–covered hair, over the funny-looking swim goggles, to her oh-so-kissable lips. "Believe me, I noticed."

Woody did another flyby, then landed on a box. He made *churring* sounds.

Kiah slowly eased to his feet, glanced at the fishnet in his hands, then to Hallie. "What are we going to do with him?"

"Release him outside?" Hallie lowered the goggles to dangle around her neck and raised a brow.

"He'll just get in again unless we find his entrance and block it."

She wrinkled her cute little nose. "Oh."

He snagged the worn-out straw hat from her head and handed it to her. "Go get him, Hallie. You can try to make him fly in my direction with the hat. I'll find the hole he's getting through after he's caught."

Hallie nodded, firmed her jaw, raised the goggles, and marched toward the bird. When she neared it, she flapped the hat.

The bird took flight.

It was good Kiah had played softball. He jumped, arm outstretched, and Woody flew into the net.

He landed with a backbone-jarring thud. At least this time he stayed on his feet.

"What's going on up there?" a stern male voice called. It didn't sound like his *daed*. It might be hers.

Hallie scrambled past him and pulled open the hatch.

"We caught the woodpecker." She took the flopping netted bird from Kiah and scampered down the ladder.

Kiah peeked out. Hallie's *daed*'s gaze widened as it slid over her loose, tangled hair. He took the net; then his eyes met Kiah's.

A heaping buggy-load of warning filled them. Kiah knew why. He was seriously attracted to Hallie. And he saw her with her hair down. Forbidden among unmarried couples.

"I'll take care of the bird." *Daed* Brunstetter turned away without further ado.

"I'll block the hole where it got in," Kiah said.

"Supplies are in the barn." Hallie's *daed* carried the unhappy bird downstairs.

Kiah climbed out. His fingers brushed a smear of dirt off Hallie's cheek. "You got dirt on your cheek. I think you need another shower. But I'll be more than glad to comb your hair."

CHAPTER 7

Their pathetic water heater hadn't had enough time to do its job, so Hallie rushed through a cold shower. This time she forced herself to comb and bind her hair before dressing. Especially since she heard Kiah whistling as he thumped around overhead. Pounding began as she slipped her dress on and ended just as she slid the last straight pin into place.

She was halfway down the hall when Kiah clomped down the attic ladder.

The whistling stopped. "Hold up a moment, Hallie. We need to talk." He sounded serious. Too serious.

She stopped. Tried to control her expression so he wouldn't see the pain. Then turned. "Is it time for the talk, take two?"

His mouth opened and shut as he blinked. Twice. "*Jah*, I guess so."

She aimed her gaze toward the ceiling. "Let me save you the time. It's nothing personal, but since you believe my sister is the scribe, there can be nothing between us and please don't mention the kiss."

He took the time to raise the ladder and close the hatch. "I might not have been so blunt. But *jah*. That nailed it."

This was her fault, but still, her lips wobbled. She tried to firm them. She swallowed a stubborn lump. *Breaking up was hard to do*... even though they were never a couple. Then she aimed a fake smile in his direction. "Of course."

"But what do you mean, since I believe she's the scribe? She as good as admitted it. She recognized my name from my letters, her name matches the initials, and she had you hand her the notes, which are no longer on your bed, I might add."

Actually, they were. Under the pillow. The notes Anna collected were her midwifery notes. Not that Hallie would ever say so.

"Plus you'd know her in a roomful of strangers." She cringed as soon as she spat the words. Okay, that was a bit snide. But she needed to keep patching the cracks in the walls, protecting her heart or else delicious Kiah would break through and that would only hurt worse in the long-term.

Getting to know him through his letters, then meeting the real live breathing version... She sighed. If only she could tell him the truth without repercussions.

"Ouch." Kiah's face clouded. "Apparently I was wrong about that, because my heart recognized you."

"I won't mention that, either." Her voice cracked. Her heart had recognized him, too. Or at least she thought it might have. Something inside her gravitated toward him.

She never felt this strong level of attraction for Toby. Never. With Toby, she was just glad to be part of a couple. With Kiah, it was something more. Something she couldn't begin to articulate, but... well, there was a heart connection.

"*Danki*. I would like to be your friend, though. We kind of need to be friends if I'm going to marry your sister."

Hallie forced the fake smile to grow bigger. "Wow. Now you're getting married. Just like that."

"No, but that's the ultimate goal in finding the scribe. *Jah*. But…" He inhaled. Exhaled. Then shook his head. "I guess that's all I have to say. Except I have a massive headache."

She erased the fake smile because she really was concerned. Based on his letters, he tended toward migraines. "I'll get you an ice pack and a painkiller."

"I already took a pain pill. But…that's what I get for thinking you were the scribe. And kissing you. I confused myself."

"I'm sorry?" She tilted her head.

"The headache," he said.

She laughed. It felt strange. It'd been so long. "You get a headache from thinking? Does your brain…Um, do you mean you normally don't think? Your brain is that rusty? Or was it the kiss that was headache-inducing?"

"Definitely not the kiss. And around you, all I can think about is…" He grimaced as his face flamed red. "Never mind. It's a tension headache, okay? But…you laughed." Wonder filled his eyes.

Not knowing what to say, she spun away. He needed an ice pack for his head and she needed to regroup. She was so tempted to admit the truth and then she'd lose the scribe position.

Not admitting to it wasn't a lie, right? Especially if she didn't deny it. Technically, she just let him believe what he wanted to believe.

Why did that feel wrong?

His hand landed on her shoulder, and he gently tugged her to a stop. "Hallie…Why couldn't you be her?"

"Why can't you believe that I am?" Her voice caught. Oh no. Did she actually say that?

His breath hitched. "It's her I fell in love with. Through the mail."

No. It wasn't. And for one insane moment she was tempted to retrieve the notes and prove it. But what good would it do?

She didn't want a relationship. Well, she did. She didn't want the pain of a broken heart ever again.

She shimmied her shoulders to dislodge the comfortable weight of his hand. "She gets first dibs anyway."

Kiah chuckled, but it sounded uncomfortable. "She called dibs?"

Why did she say that? "You don't need to sound so surprised. You're gorgeous." Wow. Her mouth was running away with her.

He gave another chuckle, but this one was tinged with embarrassment. He cleared his throat. "So, friends?"

She gulped and turned to face him. "No." She blew out a puff of air. "No. I don't think so." Because it'd be too painful. Loving a man who was in a relationship with another... That would be coveting. And a sin.

The light in his eyes died. His lips turned down. But he gave a slight nod. "You know I'll try to change your mind."

"You won't." But, oh, she wanted him to. In so many different ways.

* * *

Kiah carried the tools through the *haus* and out the back door. *Daed* Brunstetter had Jellybean hitched up to the buggy, the trapped woodpecker squawking complaints from the fishnet that was balanced over a cardboard box.

"I fixed the hole in the attic." Kiah glanced at the bird, which rewarded him with an especially raucous noise. "If he was getting in where I think he did."

"*Danki*." Hallie's *daed* studied him. "So I suppose I could let the bird loose here."

"If you trust me."

"You're Kiah Esh? From Shipshewana?" There was more than a touch of sarcasm.

Kiah nodded. Because the man knew that. But maybe he was just now matching the name on the envelope with a real living person.

"I'm Ted. I'll give you the benefit of the doubt on your bird-proofing abilities, but as far as being alone with my daughter, the way you were, and considering the way she was, no. I don't trust you."

Wise man. But... "I'm here for the scribe. Anna. Not Hallie."

Ted opened his mouth. Shut it. Confusion clouded his gaze. "Anna, huh? Not Hallie?"

Didn't he already explain this? Multiple times? "I'm here to court the scribe. That's Anna."

"That's...Anna?" There was an undefined note in Ted's voice. His head tilted. The confusion deepened.

Confusion started to bloom in Kiah's pounding head, too. Hallie's "you believe she's the scribe" comment replayed. Second and third guesses slammed through his head, making his head pound worse. But Anna took the notes. She needed them...No. He was right. Maybe. Possibly. *Jah.* He was right.

But then again, Ted wasn't daft. And it seemed he'd know which daughter was the scribe. Maybe it was Kiah who was daft. But no. Anna as good as admitted it. She recognized his name. And she'd *definitely* asked Hallie for the notes. Notes that he had seen.

Kiah mustered what he hoped was a bright smile and changed the subject to keep from insulting Ted's intelligence or making himself look more like an idiot. "I noticed bug bombs in the shed. If I pay for them, can I use them? I need to help some-one solve an ant problem." George's house was infested with the things.

Ted's brow furrowed. "Bug bombs...Ants...You don't need to pay for them. Just take them. I'm glad to supply for a need. But does this person want your help solving his ant problem?"

"His wife asked me to." Eighteen months ago. "It'd be a random act of kindness."

Ted blinked. The furrows deepened. "What?"

It sounded more like an exclamation point than a question mark, but maybe Ted had his emphasis wrong. "You know. Don't let your right hand know what your left hand is doing? When you do something in secret?"

Ted stared at him. A hard, unyielding stare. "Sometimes, random acts of kindness aren't perceived as kind and may backfire. They might be considered random acts of malice. Think about it."

Kiah considered that. But no. Anyone would appreciate being rid of pesky tiny ants. Maybe even not so tiny cats. But he wouldn't get rid of the cats without asking. No. He'd just put them outside while he set off the bug bombs. They'd be fine. "I'll do it anonymously. And George's wife will appreciate it."

Ted shook his head, picked up the flapping, still-netted woodpecker, and walked off, muttering something about young, know-it-all whippersnappers. Whatever those were. The term sounded vaguely familiar, but either the headache clouded his thoughts or the pain pill was kicking in and still affecting his brain power. But maybe after Kiah got rid of George's ants, he'd help Ted eradicate the whippersnappers. At least they were still young.

But thinking of George made Kiah remember George's cane slapping the buggy and causing the horse to bolt. Kiah hadn't checked the buggy over for loose bolts yet. He probably should, while the buggy was out.

He unhitched Jellybean and let her out to pasture, then returned and examined the buggy. He crawled beneath it to check the underside. It was rather hard to see. He needed a flashlight and maybe a few tools. Kiah rose to his knees to hoist himself out.

"What are you doing!" Ted's voice was raised to not quite a yell. He had his emphasis wrong again.

Kiah forgot he was under the buggy and attempted to sit, whamming his already hurting head on the dusty, dirty underside. "Ouch." He collapsed back to the hard ground and rubbed his head. The pounding was worse. He'd need the other half of the pill after all.

Ted planted his feet right in Kiah's immediate view. "I'm waiting, boy."

"Jellybean had a bit of a run today, and I—"

"You raced my horse? Of all the foolish, irresponsible—"

"Accidentally. I didn't mean to, but George thumped the buggy with his cane and it scared Jelly—"

"Take responsibility for your own actions!"

"*Jah*, but—"

"But nothing. And you unhitched my horse. I was getting ready to run errands and you unhitched the horse." Ted couldn't possibly sound more annoyed, which didn't bode well for Kiah's courtship of either Hallie or Anna.

Oops. Kiah cringed. He slid out from under the buggy a different way, slowly straightening to work the kink out of his back, and looked at Ted. "I'm sorry. I didn't know you were going out. I was going to check for loose nuts and bolts. I'm sure it's fine, though. I'll rehitch the horse."

"You've done quite enough. Stay away from the horse, stay away from my daughters, and set your sights on a different scribe."

Ouch. "But—"

Movement in his peripheral caught his attention. A blur shot from the eaves. Kiah looked that way barely in time to duck as Woody the woodpecker dive-bombed him.

Woody made another pass.

Moisture seeped through Kiah's hair. He reached up and touched it. Looked at his hand. *Bird poop. Ugh.*

Ted laughed as he walked away.

And Hallie stood on the back porch, witnessing this ultimate humiliation.

* * *

Hallie watched as *Daed* strolled away from Kiah, still chuckling. Was he laughing at the woodpecker's unkind poop attack or had they shared a joke?

Kiah winced, bent to pick up his straw hat, and shot a frowning look after *Daed* before squaring his shoulders and heading her direction.

She picked up her gardening tools just to give herself something to focus on other than Kiah. She needed to pull radishes for supper anyway.

He stopped at the bottom of the steps. Her breath stalled. With his hat in his hands, he looked like an old-time suitor from days gone by. So adorably cute. Except for the frown, the confusion, the...rejection clouding his green eyes, his expression. Hallie wanted to smooth away the furrows in his brow. She tightened her grip on the bucket she held.

"What's wrong?" She shouldn't have asked, really. She glanced at *Daed* leading Jellybean back to the buggy.

Kiah turned his head to look at something over his shoulder. "Your pet woodpecker hates me."

Woody *churred* his agreement.

"I need a shower."

Hallie made a sympathetic noise and tried not to glance at Kiah's soiled head. "Water's cold."

Daed and *Daadi* climbed into the buggy. "Stay away from that young whippersnapper," *Daed* called. He flicked the reins and drove off.

Kiah sighed. "I don't think your *daed* likes me. But maybe

if I help him get rid of the whippersnappers he will. Like me, I mean. Problem is, I don't think I've ever seen a whippersnapper. I've heard of them, but I can't seem to remember what they are. Are they easily destroyed?"

Hallie blinked at him. Her lips might have twitched, although she tried not to let them.

"They are very hard to destroy. Later, if my sister isn't home by then, I'll take you out to see one."

"Will I need a weapon? To protect you with, I mean."

She walked down the steps and passed him, headed toward the garden. "Just bring your wits. You'll need them."

Especially if she kissed him.

CHAPTER 8

Kiah dipped his head and plodded into the house, through the kitchen, and up the stairs. He stopped in his temporary room, shared with an as-of-now-still-unseen and unknown brother. GHB had never mentioned brothers. Or sisters. He'd have to ask Anna about it when he saw her next. She'd also never mentioned she was a midwife apprentice.

Other than the lavender ink and scent, the initials, and a few other minor details, he really had very little family details to work with. Why had she so carefully guarded her identity?

Especially when she seemed so willing to admit it when they met.

He swallowed the other half of the pain pill, grabbed a change of clothes, and headed for the bathroom Hallie had so recently vacated. It was humid in there, a difference from the rest of the house. The air was scented of lavender. Hallie's scent. He hadn't noticed it on Anna, but he hadn't gotten very close to her. Yet.

Once he stood in the shower stall some of the bottles lined up on the shelf revealed why. Lavender-scented bodywash. Lavender-scented shampoo. He popped the top open and inhaled

the fragrance. He closed the lid and put it back, then picked up
the men's bottle of combination shampoo and bodywash. Alpine
scent. Would Hallie like that on him? Uh, not Hallie. Anna. It
didn't matter whether she liked it or not. He didn't want to smell
like lavender at church in the morning. His best friend Zeke
would never let him hear the end of it.

Oh, it would be good to see Zeke again. Kiah had missed
being a sidesitter at Zeke and Gracie's wedding because of
the unfortunate timing of a violent case of the stomach flu, or
maybe it was food poisoning, that necessitated being hospital-
ized and then sent back to the comforts of home. And when
Zeke had brought his bride to Shipshewana on their wedding
tour, Kiah had been in another part of the state, training someone's new buggy horse. *Daed* had insisted no one else would do
for that job, probably hoping to distance Kiah from Zeke and
Gracie and quizzing them about the identity of the scribe Kiah
had already developed fledgling feelings for. In fact, *Daed* had
tried to keep him from coming along on this trip by misquoting
Bible verses related to searching for things in hidden places. A
not-so-vague approach to keeping Kiah from searching for his
bride in Hidden Springs.

Daed had finally relented, convinced the scribe would be well
hidden, and if not, then *Mamm*'s prediction of the scribe being
eighty-if-a-day would be accurate and result in Kiah "giving up
this foolishness" and marrying Molly as he should.

But no, Kiah had found *her*. Hallie. The woman of his
dreams. His soul mate. And she'd been standing in this shower
in much the same condition as him just a short time before. Her
soft curves caressed by the gently falling water...

Ugh. Make that the not-exactly woman of his dreams, *Anna*...
although she hadn't been in the shower a short time before. And
she wasn't the woman of his dreams. Hallie was.

Why had his heart recognized Hallie? *Gott* must be sitting

up in Heaven laughing at the predicament Kiah found himself in. Attracted physically to one sister while imagining himself in love with the other.

Imagining?

Double ugh.

He wasn't even imagining himself in love with Anna. He was with Hallie.

He twisted the knob completely over to the hot side and turned the faucet on. Frigid water spewed forth, full stream. Kiah yelped, backed out of the spray as far as he could get, which wasn't far enough, and waited for the water to warm.

It didn't warm. In fact, it stayed melted-ice-cube cold.

"Really, *Gott*? A cold shower?" Though to be fair, Hallie had warned him. Not to mention, he probably needed one. Because all he could think about was Hallie. Kissing Hallie, specifically.

Something he shouldn't have done. But he was oh so glad he had.

Besides, he'd been so distracted and humiliated he hadn't listened much past her invitation to go hunt whippersnappers tonight. Why did something about that word seem so familiar? If it wasn't for his pounding headache, maybe he could figure out why. Seemed his *grossdaadi* mentioned them a time or two. Maybe *Daed* would remember how they got rid of them.

Kiah shivered through his shower but got his hair clean— while growling about the woodpecker. He rubbed himself dry, got dressed, and headed downstairs, planning to sit in the sunshine and warm up.

Hallie stood at the kitchen counter, a bundle of dirt-covered radishes in her left hand. With her right hand she riffled through a drawer, finally emerging with a pink paring knife. Water ran from the faucet into a pink, hospital-style, plastic sponge-bath pan that had been reutilized as a dishpan.

She was either ignoring him or hadn't heard him in his

stocking feet. He couldn't think of anything to say anyway, so he snuck past. He opened the screen door as quietly as he could and padded outside.

He didn't see any sign of anyone around except for Hallie in the kitchen. And wait. Was that two people—a man and a woman—walking across a distant field? He squinted. They both carried a bag or backpack or something. And...were they coming this way?

Something flashed in his peripheral and he turned that way in time to see Woody on a collision course with his face. He ducked and stumbled backward, right into the screen door. The handle bit into his spine, reminding him of the developing bruises on his tailbone.

The woodpecker flew off, up to a branch on a tree, where he scolded, or maybe cussed out, Kiah. Not that he understood woodpecker.

"Good grief, bird! I was trying to help you. An attic is no home for a woodpecker!" Kiah spread his arms wide, trying to make his point. Not that the bird understood human.

"Kiah?" Hallie's confused voice came from behind him.

He groped for the handle and opened the door wide enough to back through while Hallie stepped to the side. "Exit at your own risk. Woody is on the attack."

"He ignored me when I was in the garden." Did she have to sound so skeptical?

Kiah shut the door. Firmly. Then he turned to face Hallie. His gaze roved over her beautiful face. Her dark blond hair. Her expressive blue eyes. Her kissable lips. He resisted the urge to peruse her further. "He probably didn't recognize you with your hair up, your *kapp* on, and without those cute blue swim goggles." He winked.

Hallie blushed. Then she glanced out the screen. "Oh. Aaron and Joy are home."

"Aaron and Joy?" Kiah turned to see. The couple crossing the field were closer now. "Who are they?"

"My younger brother and sister. They joined a group of *youngies* for a trip to Chicago to go to a Cubs baseball game."

"Nice." Kiah was more than a little envious. "And you and Anna didn't go?"

"We had to work," Hallie said simply.

"Ah," Kiah said. But he was glad they did, because the timing of his visit to meet the scribe would've been terrible if the scribe wasn't here. And *Daed* might've refused to let him make the trip for this reason again.

But Kiah's future marital bliss depended on this visit being a success.

* * *

Hallie wanted to rush out the door, greet her siblings with "I missed you" and hugs and then sit down to hear the details of their trip. She'd hoped to go but couldn't find anyone to cover her shift at the restaurant on such short notice. The responsible thing was to go to work and enjoy the trip vicariously.

She took a step forward, but Kiah was centered in front of the screen, his hand gripping the handle, effectively blocking her exit. Unless she shoved him out of the way. And, well, that involved touching.

Touching Kiah had already proved to be highly dangerous.

Of course, she could nicely ask him to step aside.

"One brother, two sisters," Kiah muttered. "Why had Anna never mentioned them in her letters?"

Well, that was easy. Anna had never written him. She had intercepted the letters from Kiah Esh, addressed to the Hidden Springs Scribe, and always delivered them to *Mammi*. Teasing her for writing another man and cheating on *Daadi*.

Mammi never denied the accusations. Because, of course, she was the logical choice for scribe. Hallie was too self-centered because she didn't want to become a midwife and because everyone walked on eggshells around her after Toby's death. According to Anna. Besides, Hallie's role as scribe was to be kept secret. Even from her sisters.

But Hallie couldn't tell Kiah that.

She shrugged.

"What else hasn't she told me?" Kiah sounded hurt.

More than he knew. But Hallie couldn't answer that, either. Revealing her secret, even accidentally, meant the scribe position would go to someone else and she desperately needed this outlet. She enjoyed writing the fun little unique tidbits once she got past the news.

"She didn't know me, though. I can understand her needing to withhold information to preserve her identity. You can't be too careful in this day and age." Kiah brightened, as if that was the sole reason. And it sort of was. Just not for Anna. "She doesn't know I'm as safe as the day is long."

Hardly safe. Hallie barely kept from snorting.

Kiah sighed heavily. "Any more members of this family that I don't know about?"

"Gideon Brunstetter is my great-uncle."

"*Jah.* I gathered that." He turned to look at her. "He's also blind. Yet you sent me to visit him anyway."

"Not completely blind. Just legally blind. And they have voice-to-text capabilities on computers so he'd be able to speak and—"

Kiah held up his hand and pressed his fingers against Hallie's lips. "I think you protest too much." His dimples flashed.

She caught her breath, then froze, afraid to even breathe.

He glanced down. His gaze landed on her lips; then his eyes widened. He jerked his hand back as if he'd been burned.

"Sorry. I...I didn't think," he stammered, his neck turning red. "I need to be very careful not to touch you. Especially since I'm courting Anna. I mean, the scribe. I mean, I might be courting someone."

And with that hurtful reminder, he turned away, once again blocking the screen door so she couldn't go out and greet her siblings without shoving past him. She couldn't trust her voice enough to ask since tears clogged the back of her throat. Whatever she said would probably emerge in an embarrassing wail.

She'd chosen to become an old maid. And eventually live all alone. Why did it seem as if she hadn't made the best choice?

His beliefs about the scribe were her fault, too. She allowed him to believe she wasn't her. That Anna was. She'd stated quite firmly she wasn't interested in a relationship. And now she needed to step back and allow him to pursue her sister.

Move away from him. *Jah*, that would be the first thing to do. She backed up, then veered toward the refrigerator, a cold pitcher of lemonade prepared and waiting inside. A plate she'd already piled full of a mixed variety of cookies. Chocolate chip walnut. Shortbread. Oatmeal raisin. Peanut butter. She also had banana bread she could slice.

Hallie glanced at the clock. Still two hours until supper. Hopefully no appetites would be ruined.

Footfalls sounded on the porch, and Hallie tried to find a pleasant expression and not a sour woe-is-me one. She turned toward the door in time to see Kiah stick out his hand, a real grin on his handsome face. A frown flashed across Aaron's face as he took in the male stranger in the kitchen. His gaze bounced from Kiah to Hallie and back.

"Hi." Aaron's greeting sounded more like a question. Cautious. Unsure. He stopped just inside the door, stance indicating he wasn't sure whether it was fight or flight.

Jah, Hallie wasn't sure what was with his hands, either. She'd never met anyone so interested in shaking hands. Maybe it was an Indiana thing. Though Zeke didn't do it. Or it might be due to Kiah's job as a horse trainer. He probably worked with a lot of *Englischers*. That most likely explained it.

"I'm Kiah Esh. From Shipshewana."

Aaron shot a *help me out here* look toward Hallie, then awkwardly shook hands. "Nice to meet you."

"His *daed* is the guest preacher tomorrow," Hallie said.

"Oh." Neither Aaron nor Joy seemed too impressed. In fact, Aaron shrugged, *so what?* clearly visible in his expression.

Hallie set the plate of cookies on the table. "Kiah, this is my brother Aaron and my sister Joy." She turned back to fetch the lemonade from the still-open refrigerator. "Kiah is here for the weekend." *Danki, Gott.* Then life could go back to normal. Was the Esh family leaving tomorrow after services or Monday morning? Either way, the end was in sight.

"Actually, I'm hoping to stay a bit longer." Kiah moved away from the door. "I need to do some serious courting."

Hallie's heart lurched. Hopefully he wouldn't be allowed to stay longer. She wouldn't be able to bear watching him court—and fall in love with—Anna. It was hard enough knowing he'd be writing directly to Anna and not to Hallie, aka the Hidden Springs scribe. Would he notice the handwriting differences?

"And I need to get over to George's and assist with the ant problem, if I can convince him and his wife to leave for a few hours. His wife asked me to do it."

"I saw them at the bus stop." Aaron dropped his bag by the door. "They were waiting to pick someone up on the next bus. Except, they were quite a bit early." He smirked. "The next bus is scheduled for six. Two hours yet."

Kiah's eyes widened and he spun around. "Really? That's great. Can I borrow a horse?"

"I'll help you," Aaron said. "You'll need me to assist with catching the cats."

Kiah turned his head enough to meet Hallie's eyes. "Can we go now? So we're sure they're not home?"

Hallie held up her hands. "I'm not getting involved in this."

"That's okay. It'll be our good deed," Aaron said. "His wife hates those ants." He seemed a little too eager.

Kiah remembered her complaints about the ants when he was there for tornado cleanup. She even commented about having to pretend the black specks in the food were pepper and not a protein source. Kiah had promised her he'd find some way to help. But he'd returned home without doing it.

Now was his chance to keep his promise.

"I'll go get the bug bombs and harness up Hallie's horse." Kiah started for the door but he hesitated with his hand on the knob. "I need a disguise so that killer woodpecker doesn't recognize me."

"Killer woodpecker? Really?" Aaron snorted.

Joy giggled as she grabbed Aaron's bag and headed for the other room and the stairs without greeting Kiah.

Hallie picked up the platter of cookies to remove them from the table. If the men weren't going to be there...

Kiah ignored their reactions. Instead he grabbed *Mammi*'s black bonnet from the hook and tied it on his head; then he pulled on her black sweater.

"Isn't there a rule about cross-dressing?" Aaron eyed Kiah's getup.

"I'll take it off when we get away from Woody." Kiah grabbed *Daddi*'s cane and pretend-hobbled toward the door. He turned back halfway out. "See you later, sweetheart," he said in a high falsetto, then ambled onto the porch.

Sweetheart? Hallie watched him go, still holding the platter of cookies in her hands.

"Is he safe?" Aaron looked at her.

"That's highly doubtful." She set the platter back on the counter. "But the jury's still out."

* * *

Kiah was certain the woodpecker eyed him suspiciously, but it didn't attack. He hitched up the horse Hallie had driven that morning, tossed in the unopened box of bug bombs, and grabbed two pairs of work gloves to protect their hands while wrestling cats. Not all of them were friendly, if Kiah remembered right. They might be even unfriendlier when they discovered they'd be tossed out into the yard for a few hours.

Aaron came out and climbed into the buggy—in the driver's seat—so Kiah walked around and got in next to him. He tried to ignore Aaron's frequent distrustful looks. It wasn't like Kiah was an ax murderer. The boy—he might be sixteen or seventeen—didn't *have* to go with him. He chose to. Though catching uncooperative cats would go easier with two. Should be quicker, too.

Kiah read over the instructions on the bug bombs twice as they rode in silence to George's house. It appeared the place was empty, and not seeing any sign of a stowaway woodpecker in or around the buggy, Kiah tossed the cane on the floorboard and stripped off the woman's sweater and black bonnet. Uncomfortable things. Plus the bonnet worked well as blinders, making it even more uncomfortable. He left the clothes in a messy heap on the seat and followed Aaron out.

Kiah looked around the neighborhood as they approached the house. Across the street, someone's curtains moved. He ignored it.

"The door's locked," Aaron said.

"It's a weak lock. Or at least it was when I stayed with them in the fall." Kiah motioned Aaron out of the way and bumped his hip against the door. It might leave a bruise, but the lock popped open. "First thing is to collect the cats." But he didn't see any when he glanced around the dim interior. Of course, they might have run and hid. They tended to do that.

"Cats like tuna." Aaron turned on the gas-powered light and headed for the kitchen.

"George's wife wouldn't give them human tuna. She has fish-flavored wet cat food."

"Whatever. There's a cat hiding under that chair." Aaron pointed. "Grab him and toss him out."

Kiah threw a pair of work gloves toward Aaron, set the box of bug bombs on the coffee table, then got down on his hands and knees. The cat hissed, showing his claws.

"Come on, cat. I've had a hard day."

The cat seemed unimpressed. With Kiah not reaching for him, he started grooming himself.

"I'm mortal enemies with a woodpecker," Kiah explained to the cat.

If the cat cared, it showed no emotion.

Kiah reached for it again. The cat flicked his tail and left, crawling under a wooden chest.

Catching cats wasn't going to be so easy. Uncooperative creatures.

From the kitchen came the sounds of pop-tops on cat food cans being opened. And from out of nowhere cats appeared. Marching, running, slinking, or sneaking past Kiah as if they hadn't seen food in days. Weeks. Months. Of course, the last two weren't true. George's wife fed her cats better than she did people. Humans got bean soup. Twice a day. Every. Single. Day. Except Sunday. The cats got a variety.

Kiah lost count of how many cats paraded by, but he thought George and his wife had ten cats and it seemed as if three times that amount headed to the kitchen. So he straightened, ignoring the hissing cat under the cabinet, and trailed the feline train. The floor was literally covered with cats.

Aaron had already opened the back door and was tossing cats out. Hopefully the cats would stay near. Kiah hated for George and his wife to lose their pets, even if they did have too many.

Unfortunately, not all the cats were willing to leave, and it took the better part of a half hour to get most of them out. Kiah was running out of time, since the house had to be vacated two to four hours, so they tossed the open cans of cat food after the cats and Kiah breathed a prayer that any cats left inside wouldn't get sick from the bug bombs.

Kiah sent Aaron outside through the back door while he set off the three bug bombs. One in the kitchen, one in the living room, and one in the bedroom.

Then he ran outside—and found an older Amish man directly in his path, holding something that appeared to be a soccer ball, except it had flashing blue, green, and red lights.

CHAPTER 9

Hallie poured herself and Joy a glass of lemonade and sat at the table. She didn't bother with the cookies since Joy was going through a phase that eliminated all cookies from her diet. She was convinced they were bad for her. It might be true, they probably were, but since she hadn't given up pies or cakes, it didn't seem there was much point in giving up cookies. But whatever.

With Kiah and Aaron both gone, the house seemed much quieter. No one else was home, except for *Mammi* and she usually took a nap in the midafternoon.

"How was the trip?" Hallie centered her glass on a coaster, running her finger through the condensation as Joy sat across from her. She tried not to appear envious. But wow, she'd really wanted to go. She'd never been to Chicago for any reason. And Joy and Aaron went with their friends and the other *youngies* to a Major League Baseball game and to the Chicago zoo. Well, one of the two zoos she'd heard were located there. Not fair. So not fair.

Joy took a sip of her lemonade and made a face. "This is sour. It needs more sugar."

Hallie blinked at her. This from the girl who wouldn't eat cookies? She glanced at the sweating glass. "I made it from frozen—you know. Just add water?"

Joy shrugged and pushed it away. "I had a lot of diet soda this weekend. Maybe it just tastes sour compared to that."

Hallie wouldn't talk about Joy's weird eating habits. She'd grow out of them eventually. Maybe. She picked up her glass and took a sip. It did taste tart. "Tell me about the trip."

"We went to Brookfield Zoo. We had to pay to get in, but they have literally thousands of animals. We were there all day— well, from the time we arrived in Chicago until it was time to leave for the ballpark—and we barely saw one-third of the zoo. We could've spent days there."

"Did you see the polar bears or wolves or—"

"No. We didn't get all the way to the arctic animals. I wanted to see the seals perform." Joy wrinkled her nose. "Maybe next time. But we did get to ride the elephants for a little while. That was scary. They are so big."

Hopefully Hallie would be able to go next time. But this was the first time the bishop had approved the trip for the *youngies*. Depending on feedback and behavior issues, it may not happen again.

Joy pulled the glass of lemonade nearer and took another sip. She grimaced but this time didn't push it away. "I'm not really a fan of baseball. It reminds me of playing softball in school. But it did get pretty exciting, and even better...Hold on a minute." Joy bounced out of the chair and grabbed her baggy purse from where she'd dropped it on the floor.

Returning to the table, Joy dumped out the contents of her bag. Forbidden makeup: mascara, blush, and lip gloss. Hallie carried lip gloss in her purse, too. Joy shoved aside personal hygiene items and an unopened box of caramel corn Hallie barely kept from reaching for. She loved that, too. *Unfair.*

Joy grabbed a baseball that rolled toward the edge of the table. "Aaron is so jealous. I caught this fly ball. And one of the baseball players signed it." She held it out to reveal a scribbled signature Hallie couldn't begin to read. "He wants it. But it's mine, mine, mine."

Not that Joy truly cared about it, but since Aaron wanted it, it would be the cause of many scuffles and arguments. Hallie knew how that worked. And even though Aaron and Joy were fraternal twins, and close, they could still fight with the best of them.

Joy tossed the ball back into her purse and slid the rest of the scattered contents in after it. "So, that man, the preacher's son, who's here…"

Hallie's heart thudded. What could she say? She swallowed the bile that rose in her throat. "Um, he might be here to see about courting Anna."

"Anna? Is someone trying to set up an arranged marriage? Or is this more like a blind date, just to see if they suit each other?"

"I guess it's more the blind date thing." Though that didn't exactly fit. But how could she tell her seventeen-year-old sister that he was looking for the scribe and she was really the one he searched for and yes, she had kept it a secret from everyone. That would kind of sound like sour grapes—especially after Anna called dibs and he'd declared interest.

Besides, she wasn't interested.

Really.

Maybe it'd become true if she kept telling herself that.

* * *

Never in Kiah's wildest dreams had he imagined being greeted by flashing toy soccer ball lights and a yard full of neighbors, both plain and *Englisch*. Some of the women walked around collecting cats.

"Put your hands up!" one of the men shouted. He wore a short-sleeve blue button-up shirt and jeans with a ball cap and a tool belt.

Kiah eyed the hand resting on the man's belt—was he licensed to carry those tools? Then he slowly raised his work-glove-covered hands high over his head as he glanced around for Aaron. There didn't seem to be any sign of him anywhere.

Except, wait. The buggy he'd arrived in was rolling away. He didn't see anyone in it. Actually...Aaron—his partner in this random act of kindness—was hunched over in the front seat as if he was trying to hide, leaving Kiah to take the credit—or blame—alone.

Kiah lowered his arms and pointed. "My buggy—"

"Arms over your head!" The middle-aged man didn't seem to care that Kiah was being abandoned. In fact, he frowned. "Hands up! Neighborhood watch!"

Huh? The neighbors watched George's house?

Kiah raised his arms again but pointed with his raised hand. "My getaway buggy is gettin—"

"Stop talking! On the ground!"

Right. Apparently it didn't matter that his borrowed buggy— and his ride—was leaving without him.

With a sigh, Kiah lowered himself to his knees.

"Flat on your face!" the neighbor yelled. Then he turned to a younger Amish man and handed him the ball. "I always wanted to say that."

The Amish man looked as confused as Kiah felt. He tossed the flashing ball aside. "Should we call the police?" A third man approached.

Was Kiah going to be being arrested? For bombing bugs? Or was it for dumping the cats outside the house? The situation was going from bad to worse. *Daed* would never let him hear the end of this. Courting anyone would be forbidden. Kiah would likely be grounded until he was eighty. "What's going on here?" George bellowed, thumping his cane on the ground and narrowly missing Kiah's glove-covered fingers.

Oh, good. George would clear this up. Kiah pushed up.

"Get down!" The older *Englisch* man glared at him.

"I killed the ants!" Kiah shouted at the dirt. Hopefully George would hear. And he'd be eternally grateful. Kiah might even get an award.

"What's that? You killed my ants? You murderer! Murderer!" And worse, George burst into tears. Great big sobs that were as loud as he talked. "My ants!"

"You're confessing? Where's the murder weapon?" An *Englisch* man who apparently watched too many crime shows ran his hands over Kiah's body. Oh, the shame. Kiah's face burned. "He's clean."

"Inside," Kiah said. "But—" His arms were yanked painfully behind his back and toy plastic rings clamped on him. Someone tugged him to his feet, repeating a bunch of words that made no sense, and shoved him toward a pickup truck with a force that hurt his still slightly pounding head. The back door was held open by another Amish man who looked as confused as Kiah felt and Kiah was pushed in. The door slammed shut. Hopefully the police when they arrived wouldn't administer a drug test, because the pain pill Kiah took had some sort of narcotic in it. At this minute, he couldn't remember exactly what, though.

Maybe it was good that Aaron had disappeared. It would be worse if he'd gotten arrested, too.

Tears burned Kiah's eyes, but he wouldn't give in to the despair. Not yet. Somehow he'd make them understand. But how was he supposed to know that killing ants was against the law here? George's wife had begged for Kiah's help getting rid of them. Hallie's *daed* should've told him they were endangered creatures. But wait, hadn't he said something about an act of malice? Toward the ants or toward George who obviously loved the pests? Either way, it was his fault that Kiah would be arrested and would lose his chance to court and marry Hallie...um, Anna...um, someone.

Somehow he'd work around this. He could court Hallie—er, the scribe—by mail, marry her by proxy, and she could join him in his grounding...No. Wait. He'd be in jail. Maybe facing the electric chair. Okay, that was a bit dramatic, but still. A lump threatened to clog up his throat.

More neighbors arrived, and after talking to some wildly gesturing *Englisch* woman, and making a phone call, a couple Amish men entered the house.

Ted would never forgive him for involving his son in this huge misunderstanding, aka "crime." When *Daed* found out, he'd be sent home on the next bus. Either way, his future plans were doomed. Doomed.

* * *

Hallie glanced at the clock again. Supper was prepared and ready to set out, and *Mammi* waited at the table, working on finishing her knitted gift for the new baby whose birth *Mamm* and Anna were assisting. First babies sometimes took forever, so Hallie wasn't surprised they weren't home yet. However, *Daed* and *Daadi* should've been home from *Daadi*'s dentist appointment by now, and even though the buggy Aaron and Kiah had used was visible through the open doors in the barn and the horse was in the pasture, she hadn't seen either one of them. Aaron had probably called a friend or was doing his chores, but it seemed as though Kiah would've been underfoot by now. Unless he was helping Aaron. His *daed* was studying for his sermon in the morning while his *mamm* read a book and drank lemonade. They were both in the living room.

Joy was upstairs unpacking, and with nothing that urgently needed doing, Hallie told *Mammi* where she was going, slipped on her tennis shoes, and headed to the barn. Not that she missed Kiah. Really. Okay, she did. But she'd just peek in on him and not talk—make that flirt—because he planned to court her older sister. Talking should be okay because that was innocent getting to know a stranger. A friend.

Entering the barn, she breathed in the familiar scent of dust and animals. The hog grunted, the hens clucked, a calf bawled. She didn't hear any human noises, though. The big area where the buggies were kept was empty of people, so she headed down to the stalls and pens. The hand-operated water pump squeaked. It came from the cow barn. She peeked in from the top of the four steps leading down. Aaron stood at the other end of the room priming the pump. He was alone. Except for a cat she'd never seen before. Must be a stray.

"Where's Kiah?" Ugh, she shouldn't have blurted it out like that. Now Aaron would think she was interested.

Aaron glanced up as water gushed. "Um, I don't know. Best case, he's at George's. Worst, he's in jail for breaking and entering."

"What?" That came out a little loud. Breaking and entering? She frowned.

"There was a crowd of neighborhood watchers waiting when I came around the house. I sort of went around, got into the buggy, and left. I didn't do anything wrong. He's the one who broke in." Aaron looked defensive.

"You left?" Kiah was a guest, even if he was a criminal.

Aaron huffed. "I'm not going to jail for this."

"Did he rob someone?" Hallie clenched her dress in her fists. How could Aaron abandon him?

"No! We were setting off bug bombs. You know that." Aaron shook his head. "George's wife has been asking for help with their ant infestation for eons. Everyone has been afraid to step in and do it on account of upsetting George."

For good reason.

So Kiah wasn't a criminal. Hallie sagged in relief. George's door stuck. He usually didn't have it locked. "Hitch up the horse. I'm going after Kiah."

"You might need a bail bondsman." Her brother got a long-suffering tone in his voice.

"A what?" What on earth was a bail bondsman?

"Money. To bail him out of jail." Aaron turned his attention back to the pump.

Why didn't they just call it money? "I have twenty dollars."

Aaron looked at her and rolled his eyes. "Thousands."

Thousands? "You're kidding."

He shook his head.

"I'll take his *daed* with me. But he's studying for his sermon tomorrow. Maybe the bishop?"

She whirled and ran out without waiting for Aaron to answer.

Kiah. In jail.

This was bad.

For Kiah.

Very, very bad.

CHAPTER 10

Kiah slumped in the front seat of the pickup. His shoulders and upper arms hurt from being twisted behind his back at an awkward angle. At least until the plastic kids' handcuffs broke. He'd owe some kid a new toy. Not to mention his backside he'd already hurt by falling downstairs. And his head...This had been a very bad day overall. Except for meeting Hallie. Anna. He grimaced. No. Definitely Hallie. She seemed very right while something about Anna seemed off.

Tears burned his eyes, but he blinked them away. This was beyond shameful. If any of the Amish witnessing this remembered him from November, they would think that the helpful volunteer from Shipshewana had been scoping out the area for a crime spree.

The two Amish men exited the house, hands over their noses and mouths and coughing. They approached another man, this one *Englisch*, and said something Kiah couldn't hear through the buzzing in his ears mixed with George's loud wails from where he stood in the middle of the front yard. Lips twitching, the neighbor who seemed to be in charge approached the vehicle. As he opened the door, he schooled his expression, a stern mask falling over it. "Explain yourself, boy."

"I didn't know ants were endangered. I meant to do an act of kindness and help George get rid of pests. His wife had asked me to. But, uh, that went terribly wrong."

"Hmm. Ants aren't endangered. You had someone else with you?"

Oh no. He didn't want to get Aaron in trouble. "All he did was help catch the cats. There were, like, thirty of them. Or more. I lost count. Wait. Was that the crime? Catching cats?"

The man's lips did twitch. He glanced down at a cat that appeared, purring and rubbing against his leg. "No. Breaking and entering is, though."

George's wife touched the man's forearm. What was her name? Mildew? No. That couldn't be right. Mildred? Maybe.

"The door was unlocked, Ashton. It just sticks. This boy is welcome here. He fixes things."

"He's a murderer! Murderer!" George shouted to someone on the other side of the front lawn with what could only be perfect timing.

"I can fix your front door," Kiah said. Should he offer to catch ants and replace them? Perhaps a nice little ant farm would suffice instead. Especially since those ants would be confined.

"See? He fixes stuff." Mildred smiled up at her neighbor Ashton and patted his arm. "Let the boy go."

Jah, please, mister, please.

Ashton motioned with his head for Kiah to slide out. As Kiah straightened, Ashton returned to his position in front of him and looked him in the eyes. "Normally the police would be called for this, but considering this involves Amish George…" The man chuckled. "In the future, don't enter someone's house without permission."

"Yes, sir," Kiah said.

"He had permission," Mildred said. "Though, I thought he'd get to it a lot sooner than he did."

"And definitely get permission before setting off bug bombs in someone else's home." The man glanced over his shoulder at George, who was still shouting *murderer* and probably enjoying the attention way too much.

"He had permission for that, too." Mildred smiled at Kiah.

A buggy rattled to a stop on the other side of the street. Great, more gawkers. Kiah kept his focus on the neighbor man. "Yes, sir," he said again. He thought again about Ted's cautions. Had this reaction been what Hallie's *daed* had warned him about when he'd talked about random acts of malice? If so, why couldn't the man have been more straightforward? Although, Kiah probably wouldn't have believed him if he'd said that George would have a meltdown over exterminated ants. It was a good thing George wasn't aware of the previous killing spree he and Henry had gone on, stomping and squishing ants, when they'd stayed with George and Mildred after the tornado.

Movement in his peripheral vision caught his attention. He turned his head that way as Bishop Nathan and Hallie came around the front of the pickup. Hallie's eyes were red-rimmed as if she'd been crying. Oh, he hated that. He made a quick move toward her, but then stopped himself. Not only would it be frowned upon, but he was planning to court the scribe.

The bishop wore a concerned expression. His brow was furrowed, his mouth set in a frown. "Hezekiah Esh. What kind of mischief are you up to now? First you come to steal our scribe and—"

"He's a murderer!" George hobbled across the yard, leaning heavily on his cane as he approached. Loudly.

"That's pretty much it. I meant to help them out by eliminating their ant problem, but it seems to have gone horribly wrong." Kiah grimaced as he looked at George.

"Go to the ant, thou sluggard; consider her ways, and be wise: Which having no guide, overseer, or ruler, Provideth her meat in the summer, and gathereth her food in the harvest," Bishop Nathan murmured. "George's favorite verse."

"Indeed." Mildred nodded. "This boy did me a huge favor, but George does love his ants."

"How can you fix this?" The bishop's voice was quiet. He eyed Kiah.

Kiah sighed. Why should he need to fix it? It was a favor! "An ant farm would seem to be a necessity as soon as I find one. Not sure how to go about doing that."

"Mm-hmm." Bishop Nathan made a sound of approval. Or agreement. Maybe both. "It might be easier than you think." He hitched an eyebrow. "Our schoolteacher—whose name happens to be Ginny Hannah Baer and could be your GHB—has an ant farm at the school. She needs to find a home for the ants. School will be closing soon for the summer, and every one of the scholars seems to think they've studied enough about ants. They are quite tired of them."

Was that the bishop's way of saying that Anna wasn't the scribe? Or was he tossing a red herring at Kiah? Because he'd seen the notes. And the purple pen.

Mildred leaned close. "Don't tell George the scholars are tired of ants. He won't take it well."

"Well, you say? No. The cats stay out of the well," George bellowed, shoving his finger into Kiah's chest hard enough he moved back a step. "You let my cats loose." He leaned on the cane as he bent and picked up one that made figure eights around Ashton's legs. "Poor babies. You trying to murder them, too?" He glared at Kiah. "Don't you dare put them in the well."

Kiah sighed. "And here I thought vindictive woodpeckers and whippersnappers were the worst of my troubles today."

Hallie made a sound that might've been a giggle.

Kiah looked at her.

The bishop's eyebrows shot up as he swiveled his head around to stare at her. Then he glanced back at Kiah.

And he made another weird humming noise.

* * *

Hallie dipped her head to hide the heat burning her cheeks, but she peeked through her lashes at the very intriguing Kiah Esh. How could one person manage to find so much trouble in such a short amount of time? And without even trying. He was more exciting than Toby, *Gott* rest his soul.

If she dared to write about this, the readers of *The Budget* would be in stitches. It would also give her identity away…Maybe. She looked around. There were other Amish there. Lots of them. *Jah*, this would be in the next issue.

"I think we need to go somewhere and talk about this," the bishop said, glancing at the group.

This meaning Kiah? Or George? Hallie frowned. Or did the bishop mean to scold her for crying over Kiah when she stopped by to get him?

"George, I believe it takes a few hours before the fumes clear enough for you to enter your house," Bishop Nathan continued.

"A feud, you say?" George shouted. "There's a feud in my house?" He turned away from the group and took a step toward the house. "You stay out here, Mildew. I'll take care of it." He trotted off, muttering something about how worthless the neighborhood watch were for allowing a feud in a crime scene and how they should've put that yellow tape up. As if neighborhood watch had yellow crime scene tape.

The neighbor in charge shook his head, muttered something about "Amish George," and walked away.

Bishop Nathan frowned. "Did he lose his hearing aids again, Mildred?"

Mildred sighed. "No. He refuses to wear them. People are too noisy and his hearing is perfectly fine without them, thank you very much."

"And calling you mildew instead of your name?" the bishop asked gently.

"It started in November, right after the tornado. He thinks it's a pet name. Plus, he's trying to grow mildew, so I can live with my namesake, bless his heart. As if the ants, cats, and an enforced bean soup diet aren't enough." She flung out her arms and looked at Kiah. "Fix that!"

Kiah's eyes widened. "Me? How?"

And that was a good question. How, indeed. Hallie nodded in agreement.

Bishop Nathan shook his head and echoed Mildred's sigh. "I'd invite everyone to my home, but with my wife's undiagnosed freezing issues, we'd be more comfortable elsewhere." His gaze met Hallie's and his brow rose.

What? Hallie stared at him a couple of seconds before it hit. "Oh. Sure. *Jah.* Come to our house. *Daed* would insist." That last part was true. He would. And hopefully he'd be home.

"We have guests. George's brother, Herbert, and his wife, Margaret. His hearing is as bad as George's," Mildred said. She gestured toward another elderly couple standing by George's buggy holding a couple of cats and glaring at Kiah.

A few neighbors left the "crime scene."

"There's two of them?" Kiah blurted; then he coughed, his neck turning red.

Mildred patted his arm. "I know, boy. It's enough to make me go deaf in my left eye." And she winked.

Kiah chuckled and glanced at Hallie. "I like that. In fact, I'll probably use it. Deaf in my left eye."

Mildred giggled like a schoolgirl. "Be prepared for some strange looks, but consider it yours."

"What do you mean, it's poisoned? That ant murderer tried to poison me and Mildew, too?" Shouting began afresh as a few remaining gawkers apparently tried to keep George from entering the house.

"Mildred, you go round up your husband and guests and meet us at Ted Brunstetter's place." The bishop gave her a sympathy-filled look; then he turned to Kiah. "You can ride with Hallie and me. However, she brought the two-seater, so you mind your manners."

"My manners?" Kiah frowned.

But Hallie was driving and unless Kiah sat between her and the bishop . . .

Oh. He would be. The bishop wouldn't put himself into a compromising position. Which meant that Kiah's arm and leg would be pressed up against hers. She'd feel his heat, and those weird sparks . . .

Her face burned.

Her heart pounded.

Her brain would freeze. She wouldn't have one coherent thought.

And she couldn't wait.

* * *

Kiah followed Hallie and Bishop Nathan to the buggy, his thoughts in turmoil. Did the bishop intend to tell *Daed* about his good deed gone wrong? Would he get into trouble for it? He sighed. Probably he would, but what kind? A simple frown, as in now you know better, or a real, honest-to-goodness, how-could-you-be-so-stupid-and-embarrass-me-this-way type scolding? Hopefully it wouldn't be the latter. He'd die of embarrassment if he got scolded in front of Hallie. He'd already made a fool of himself way too many times. Good thing she wasn't the one he needed to woo.

Just the one he wanted to.

The bishop stopped so abruptly Kiah almost ran into him. He turned and extended his hand toward the buggy door. "You're in the middle."

"The middle?" Kiah blinked at him. Then he glanced at the buggy. "Oh. Okay." He climbed in and slid over; then as the bishop got in beside him, realization filled him. He'd be brushing against Hallie. Possibly more. He scooted closer to Hallie, and closer still, until the whole side of his body pressed against her. She caught her breath sharply. Sparks shot through him, like fireworks going off in quick succession. So, this was why Bishop Nathan told him to mind his manners. Why couldn't he have said so? Kiah expelled a breath, then focused on regulating his breathing. In. Out. In. Out.

It didn't work. He was still uncomfortably aware of her body against his. And he didn't need to look at her to know her cheeks were reddening.

Bishop Nathan's body pressed against his other side without nearly the same reaction. That just felt like a serious violation of personal space.

His arm trembled with the sudden urge to wrap it around Hallie's shoulders in a side hug. Maybe lose the bishop somewhere, pull Hallie nearer, and kiss her sweet lips, taking the time to savor, to enjoy, teasing a response from her...

Stop it! He planned to court Anna. He shouldn't think this way about Hallie.

She'd frozen in position. Not moving.

Bishop Nathan cleared his throat. "Any time now," he said dryly.

"Oh!" Hallie gasped, but she made a clicking sound, and the

horse moved forward. One step. Then her hands shook the reins slightly and the horse stopped.

Bishop Nathan muttered something about young love, which couldn't be true because Kiah was in love with the scribe. The connection he had with Hallie was just physical attraction. An attraction that was missing with Anna, but if she really was the scribe, it'd come in time. Maybe. He hoped.

Hallie let go of the reins with one hand and grabbed hold of the loose tie hanging from her *kapp*. She dipped her head and shut her eyes as if she was praying, then opened her eyes, looked up with a sigh and a firming of shoulders, and whispered, "You can do this."

Was she worried about driving? Or maybe her senses were as scrambled as his . . .

This was bad. Very, very bad. Probably all his fault for kissing her to shut her up, because . . . well, now all he could think about was her, her lips, her curv—

"Ahem." The bishop cleared his throat.

Kiah glanced at the bishop. Was there a chance the man might be able to read Kiah's mind and know the direction his thoughts were going?

Bishop Nathan's eyes twinkled.

Kiah looked back at Hallie. Would it be too much to hope she was as aware of him now? Hope? No. No. No.

But Hallie still sat there, hands shaking as they held the reins, as if it were the first time she'd had control of a buggy.

She did a little shimmy, drawing his attention down . . .

He jerked his eyes back up as the buggy lurched into motion. Hallie's teeth bit into her lower lip. He forced himself to look away. Mind his manners, indeed.

The trip to her home seemed to take forever as painfully aware of her as he was, but finally they arrived, right behind an extended-cab, bright red pickup with a broken-down buggy in the bed and hauling a horse in a trailer.

Kiah groaned. His day was about to get much worse. He really should've been firm about checking the buggy out earlier.

Hallie's *daed*'s face was almost the same color as the truck when he emerged from the back seat. He approached the buggy, finger trembling as he pointed it toward…the bishop. Probably Kiah by proxy.

"That young whippersnapper…my buggy…wheel came off…"

Those whippersnappers must be serious pests. Wait. He was missing something important. He wrinkled his forehead. George was a *young* whippersnapper?

Bishop Nathan climbed out, followed by Kiah. "Calm down, Ted. He'll fix it." He jerked his thumb toward Kiah.

Or were they saying Kiah was a whippersnapper? He gulped. That almost made sense.

A blur flew toward him.

The woodpecker?

Kiah stumbled backward, twisted around, and gently pushed Hallie back into the buggy seat; then he climbed in and shut the door.

She stared at him.

"Park in the barn. I need my disguise. And you must show me what a whippersnapper is. Tonight."

CHAPTER 11

Hallie stared at Kiah from where she half lay on the buggy seat. She struggled to sit upright, her hips still burning from Kiah's light grasp, even though grabbing her there was probably unintentional. No Amish man would deliberately handle a woman there, and definitely not an unmarried one in front of her *daed* and the bishop. She glanced out at the gawkers.

Kiah leaned across, his body pressed against hers, grabbed the reins, and made a clicking sound. The horse tugged the buggy toward the open barn door.

She pressed back against the seat and the buggy wall. Away from him. She wanted to move nearer. "Have you no boundaries?"

He looked at her. "What?" Then his eyes widened and red flooded his face. He shoved the reins her direction and scooted to the opposite side of the buggy after she took them. "Apparently not when I'm around angry woodpeckers."

She coughed to hold back a giggle at the swooping bird as she parked in the dimness of the barn. "You shouldn't have helped me."

"Apparently not. But how was I supposed to know Illinois woodpeckers are vicious and carry a grudge?"

"I would've warned you if I'd known."

He eyed her. "The way your *daed* warned me about George? That random acts of kindness could be construed as random acts of malice?"

"You should've listened."

Kiah rolled his eyes. "It's ambiguous. Besides, who could've known a grown man would have a huge meltdown over ants?"

"The poor man. Though his infestation was terrible." She shook her head.

"You think?" He opened the door and got out. "I'll unhitch the horse while you get my disguise from the buggy Aaron drove since he parked outside."

"Do you want me to take it in?" Hallie climbed out and stopped beside him. "Or are you going to wear my *mammi*'s bonnet and sweater in front of the bishop and all of our parents?"

Kiah stared at her a moment, then slumped. "I'd be in serious trouble if I did. And I'd lose the opportunity to court you. Uh, Anna. I mean the scribe."

That wouldn't be a bad thing. Anna was a serial dater whose goal was to go out with all good-looking men at least once before she decided who was the best and settled down. Anna who laughed off the string of broken hearts she left behind. But Hallie nodded and shrugged, ignoring the pangs of regret and rejection. She'd brought this on herself. "Anna has a mind of her own. She'd probably let you court her anyway."

He gazed at Hallie a moment, then looked away as his smile flickered on, then off. "Good to know. Because unless you can think of an alternative, I'll either have to run for the house and risk another attack or stay out here until nightfall. And the bishop wants to rake me over the coals, I think. For that matter, so does your *daed*. He'll be followed by mine." He sighed. "I'd ask you not to tell Anna anything that involves me, but chances are good she'll find out anyway. And it's probably not wise to keep secrets from one's possible future spouse."

"Probably not." She'd really rather not talk about him marrying Anna. The idea hurt.

"Except our kiss. That might hurt her and since it won't happen again..." His gaze dipped to her lips.

Her lips tingled in response.

He gulped and looked away quickly. "Well, at least it shouldn't happen again. So if I forget myself and try, you tell me no."

She hitched an eyebrow. What if she didn't want to tell him no? Well, she didn't want him kissing her and Anna both. Comparing them...

"What's this about you kissing my sister?" Aaron emerged from the stables and came into the buggy room, fists clenched at his sides. "You just got here for pity's sake."

Kiah groaned. "It was a massive mistake."

Oh, that hurt. But, "*Jah*, it was." She looked at Aaron. *Please, don't tell.*

Kiah frowned as if her agreement hurt him, too. "It meant nothing." He sounded a little doubtful.

"Absolutely..." Not. She wanted it to mean something.

"I think you should wear the disguise. I'll bring it in for you. I'm sure everyone will admire your bravery," Aaron said, smirking.

Hallie snorted. But wait. Was Aaron trying to get Kiah sent home in disgrace?

Kiah's brow wrinkled. He stared at Aaron for a long minute, his frown deepening before his gaze shifted to Hallie. Lingering. Softening. "I guess I'll just take my chances with the bird," he said quietly. "At least that is good for comic relief." He glanced back at Aaron.

Aaron pressed his lips together but said nothing. The glare he aimed at Kiah said plenty. Not telling Anna about the kiss must really bother him—either that, or kissing Hallie did. And even if Kiah didn't wear the disguise into the house, people would find out that he used the disguise. In fact, Aaron would probably mention the kiss, too. Either way, Kiah would get into trouble for both.

Unless she could think of some way to ease Aaron's anger at Kiah. But without knowing the particulars, it was hard to guess. Kiah might've done something at George's that upset Aaron.

"You're right…The disguise is good for comic relief," she finally said. "*Daed* and I both can explain the vindictive woodpecker. And with it being supper time, if you're covered you won't need to shower again."

Aaron muttered something about a cold shower under his breath. He turned on his heel and left. He returned a minute later and shoved the clothes into Kiah's arms; then he left again. A cat Hallie didn't recognize jumped out of a buggy and stalked across the room, tail flicking, and followed Aaron.

Kiah groaned and set the bundle of clothes on a buggy seat. "I think we accidentally kidnapped some of George's cats. And when he finds out…" He sighed. "Today has been a terrible, horrible, no good, very bad day. Except for meeting you. For the second time." His smile wobbled.

"You mean meeting Anna." Hallie tried to keep the jealousy at bay, but it still ate at her.

Kiah looked at her. "No. I meant you. I know I shouldn't, but I do." He cringed. "But that is top secret. Although I'll probably tell her. It's because I met you first. Or because I was so sure you were the scribe." He shook his head. "I was so very sure." He sounded a bit sad. Actually, a lot sad.

Hallie bit her lip to keep from blurting out the truth. Truth he wouldn't believe, especially now. Besides, what good would it do? If she confessed her identity and the bishop found out, then she'd no longer be the scribe. And even though the column was mainly news, there was still the way writing it calmed her, fed her creative outlet, gave her clarity of thought, and maybe, for a little while, took her focus off her losses and gave her a reason to get up in the morning. A need that corresponding with Kiah had met, too.

But now…he'd no longer write to her. He'd write directly to Anna. Except, when she wrote back he wouldn't recognize the handwriting. And then what?

The confession formed on the edge of her tongue again. Started to tumble off. "Ki—"

"Hold that thought." He shrugged into *Mammi*'s sweater, tied her black bonnet on, then unhitched the horse.

Outside, something snapped. Had Aaron stayed to eavesdrop? Had the bishop? Hallie glanced over Kiah's shoulder toward the open door but didn't see anything.

"I know what you were going to say, and you're right. You and your *daed* know the truth about the evil bird, and even though your *daed* may not want to admit it, he won't lie to the bishop. Or at least most people won't. It's probably better if I'm honest and up front about using a temporary disguise anyway. Maybe even about kissing you. But, well." Kiah turned to her. Glanced at her lips again. "I don't think they'd want to hear about how amazing it was, how I want to do it again, and again, and again, and, and actually tease a response from you this time. Make you forget about that other guy—"

"Kiah," Hallie croaked, her face burning. That wasn't what she was going to say at all. But…A shadow fell across the doorway.

He groaned. "You're right. I talk too much."

No. But, well, actually, *jah*.

Especially when the bishop appeared in the opening.

* * *

Kiah's tongue seemed to be on the fast track to disaster. He swallowed hard and gripped the horse's halter. Why couldn't he control anything about himself around Hallie? His thoughts, his words, his actions. Time to face facts. Everything was out of his control, including his relationships with Hallie, Anna, the rest of the Brunstetter family, not to mention his own family. Only *Gott* could fix this mess, and Kiah didn't even know if *Gott* wanted to hear from him, much less come to his aid. He probably should've taken the time to pray about the scribe instead of jumping on the "I love her and want to marry her" wagon and then rushing off willy-nilly to find her.

Okay, yeah, he was jealous of Zeke, meeting and marrying his one true love seemingly without any hassle. And Hallie had caught his heart's attention the sad day he'd first met her—at her boyfriend's visitation. He'd written the scribe, picturing Hallie in his mind's eye as the one receiving, reading, and replying to his letters. He'd spilled his heart out to her. Imagined she'd done the same with him. And everything was all burnless sunshine and thornless roses. He'd come to Hidden Springs, find her, and they'd live happily ever after. Amen.

Except, none of what he'd imagined had been truth. The sunshine burned. The rose's thorns were painful.

And the embarrassment on Hallie's beautiful face had turned to horror as she looked past him. He belatedly turned to find nothing. No one. Though it was rather frightening to imagine she'd seen something that wasn't there. He hadn't heard anything beyond his own rambling thoughts. He walked that way and peered out. The bishop was crossing the driveway, heading to the house.

Kiah's stomach clenched and threatened to hurl as he mentally replayed his last spoken words. There was no way the bishop could have misinterpreted his intent. He was already in hot water, and this seemed like the final blow to his dreams. He'd be sent home in disgrace without the love of his life.

"I'm pretty sure he heard that whole conversation," Hallie said, her voice strangled, as she appeared beside him.

"Did he? Wouldn't he have stayed to lecture us? Or…Oh no." He grasped Hallie's hand. "He's going to get our parents. I never should've taken that pain medication for my headache. It eliminated the pain, but it has something in it that kills my brain cells." He needed to somehow do the right thing by Hallie.

Hallie squeezed his fingers and released them. "Your parents will know about your migraines and how the medication affects it. Don't worry."

His eyes widened and he jerked to stare at her. "How do you know about all that?"

"I…uh, I suppose you must've mentioned it." Some of the color faded from her cheeks. She looked away.

Kiah couldn't remember mentioning it, but his thinking and his recall were foggy at best. So he might've. Or Anna might've told her, too. It felt kind of good to think that Anna might've talked about him with Hallie. Or maybe even shared his letters. Confessed her love for him. "Did Anna let you read my letters? Did she ever mention me?"

Her chest rose and fell with her deep breath. "No. She didn't. Not really. Other than when a letter arrived, she'd tell us and giv—" She clamped her lips together. "I need to get supper on." And she walked—almost ran—out the door and toward the house.

The horse snorted in his ear. Kiah startled, turned, and ran his hand over the horse's nose. He sighed. "What do you think? 'Not really' means she has mentioned me some, right?"

The horse bobbed her head. Whinnied. Maybe voiced her agreement.

Kiah grimaced, put on the disguise, then slowly guided the horse to the pasture. His stomach growled, but he wasn't in a big hurry to go to the house. Who knew what kind of hornet's nest he'd be walking into?

* * *

Hallie avoided glancing at the bishop and the other visitors as she dashed into the house. George, his wife, and their guests had arrived, and he shouted greetings at Kiah's parents. *Mammi* stuck her needles into her handwork and placed it on the hutch. *Daed* and *Daadi* washed up at the sink, having already unloaded the broken-down buggy from the pickup and the horse from the trailer. Someone had pulled the table out to its biggest size and brought in benches and chairs. Even if *Mamm* and Anna weren't home, there'd be sixteen people circled around the table that seemed crowded with ten.

Mamm hadn't exactly planned for sixteen people when she'd cooked the small roast for sandwiches. And neither had Hallie when she'd made deviled eggs and picked radishes. But they'd just have to stretch what they had.

Of course, George might not stop shouting long enough to actually eat anything and his fondness for bean soup was legendary. Hallie peeked over her shoulder as she set a loaf of bread on the counter to slice. Kiah's *daed* was making feeble attempts to answer George's onslaught of questions, but all that accomplished was a demand to speak up and a commentary on how everyone muttered.

Mildred sat at peace, a smile on her face, as if now that the bishop knew about George's many idiosyncrasies all her problems would be solved. And maybe they would be.

Bishop Nathan quietly wrote something in purple ink on a piece of paper *Mammi* must've given him when he came in.

The angry red was slowly fading from *Daed*'s expression. He offered Hallie a fleeting smile as he left the sink and headed for the table.

Joy bounced into the room, grabbed the platter of deviled eggs, and turned to carry it to the table.

Hallie returned her attention to the bread.

And then the door opened.

Gasps filled the room.

Hallie turned as Aaron came into the room. Kiah followed, wearing *Mammi*'s sweater and black bonnet. He carried *Daadi*'s cane.

And the room erupted.

"What in blue blazes," George shouted as Kiah took the bonnet off. "It's the murderer! He's a she! I mean she's a he! I mean what is it…" His voice trailed off.

"So that's where my cane went," *Daadi* whispered.

Mammi dropped the stack of plates she'd gotten out. They shattered at her feet. She'd abandoned her wheelless walker somewhere.

Kiah's *daed* half rose to his feet, then collapsed back into his seat, his face a mottled reddish-white combination. "Hezekiah James Esh!"

CHAPTER 12

Kiah hung the bonnet-slash-blinder on the hook, then tugged off the black sweater and placed it beside the evil bonnet. He braced himself, gaze down, to turn to face *Daed* and *Mamm*. Oh, he dreaded to see the expression on their faces.

Lord, help.

Okay, the prayer was a bit belated. He probably should've taken the time to pray as soon as he got out of bed that morning. But how was he supposed to know the day would turn out as it had? And him appearing to be a blathering idiot when he so wanted to make a good impression on Hallie and her family.

Being accused of murder and maybe almost getting arrested, kissing the right-but-wrong girl, being attacked by a woodpecker, making enemies right and left, and embarrassing his parents. There was probably more he could add to the list.

Should he go on the defense from the start? Or wait and see what happened first? Oh, this trying to do the adulting thing was hard.

Almost complete silence greeted him when he turned. Almost, because George was sniffling and muttering nonsense to anyone listening. Kiah peeked up. *Daed*'s mouth worked like a fish out of water, but thankfully his lecture was not verbalized. Tears filled *Mamm*'s eyes, along with a heaping helping of shame. That hurt the worst.

Or maybe the reaction of the local bishop and Hallie's *daed*, because he had just ruined his chances with Hallie—er, the scribe.

Hallie pulled a broom and dustpan from a closet. "He helped me catch a woodpecker that'd somehow gotten into the attic and now the bird is holding a grudge."

Her *daed* chuckled. "Funniest thing I ever saw. It targeted Kiah like he had a bull's-eye painted on the top of his head. Dead center. I'd be tempted to cover myself, too."

The troublesome *mammi* took the broom and dustpan from Hallie and started sweeping up the broken plates. "The boy went a bit overboard, wouldn't you say?"

"If … if that is true, then why isn't the bird targeting the girl?" *Mamm* asked, sounding a lot doubting and a little bit accusing. She pointed at Hallie.

"Um." Hallie turned an interesting shade of pink and turned away.

"She wore swim goggles and her *daed*'s old straw hat in the attic. The woodpecker probably didn't recognize her without the accessories," Kiah said. No way would he mention that her beautiful long hair was loose and tangled and begging for him to touch it. To comb it.

Hallie's *daed* gave him a grateful look. Kiah smiled. He'd done something right. *Finally.* Maybe if he got rid of the pesky young whippersnappers and fixed the buggy, then he'd be back in the man's good graces.

Mamm made a disbelieving snort and frowned. "Am I really supposed to believe that Illinois woodpeckers have such a good memory and are out for blood? I wasn't born yesterday, Hezekiah."

"Believe it or not," Hallie's *daed* said. "Apparently, this bird is dead set on living in our attic." He glanced away from *Mamm* and looked at Kiah. "But don't think this excuses you for wrecking my buggy."

"I'll fix it. Monday." Kiah met *Daed*'s eyes. Hopefully he'd agree to let him stay. A week of daily courting should be enough to win the scribe's heart. And to fall in love with her, if she was Anna.

Not to mention, out of love with Hallie. Or at least get over his massive crush on her.

"Wrecked buggy, you say?" George shouted. "I repair buggies!"

"You also break them," Kiah muttered. But no one paid him any attention.

Instead, the bishop slid a sheet of paper toward Kiah's *daed*.

"We're leaving bright and early on Monday," *Daed* said harshly, ignoring the bishop. "You've done quite enough—"

The bishop rattled the paper.

Daed looked down. There was a long silence while he read and reread whatever was scrawled in lavender. Then he looked at Bishop Nathan, his eyebrows raised. "Are you sure?"

The bishop nodded. "We all need something to do, someone to love, and something to hope for."

"He needs to get his head out of the clouds." *Daed* sighed. "He's just determined he's going to find and marry that scribe when he has a perfectly good girl waiting at home."

Except, she wasn't perfectly good and more than likely she wasn't waiting.

Hallie caught her breath.

Joy giggled. "That's silly. *Mammi* is already married."

Kiah frowned and looked at the older woman sweeping up the broken glass plates. "What?" His vocal cords threatened to strangle him.

The disturbing *mammi* met his gaze, fluttered her lashes, and winked.

Seriously? Kiah's stomach twisted into knots.

"I told you she'd be eighty if a day," *Mamm* said. Then she gasped as if realizing that could be considered offensive.

"Not quite. I'm seventy-six," Hallie's *mammi* said. "I'm just beginning my second childhood." She winked again.

"But...but Anna's the scribe," Kiah stammered. He looked at Hallie for help, but she was busy at the sink doing something and didn't look at him. His gaze slid to her sister Joy. Then Aaron. There had to be an ally here somewhere. Or maybe he could just escape back out the door—except the woodpecker was waiting there.

"Are you sure, sugar?" The unnerving *mammi* carefully shuffle-stepped around the piles of glass shards and pinched Kiah's cheek. She added more eyelash flutters and a girlish giggle.

He flinched. No. He was sure of nothing by this point.

"Scribe?" George shouted. "You don't need no scribe! Come by Monday and I'll teach you your letters. And you can help catch all my cats that haven't come home." He pounded the floor with his cane. The floor vibrated.

"And that's why I raced the horse." Kiah attempted to give Hallie's *daed* a meaningful look, then stared pointedly at the thumping cane.

"So you admit it?" Her *daed* glowered.

Apparently, the meaningful look failed. Kiah frowned. He didn't want to come out and accuse George of deliberately sabotaging the buggy. At least not now. Maybe when they were alone.

Hallie carried paper plates to the table, then took the broom that her *mammi* had abandoned and swept the glass shards into the dustpan while Joy filled glasses with lemonade.

"It's tart," she warned as she set the glasses on the table.

"It is," Hallie agreed. "I thought it was lemonade, but maybe it was limeade instead. I didn't look at it that close."

Kiah glanced at the glasses. The liquid did have a slight greenish tint. Of course, he probably did, too. Hopefully tomorrow would be a much better day. He couldn't think how he could possibly mess up more on the Lord's day. Especially since he'd be sitting for hours on backless benches, listening to preachers—including *Daed*—drone on and on about something they read in the Bible and getting lost on a thousand and one rabbit trails and maybe not reach their intended destination but fudging enough to make it appear they did.

Kiah leaned against the wall, not sure where to sit. Next to his parents? Or could he finagle a seat next to Hallie?

Hallie's *mammi* opened the refrigerator and peered inside. "Do we have any crackers?" she asked. "There's some cream cheese spread." She pulled out a shiny mixing bowl.

"That sounds good." Joy got a box of crackers out of the cupboard and arranged them on a platter as her *mammi* got out the mixing bowl.

"When did *Mamm* buy cream cheese?" Hallie asked.

"Who cares? I think we're ready to eat," Joy said.

"Feet?" George bellowed. "What about feet?"

Mildred stood, looked George in the eye, and pointed to the chair she'd been sitting in. "George, you old whippersnapper. Sit."

Kiah stiffened, staring at George. *Old whippersnapper... young whippersnapper...* Oh, shoot. He was a fool.

"Now, Mildew," George began.

Bishop Nathan cleared his throat. "Let's pray!" He shouted it loud enough even George could hear. And George plopped into the chair. Something cracked. But if it was the chair, it didn't fall apart.

Kiah scurried for an empty seat, closed his eyes, and bowed

his head for the silent prayer. Someone sat on the bench next to him. An arm brushed his. And judging by the way his pulse skittered out of control, it was Hallie.

Hallie, who planned to take him out to show him a whipper-snapper. Hallie, who claimed she knew how the pain medicines affected his head. What would she be doing, really? The Amish equivalent of a snipe hunt?

He gulped. He hated being made fun of. Hadn't enough people laughed at him today? But being made fun of, especially by her, really hurt because her opinion mattered more than it should.

He opened his eyes and peeked at her. Her hands were folded demurely on her lap, tan against the lavender material. Her scent filled his senses. The picture of innocence.

And it took all his strength to keep from reaching for her fingers, staring into her blue eyes, and demanding answers.

* * *

Hallie should've headed for a different seat, letting either Joy or *Mammi* snuggle up close to Kiah. But at seventeen, Joy was too young for Kiah, and *Mammi* was flirting way too hard, even though *Daadi* was getting a certain gleam in his eyes when he looked at her. Now, with Hallie pressed up against Kiah's side on the backless bench, she hoped Anna wouldn't come home that night, that she could sneak out with Kiah under the guise of showing him his reflection under the light of the moon in Hidden Springs—the actual springs the district was named for. And she and Kiah could flirt, talk, and maybe play in the water, and her long-dormant senses could come alive…

But that'd be dangerous and stupid, playing with fire when it was certain she'd get burned. Unless he truly realized the truth by then.

Not only that, but there was also probably an unwritten rule in the world of sisterhood about going after the same man. Especially when Anna called dibs. Honestly, Hallie didn't want the pain that came from loving and losing. Loving and leaving. Loving and... loathing. Okay, maybe that last word was a bit too strong. But she had come to sort of loath Toby after learning about his buggy racing during a tornado. The recklessness that had been a bit exciting was now a deterrent.

It also seemed as if Kiah was a bit too still. Sure, they were praying—or supposed to be—but was he even breathing?

She opened her eyes and peeked at him.

His head was turned toward her. Green eyes open. His gaze collided with hers. Locked. The pain and misery reflected in the depths rocked her to the core. He exhaled a shuddery breath as moisture pooled on his lower lashes; then he blinked and looked away. And shuddered again.

Poor man. Was the headache still that bad? Or... was he repulsed by her closeness when he was so fixated on wooing Anna?

No. That didn't fit. Not with the way he'd been pushing boundaries since they met at zero-dark-thirty that morning. It was her—Hallie, the real scribe—he wanted... and he'd said so, multiple times.

Oh, Kiah—

"Amen," Bishop Nathan boomed.

Hallie jumped to her feet. "Coffee, anyone?" She'd say her silent prayer while reaching for mugs from the cupboard. "*Mammi*, why don't you sit by Kiah, seeing as he wants to court you?"

Mammi giggled again. *Daadi* grunted, but there was a twinkle in his eye. "Flirt all you want, young man, but I'm confident in the knowledge of whose arms she'll be spending the night in."

Kiah's face reddened. He rested his hands flat on the table, but they shook. "I saw the notes," he said quietly, not looking at anyone.

The bishop frowned and looked at Hallie.

"They were on the bed upstairs," she said.

Kiah nodded. "*Jah*, and Anna came and took them. I saw them in her hands. She needed them for the birth somehow. I may have a migraine and be on pain pills, but I am not stupid."

"I'm not going to ask why you were in my daughters' room," *Daed* said darkly, staring at Kiah. "Or if it has anything to do with her hair being down and tangled."

Bishop Nathan's eyebrows shot up.

Kiah's *mamm* gasped and covered her mouth.

His *daed* turned a dangerous shade of red and stood, knocking the chair backward. "So help me, Hezekiah James Esh! I won't be shamed this way. You will marry the girl—"

Kiah's hands flexed. Balled. A muscle jumped in his jaw. But what girl was his *daed* referring to? Molly or Hallie?

Hallie caught her breath. "No. No, it has nothing to do with it. I showered after work and that woodpecker in the attic interrupted me before I got my hair secured."

"That woodpecker. Again," Kiah's *daed* scoffed.

Hallie pressed her fingers against her eyes and bit back words she wanted to say. She shouldn't back-talk a preacher even if he wasn't from their district. Even though his words were heavily laced with sarcasm and judgment. Kiah always spoke highly of his *daed* in his letters.

The bishop shook his head. "Simmer down. I believe Hallie. Ted already verified the bird's existence. No one is getting married." He looked at *Mammi*. "And you stop teasing the poor boy, Gloria. You may or may not be the scribe, but either way, you're married and should know better."

Mammi giggled again.

George pounded his fist on the table, drawing everyone's attention. "This cream cheese spread is poisoned!" he shouted. His plate, as well as his brother's, was piled full of food, and nothing had been passed to the next person. The serving dishes, significantly emptier, crowded the space around George's place. "This is why bean soup is best. Hard to ruin that," he bellowed.

"Except that is what I got food poisoning from," Kiah muttered.

His *daed* made some answering remark under his breath that Hallie couldn't hear. Then he sighed loudly. "I'm sorry. I will be having a chat with Hezekiah about his behavior. My son doesn't wear his heart on his sleeve. Nor does he censor his words. He apparently displays them everywhere."

Hallie kind of liked that about him. At least what he said about her. She might not appreciate him talking to her sister that way, though. Oh, that thought hurt.

Kiah's face flamed red. "Sorry if I've been rude." He kept his eyes downcast. "And I didn't mean to embarrass you with my behavior, *Daed.*"

His father's expression softened. "I'm sorry, too, son."

Kiah glanced up and he and his father smiled at each other. That was nice.

Hallie went around the table and picked up the mixing bowl with the cream cheese spread. She sniffed it, but all she could smell was the strong odor of male cats probably coming from George. She sneezed as she walked away. Once safely away from the stench, she ran her finger around the top edge of the bowl, collecting some of the creamy mixture, and stuck it into her mouth. It tasted sweet—honey? And a sourish-tangy—yogurt? A recipe that Anna had cut out recently for a homemade facial mask flashed through Hallie's mind. If this was it, then it also had oatmeal, hot water, and an egg white. It shouldn't be poisonous, but she didn't want to shout out that it was a homemade facial mask. She'd hate to see George's reaction to that. She returned the bowl to the refrigerator and whispered what she thought it was to Joy, who was putting George's "spread"-covered crackers into the hog pail, otherwise known as the slop bucket. Joy giggled. Hallie would tell *Mammi* what it possibly might be later. But in the meantime, she had to relieve George's worries and she didn't know how without laughing. Without him misunderstanding even more since he was hard of hearing. Without making *Mammi* look foolish for serving it in the first place.

Gott, help me...

Thinking hard, she backed away from the refrigerator and stepped in a wet spot where Joy had sloshed limeade. Her right foot twisted sideways and slid out from under her and she went down, landing hard on her rump. She tried to grab *Mammi*'s walker, but crashed into the support bar and it tipped, hitting her forehead and landing with a clatter of metal against the old tile floor. "Ow!"

Kiah was out of his seat and already kneeling beside her. "Oh, Hallie. Are you okay?" His cool hand pressed against her head where the walker hit.

"And that is why canes are safer than walkers, Mildew," George shouted. "Now let's go home, eat bean soup, and pet cats while we watch the ants..." His voice trailed off and he whimpered.

"Oh no," Kiah whispered. He shot to his feet while Hallie reached for her throbbing ankle. Was it already turning red? "George," Kiah said on an exhale; then he repeated the name much louder. "I'll replace your ants. And your cats. I'm sorry."

"Don't do us any favors," Mildred said.

"Flavors?" George asked. "Vanilla is best, I think. Two big scoops. In a cone." He sat down again.

Kiah groaned and looked at Hallie, his gaze resting on where she poked at her ankle. It was swelling. He knelt again, gently lifting her foot into his hands. Weird tingles shot through her. "I hope you have ice cream," he murmured.

She winced when he found a particularly sore spot. "We don't." She gasped as he prodded that spot. "But I'm not putting ice cream on my foot anyway. It does sound really good, though."

He chuckled. "Ice might be helpful." He glanced at someone and lifted an eyebrow.

"Go ahead," the bishop said.

And with that, he scooped her up in his arms.

She stiffened, then not knowing what else to do, looped her arm around his neck. "Don't drop me."

"Not a chance." He carried her out of the kitchen, into the living room, then carefully laid her on the spare bed that *Mamm* and *Daed* were using with his family visiting. He adjusted the pillow, took the ice pack from a wide-eyed Joy, carefully placed it on Hallie's ankle, tossed a fuzzy throw over her legs, then bent and brushed his lips across her forehead.

Tears filled her eyes as he backed away. Toby had never been so sensitive to her needs. Some kind of strange feeling washed over her. Why did Bishop Nathan have to make the scribe be secret? Kiah could've been hers.

She watched him merge into the crowd of witnesses—which didn't include George, who still hollered for ice cream—and gave in to the tears caused by a mixture of pain, embarrassment, shame, and longing.

If only he could've kissed four or five inches lower.

* * *

Kiah turned to face the gawkers and met a variety of expressions. A knowing smirk from the troublesome *Mammi*, the one who claimed he'd marry Hallie. *Jah, please.* Confusion—and maybe respect—from Hallie's *daed.* Love from his *mamm.* That warmed him. More confusion from *Daed.* Anger radiated from Aaron. Joy seemed smitten. Hallie's *daadi* beamed—at his wife. Which was as it should be. And the bishop's expression was unreadable, but the furrows in his brow seemed to indicate they'd need to have a chat. Which probably meant he would be in trouble. But what else was new? Of course, he might just be thinking hard.

Kiah's attention shifted back to Aaron. How'd he get on his bad side? They'd barely met, but he'd thought they'd bonded over the shared ant-murder, cat-freeing experience. But Aaron did overhear Kiah admit to kissing Hallie and still planning to court Anna. That might have done it.

"These deviled eggs are great!" George bellowed from the kitchen. "You should get the recipe, Mildew."

"You wouldn't let me make it," Mildred shouted back.

"Give me back that platter," George yelled. "I want more of those eggs."

Someone behind Kiah gasped.

"He won't leave anything for the rest of us," Hallie's *daadi* said. "I suggest we get back in there."

"Joy will fix you and Hallie a plate," her *mammi* said, looking at Kiah. "You stay and keep our girl company."

"And keep your hands off," Aaron growled.

"Of course." Kiah forced a smile. "No worries." He faked a British accent, which probably sounded ridiculous in Pennsylvania Dutch.

Joy giggled. "I'll fix your plates. You cozy up to Hallie and wait."

"Not too cozy," Aaron shot back as he left the room.

Right. Kiah pulled a rocking chair over and sat beside the bed. He glanced at Hallie and the tears beading on her lashes. That ankle must really hurt. "Hallie." He said her name on a sigh. "Don't cry." He barely stopped from reaching for her. And he didn't even carry a handkerchief. Massive fail as a hero.

"I don't think I'll be hiking tonight." She grimaced. She swiped her fists over her eyes.

It took him a minute. "Oh. Well, I figured out what a whipper-snapper is. A know-it-all jerk. And your *daed* was calling me one." That hurt more than a little. He'd wanted to make a good impression.

Hallie looked away. "Actually, it's a young and inexperienced person considered to be presumptuous or overconfident."

He touched her chin, turning her face back toward him, and wiped a stray tear or three from her cheeks. "Which makes me wonder what your plans were for tonight. Something naughty like skinny-dipping in the pond?" He attempted a smile. "Or a snipe hunt, where I'm left abandoned, holding the bag in the woods, feeling and looking like a fool?"

He'd listen to what she had to say, but what he really wanted was the truth. What did she think of him? How massive was his fail?

Any chance of recovery?

CHAPTER 13

Hallie's face flamed red, and she lowered her lashes to keep from seeing the pain in Kiah's eyes. Another tear escaped. She brushed at it and sniffled. She hadn't intended to make him feel bad, and now she wanted to comfort him. Taking him hiking had seemed innocent at the time—or maybe not so innocent. When she and Toby used to go off alone, they'd had more than a few stolen kisses, but Kiah was not Toby. Kiah wanted to court her sister—well, actually Hallie, but he thought the scribe was Anna. And Hallie and Kiah were relatively new acquaintances—in person—and shouldn't be kissing. Even though he had kissed her ever so briefly. Just a tantalizing touch. Enough to make her want more. It'd been ever so long since she'd been kissed.

"Well?" he asked quietly.

Hallie looked up, struggling to redirect her thoughts and find answers, but Joy chose that moment to reappear with a silver-plated serving tray holding two glasses of limeade and two plates with a selection of food. Two slices of bread with roast beef, sliced cheddar cheese, and lettuce, next to a small pile of radishes, carrot and celery sticks, and half of a deviled egg.

"There were only enough eggs left for a half each. George really liked them," Joy explained.

"*Danki* for bringing us food." Kiah stood and pulled over an end table for Joy to set the tray on. He placed the small table between the bed and the rocking chair. That should make Aaron happy, having a physical barrier between her and Kiah, but Kiah probably was considering the ease of them both reaching food and beverage when he did it. His courtesy and kindness was so sweet.

Hallie struggled to sit up. Awkward, especially since it shifted her ankle and the ice pack. She caught her breath at the rush of pain.

"You're welcome." Joy giggled. "This is so romantic."

What? Hallie lifted a shoulder and glanced at Kiah. He looked as confused as she felt. What was romantic about a painful, twisted—and possibly sprained—ankle?

Joy gave a little finger wag punctuated with another giggle and left the room.

"Well, she's appropriately named," Kiah said, looking after her.

"I guess." Hallie twisted her fingers together. "Her real name is Angel Rejoice."

Kiah startled. "There has to be a story behind that. And why was Anna named Genesis Hosanna? And how did you end up with a normal name like Henrietta?"

Well, that last question was easy. She hadn't. She took a deep breath. "Well, *Genesis* means beginning and she was my parents' first child. *Hosanna* means 'praise and adoration' so they were giving thanks to *Gott*."

Kiah smiled. "I like that. And Joy?"

"Somehow the midwife missed that *Mamm* was carrying twins. Aaron was the first—and only—boy, and then there were serious complications and *Mamm* said that *Gott* sent an angel to save her and the babies and my parents rejoiced. I don't know if it was a real angel or not, but someone did show up unexpectedly who knew exactly what to do."

He blinked. "Wow. Just wow." He picked up his glass, took a sip of limeade, and wrinkled his nose. "This *is* tart. But good." He took another sip. "So, why were they so uncreative with your name?"

Her face heated. "They weren't," she mumbled.

He set the glass down, picked up his plate, and assembled his sandwich. "Sorry, Hallie. No offense. Henrietta is a lovely name, really. Old-fashioned but lovely. However, compared to your sisters' names, it is uncreative."

The bishop never said she couldn't tell people her full name. "*Jah*, but my na—"

He waved her words away. "Back to the topic at hand. The whippersnapper thing. Was it a snipe hunt?" He took a bite of his sandwich.

"Hallelujah. And no. Probably closer to skinny-dipping in the pond." *Jah*. She was going for shock value. Especially since he waved away her important name confession. Still, her face burned.

His eyes bugged as he stopped chewing and stared at her. He set the sandwich down. Swallowed, coughed, then took a swig of limeade and coughed again. "Henrietta Brunstetter!"

"Hallelujah," she mumbled.

"What did you say?" His voice was garbled.

"Hallelujah," she repeated. Stronger. More certain. Because he needed to know that much of the truth.

"Not that. Skinny-dipping? Really?" A high-pitched squeak punctuated the words. His gaze started to dip toward her assets, and he forced it back up. Red stained his cheeks.

"Of course not really. Sheesh. What kind of girl do you think I am?" She scowled at him.

"Hey. You're the one who said it." His tone was a cross between relieved and disappointed.

"You asked, plus you mentioned it first, and I said it'd probably be closer to it. But we wouldn't be skinny-dipping and it isn't a pond."

Kiah puffed out a breath and picked up his sandwich again. "You are so frustratingly confusing."

Hallie shrugged. Her emotions were a confused tangle, too. But she didn't care to go into that. She liked Kiah, a lot. She wanted Kiah to pursue her. But she didn't want the pain that came from loving and losing. She picked up her plate and eyed her food. "I need to pray." For more than one reason. "I sort of forgot to when the bishop called for prayer."

He sighed and put his sandwich down again. "I did, too. I was too busy wondering what you were going to show me about a whippersnapper since you could have just reminded me what it was. And now I'm intrigued and still wondering. But let's pray first." He bowed his head.

Hallie silently said the Lord's Prayer from memory. Likely the same prayer Kiah said. But then she added, *Lord, I don't know what to do about Kiah. Make it clear. Better yet, remove my strong attraction to him. Especially since he plans to court Anna.*

Warm fingers closed on hers and gently squeezed. "Amen," he said, pulling away and picking up his sandwich again. "So. The whippersnapper thing. Explain yourself."

"I don't know if I can. I thought I could take you to Hidden Springs and let you see your reflection in the water by the light of the moon." She squirmed. It sounded rather juvenile out loud. "It's supposed to be a full moon tonight. And then maybe go wading." *And do a lot of kissing.* Which would be forbidden. Her cheeks burned. Good thing he couldn't read her thoughts.

"Hidden Springs? You mean there is an actual spring here?" Kiah asked.

"Well, duh. How do you think the town got its name?"

"And is it hidden?"

"Very secluded."

His eyes lit up. "I'd like to see it."

"Maybe Anna will take you."

The light in his eyes died. He made a noncommittal grunt and turned his full attention to his meal.

After another moment, she did, too. But her heart hurt. Kiah apparently felt the same connection to her that she felt to him, but with his intention to court Anna, it could— would—go nowhere. Hallie refused to be a plaything for a man pursuing another woman. Or married to another. That was a recipe for disaster. Best to cut their "friendship" off at the bud now.

Then again, Kiah would eventually learn the truth that Anna wasn't the scribe and Hallie was...

But Anna had called dibs.

She wished things were different. Wished Anna hadn't called dibs and wished her heart was ready to love again and wished that Kiah was free to pursue her.

Her appetite destroyed, Hallie forced herself to eat her food. She'd be hungry later if she didn't. She'd just finished and had set the plate down on the tray when Joy popped back into the room.

"Dessert?" Joy looked at Kiah. "We don't have ice cream, but we do have pie and cookies."

He shook his head. "No, *danki*."

"I don't want any, either." Hallie picked at a thread on the throw blanket draped over her legs.

Kiah glanced at Hallie, and with another sigh, pushed to his feet. "I'll go see if I can get started fixing your *daed*'s buggy. Or maybe help with chores. Or something." He plodded from the room, shoulders slumped.

Joy and Hallie both watched him go; then Hallie blinked at

another round of stubborn tears. Silly of her. She'd made the right choice.

Joy turned and picked up the tray. "You *had* to go sabotage that potential relationship. He made it more than plain that he likes you."

"He's planning on courting Anna." And that said it all.

Joy's mouth opened and shut. She stared at Hallie for a long silent minute.

Hallie sniffled and pretended to shift the ice pack on her ankle. Maybe Joy would believe the tears were from pain and not a fresh crack on her already broken heart.

"You *need* ice cream. Chocolate, I think. I'll mention it to *Daed*. And Kiah shouldn't be courting Anna," Joy said finally. "He only has eyes for you."

But Joy hadn't seen Kiah and Anna together.

Hallie had.

Kiah was a flirt. And Anna had turned on her answering flirt to full-blown.

* * *

Kiah trudged through the kitchen, his gaze skimming over the group still sitting at the huge wood table. Pies and cookies had been passed around and coffee poured. Conversation was at a minimum and even George was silent except for lips smacking.

Kiah stopped beside Hallie's *daed* and crouched down. "May I take a look at your buggy and see if I can fix it?" Given the circumstances, and considering that "acts of malice" remark from earlier, it probably was wise to ask permission first.

The older man frowned. "Well, now, I'm not rightly sure if I can trust you—"

Ouch. But Kiah could see why.

"Go ahead and let him, Ted," the bishop said with a hint of contemplation in his expression. "He needs to be responsible."

Not only that, but it'd also be a good way to get his mind's focus off Hallie. Maybe.

Ted's frown deepened, but he shrugged. Grunted.

Kiah decided to take that as agreement.

He was halfway to the barn before he remembered the woodpecker. And by then it was too late. The harsh churring sound came moments before the bird did a flyby, buzzing right past Kiah's ear. Thankfully, the bird either had bad aim this time or he didn't intend to connect, but Kiah did duck as he quickened his steps to the safety of the barn.

He found Ted's toolbox on the workbench in the corner of the tack room and dug through it for things he might need to replace the wheel; then he leaned the wheel nearby and started to jack the buggy up with an antique wagon jack.

"I saw the bird. We all did." Bishop Nathan's voice came unexpectedly from behind Kiah. "Except possibly George."

Kiah let go of the handle and spun around. "*Danki* for the complimentary heart attack."

Though really he had expected the bishop to search him out. He just hadn't expected him to abandon his pie to do so.

The bishop chuckled. "At least your folks believe you now."

That was a plus.

Kiah turned his attention back to the buggy and the jack. He might not know much about buggy repair, but he did know how to replace wheels and tighten bolts. "What did you need to discuss with me?" Best get this scolding or lecture—whichever it will be—out of the way.

"Why exactly are you looking for the scribe? I want the whole story."

Hadn't he gone over this at the bishop's house at noon? He

couldn't remember for sure what was said. "Well, it all started with a girl."

The bishop made a noise that might've been a snort. "All terrible stories do."

What? Kiah glanced over his shoulder at the bishop.

Bishop Nathan raised his eyebrows. "Go on."

"My girlfriend stepped out on me when I was 'chasing storms,' her words, in Illinois. Really, I was here to help with cleanup."

"I remember why you were here." The bishop knelt beside him and riffled through the toolbox as Kiah fitted the wheel back onto the buggy.

"Can you find a roller axle in there? Please. Oh, and I need a clip, too."

"Sure. When did you meet Hallie?"

"I met Hallie at her boyfriend's funeral. We didn't talk much, but I remember her. My heart connected. I imagined she was the scribe and started writing to her—the scribe—after the storm."

"Hmmm. And you still think she's the scribe?" The bishop handed him a few roller axles and a clip. "You said your heart recognized her?"

So he'd told Bishop Nathan he thought the scribe was Hallie. His face heated. "*Jah*, I honestly believed Hallie was the scribe. I wanted her to be. I connect with her somehow. But then Anna recognized my name. She took the notes I'd seen in their room when I delivered the laundry for their *mammi*. She had a purple pen." But then so did Hallie. "Anna's initials are GHB."

"Purple pens are popular in this house."

"*Jah*. Very." Kiah finished installing the old wagon wheel, which thankfully wasn't damaged. At least not that he could see.

"So are you here for Hallie or Anna?" A hardness appeared in the bishop's voice.

Kiah straightened. "I don't know." He didn't know, but he needed to be honest. He found a beat-up flashlight in the toolbox. It worked, so he took it and shimmied under the jacked-up buggy.

"Explain yourself." The hardness was still present in the bishop's tone.

"I'll try." Kiah attempted to formulate his thoughts. "Like I said, my heart connected with Hallie both then and now. But then it connected with the scribe in the letters. I came here for Anna—for the scribe—so I need to give her a chance, but I also want to keep the door wide open with Hallie. I don't want to pit them against each other, but in case Anna and I don't connect like Hallie and I do . . . Well, I'd like to keep that door open."

"That will be difficult to do. Not like you can keep them secret from each other," Bishop Nathan said. "Of course, I would discourage that if you could."

"I wouldn't think of trying. I intend to be completely honest with both of them." Kiah flashed the light over the undercarriage, but he didn't see any problems other than a loose bolt or two. Not that he'd recognize many. He tightened the bolts.

"You do realize they are sisters and you could cause problems with their relationship with each other. This has the potential of going very badly with this whole family."

"The story of my life." Kiah frowned and slid out from under the buggy. He turned the flashlight off and returned it to the tool-box. He sat cross-legged across the metal box from the bishop. "I dream big, put my heart into something, and it turns into sawdust in my hands. Like with my ex-girlfriend. I designed and built a tiny house for her because she said she wanted one when we married. But then she hated it, so I put it up for sale, but that doesn't matter. The point is, I already messed up so much here in less than twenty-four hours. I'm just tired, you know? Tired of figuring out how to get back up and keep going."

"When it seems there is nothing left, there is still hope," the bishop said.

Kiah didn't know how much hope there was. Probably not a whole lot. But he didn't want to disagree with the bishop.

He could look for the silver lining in the cloud now, he guessed. "To be even more honest, Hallie and I took a walk this morning at the park on the trail. We talked about so many different things. And she answered every question the way the scribe did. Every single one. What do you make of that?"

Bishop Nathan made a noncommittal grunt.

Kiah puffed out a breath. Okay. Looking at the bright side...

The woodpecker was still there but at least the buggy was fixed and the horse didn't seem worse for wear. Now, how could he fix things for Mildred and George? George who believed Kiah was worse than a mess-up and also illiterate. How was he supposed to fix that?

"George thinks I can't read or write." *Jah*, he was grumbling.

The bishop blinked. Kiah supposed that was a bit random.

"Always listen to the opinion of others. It might not do you any good, but it will them."

Kiah frowned. "So I need to pretend to be illiterate?" The bishop was encouraging him to lie?

"No. But you need to show up for your lesson. It might do you a world of good. And get the school's ant farm for him. Every time you break your word, you put a crack in your character."

He *had* promised to replace George's ants. Kiah glanced around and spied a cat stalking a mouse. And he'd promised to replace his cats. If either was even possible. "How many cats did George have anyway? What was the teacher's name and where is the schoolhouse?"

"Ginny Baer. But the school is closed on weekends. You'll need to go Monday on the way to George's. I'll draw you a map." Bishop Nathan puffed out a breath. "As for cats, I'm not sure George even knows how many there are. Were. I'd say too many, but he collects all the strays and unwanted litters and gives them homes, which is commendable. Of course, they procreate...But I digress."

"Commendable, *jah*, but there are still too many," Kiah said. Their house stunk.

"As for why I came out here, I need you to walk down to the corner Amish grocery. It's more of a bent-and-dent type of establishment, so you never know what they'll have. But anyway, George is demanding vanilla ice cream, and Joy said something about Hallie needing a whole pint of chocolate ice cream, but that seems a bit excessive. Anyway, I was thinking one of those cartons with three flavors, but they may not have it. Just whatever they have is fine." He pulled a crumpled ten-dollar bill from his pocket. "Here's some money to pay for it. Turn left at the mailbox and walk about an eighth of a mile. You could bike if you wanted"—he glanced at the purple girls' bike, then the bicycle built for two—"though maybe not. It's located at the mailbox that looks like someone played softball with it. Name on the box is Zook. The store is not marked, but it's located in the shed. There's a red hitching post outside the front door."

Right. Kiah had noticed that mailbox on his way to town that morning. And an eighth of a mile was nothing to an Amish man. But the bishop would buy ice cream to placate George? Or was this an attempt to get Kiah off the premises for some reason? Maybe to discuss his many shortcomings with both his parents and Hallie's *daed*? As if Kiah hadn't made those abundantly clear on his own.

"As for Anna and Hallie, I suggest you choose one or the other to focus on. Whichever one you choose will destroy any chances with the other, so take your time, pray much, and choose wisely. Love is a wonderful thing, but it gets along best when it has brains to direct it."

Kiah frowned. Was that another thinly veiled insult? But that reminded him..."The Bible says, 'He shall direct thy paths.'

How do I know when He is directing my path? It's not like He comes down from Heaven, points, and says, 'This is the way, walk ye in it.'"

Bishop Nathan surveyed him for a long, silent minute before he cleared his throat. Twice. "Actually, it says, 'Trust in the Lord with all thine heart; and lean not unto thine own understanding. In all thy ways acknowledge Him, and He shall direct thy paths.' Are you trusting *Gott* with your whole heart and acknowledging Him in all your ways?"

"Honestly, probably not."

Another long silence. Then the bishop nodded. "There you go. When you do, He will. But it won't be with a bright neon light blinking an arrow like with some road construction signs. It will be more of a still, quiet voice that you'll need to listen for."

Well. That was helpful. *Not.* Kiah rose to his feet. "I'll get the ice cream, then. Right at the mailbox?"

"No. Left. Eighth of a mile. Zooks'. Red hitching post. But before you go, help me up. I'm not as young as I used to be." The bishop extended his arm.

Kiah grasped the bishop's hand and, when he had his feet positioned, gave him a tug.

"*Danki,*" Bishop Nathan said. "One would think I'm an old man. I'm not. Only fifty-three. But my knees are giving out." He chuckled. "But then again, I'm double your age."

More than doubled by slightly less than a decade, but Kiah just gave him what probably was a sick-looking grin and a tiny nod. "I'll just go get that ice cream. Is one carton enough for everyone?"

The bishop wrinkled his nose as his brow furrowed. "Maybe two. The kind with chocolate, strawberry, and vanilla, if they have it. If not, whatever they have." He repeated himself there. "Go on now."

Kiah nodded and started the hike, thankfully without a

woodpecker tagging along. Basically, vanilla for George and chocolate for Hallie. Everyone carried those flavors, even if they didn't have the three flavors together. And if Hallie needed a pint for herself, he'd get it for her with his own money even if it was a bit excessive. Her happiness was important to him.

That probably said volumes about which sister he should pursue, but if Anna was the one he came for—though it didn't seem likely—then it seemed wrong to throw her over for her sister. Especially if the sole reason for wanting to please Hallie came from a simple desire to erase the lingering sadness in her eyes. Or that was what he sort of told himself. Sadness he understood, because he mourned for two weeks when he and his girlfriend Molly broke up. Although, truthfully, the grief might've had more to do with his best friend Zeke marrying and moving away than the breakup, especially since Molly had stepped out on him.

Whichever the case, two weeks later, he'd realized that life goes on. And he needed to move on with it. So he did. With the unattainable, aloof Hallie that he'd met at her boyfriend's funeral replacing his unfaithful girlfriend in his mind's eye, and even more so when he started writing the scribe. Befriending the scribe. Falling in love with the scribe.

The scribe was Hallie. She *had* to be.

Except maybe she wasn't.

His brain had considerable trouble accepting that. His heart flat-out refused to try.

And that also spoke volumes about which sister he should pursue.

But he told everyone he was here to find and court the scribe. And if he didn't, he'd be a liar. So he had to at least make an effort. Or at least make sure the scribe truly wasn't the flirting *mammi* inside like Joy seemed to think. Might not be a bad idea to grab on to some extra confirmation that Anna was the scribe before he got in too deep with her and burned bridges he wished to cross later. Or rather prove that Anna was not the scribe while developing his friendship with Hallie. That would mean following the bishop's advice to wait and pray while also keeping Aaron—and Hallie—happy by not playing both sisters. And somehow it might keep the door wide open with Hallie.

He stopped as he arrived at a badly dented, misshapen, beat-up mailbox. It did look like it had been used for how-to-swing-a-baseball-bat practice. The name on the box in gray stick-on letters was ZOOK. And there was a red hitching post outside the shed. A horse was tied to it. And a crooked sign on the doorknob read OPEN.

Kiah stuck his hand into his pocket to verify he still had the crumpled ten-dollar bill; then he went inside. An unmarried Amish man picked up two bags of groceries and turned toward the door. Kiah scanned the cluttered shelves and turned toward the man. "I'm looking for ice cream."

The man jerked his head toward the left. "It's in a cooler in the other room. Be warned. They have weird flavors such as bubble gum ice cream and birthday cake ice cream."

"I just need chocolate and vanilla," Kiah said, and he headed down a store aisle.

"Good luck with that," the man said. The door clanged shut behind him.

Moments later, Kiah stared down into the white cooler. There was nothing even vaguely resembling normal. He thumped a carton. "Dill pickle ice cream? Really?"

"Seventy-five percent off," a young Amish woman chirped as she walked past. Her dress was slightly darker than dill pickles.

"*Danki*, but I'll pass."

"You and everyone else." She tilted her head and surveyed Kiah. "I saw you at the restaurant. You came to see Hallie. I'm Mandy. I'm a sister of one of her best friends."

"*Jah*. Nice to meet you. I'm Kiah Esh, from Indiana. I'm here for the weekend at least, maybe a little longer." Kiah thumped the carton again. "The bishop sent me for chocolate and vanilla."

"I suggest pudding. We have sugar free." She made a slight face and pointed to a row of off-brand instant pudding.

Kiah surveyed it. "My *mamm* can make it from scratch." But it wouldn't be sugar free. Did that matter?

Mandy rolled her eyes. "Any self-respecting Amish woman can. The question is: will she want to this late on a Saturday evening?"

Oh. There was that. Kiah rubbed his chin. It felt a bit prickly. "I don't know. The bishop specifically said ice cream." He glanced at the dill pickle flavor and grimaced. "But I don't think he expected that."

"Well, since the bishop is involved..." Mandy leaned close enough he could smell something floral and lowered her voice. "We have some other kinds in the back. They won't be seventy-five percent off, though."

Kiah brightened. "Sold!"

"And you have to promise not to tell. My boss likely will fire me and I just got hired today after the restaurant fired me. The boss really wants the dill pickle ice cream gone."

"I promise. But won't he find out when I pay?"

Mandy frowned. "Maybe if you buy a carton of dill pickle ice cream, he won't mind so much."

Um, no. "Bishop Nathan asked for chocolate, vanilla, and straw—"

"We have eggnog, birthday cake, and fudge mint." She swung around to go back where she came from.

"I hope he's prepared to be disappointed. Eggnog and fudge mint are at least the right colors. And fudge mint actually sounds good."

She turned around long enough to make a gag face.

Okay. That didn't seem promising. Kiah watched her go. She was a terrible salesperson. But that aside, only he could fail at ice-cream shopping.

* * *

Hallie shifted the ice pack on her still-throbbing ankle. *Daed* would probably ask *Mamm* to look at it when she got home since a midwife was also called upon for a wide variety of medical needs. In most cases, the Amish trusted a little-trained member of their own community more than they did a highly trained *Englisch* doctor. Another reason why she hesitated to follow *Mamm* and Anna into midwifery. She didn't want to be responsible for the accidental death of someone who might've lived if they'd gone to a professional.

And Anna called her selfish.

She made a tiny snort, then turned her attention to her red, swollen ankle. Picking up the ice pack, she made a tiny, cautious flex of her foot and almost howled from the pain. Hopefully it was only a sprain and not a break.

"Hezekiah Esh." Bishop Nathan appeared beside the bed.

Hallie quickly dropped the ice pack back into position and yanked the fuzzy blanket over her legs. Neither the bishop nor Kiah should see her ankles. She flopped back against the pillow and glanced up, *expecting* to see Kiah sitting on the chair he'd abandoned. Instead, only the bishop was in the room and looming over her.

Her face heated and she directed her gaze back toward the blanket. "He's fixing the buggy, I think."

"No. He finished, and seemed to know what he was doing, though I'm not sure how well he did," the bishop said as he shrugged. "I'm not a buggy repairman. He went to the store for ice cream."

She blinked. "For George?" Since he was still yelling in the other room.

"Mostly for you."

What? She peeked back up. "I didn't ask for ice cream."

"Joy did on your behalf. A pint of chocolate, she said." He chuckled. "I sent him to Zooks' Salvage Grocery, but I cringe to think what he returns with."

Jah, Zooks' didn't have normal ice cream on a regular basis. Actually, she'd never seen any of the popular flavors there. Last time she was there they had a truckload sale of dill pickle ice cream. She giggled.

The bishop sat in the chair Kiah had abandoned. "I haven't seen you with this much life in your eyes for over a year."

Eighteen months, to be precise. Since before Toby died because he'd started to micromanage her. His will only. She'd shared that with Kiah in a letter, not using any names, of course. Kiah had advised the highway option—whatever that meant. She'd gotten the letter explaining it after Toby's death. Hallie pursed her lips and picked at the blanket. "Nothing will come of it," she mumbled.

"Don't tell me you aren't interested. We both know you are. I heard you and Kiah talking earlier in the barn. I heard that you scolded him for reckless driving." He didn't mention the kiss. "I heard that you and Kiah walked three laps on the walking trail, talking the whole time. About what, I wonder." He hitched a brow, though his eyes had a knowing look.

"Twenty questions. More actually. Almost everything we discussed in the letters. And *jah*, I answered honestly." Hallie looked away from the bishop's penetrating gaze. "I decided I don't want to ever marry. Love is too risky. Besides, Anna called dibs."

Bishop Nathan snorted. "Dibs smibs," he muttered. "Hallie, consider this," he continued in his preacher voice. "If you don't get out of the boat, you'll never walk on water. There's an old saying that goes like this: 'nothing ventured, nothing gained.' Do you know what this means?"

She tugged at a string and lifted a shoulder. She could offer a reasonable and probably correct guess based on simple logic, but she didn't want to. She also didn't want to have this conversation, especially with Kiah's parents and her *daed* right in the next room where they might overhear. Though, honestly, the talk was long overdue. She'd been rather vocal on her plans to never marry.

"It means playing it SAFE is RISKY."

Did he have to loudly emphasize those two words? That reminded her of Toby's risky ways. And her desire to be safe. Except safe was now very lonely. Hallie cringed. She needed to get the attention off of herself. And fast. "I think Kiah is risking enough for both of us."

For a blessed moment, Bishop Nathan was silent. Good. Maybe he'd end this uncomfortable discussion. "Stop lurking at the edge of life and step into the glow of the campfire."

That triggered the memory of the secret wish she'd written in her journal early that very morning. And the sun had come up today in more than one way.

Or maybe not. Hallie shifted. Would her ankle support her if she stood and tried to make a run for it?

As if reading her mind, the bishop stood. "What if He wants to bless you beyond your wildest imagination?"

"My sister has dibs," Hallie reminded him. Not that he'd listen.

"We both know better. But that aside, He who holds us in His hands has no problems. Only plans. Remember this, Hallie: Don't accuse *Gott* of ignoring your questions if you've been avoiding His answers."

And with that, the man of *Gott* strode off.

CHAPTER 14

Kiah carried the thin grocery bag with *thank you* printed on the plastic three times in red up the Brunstetters' driveway. He kind of hesitated to give the bag to Bishop Nathan, especially since the owner wouldn't let him buy the fudge mint and the eggnog ice cream without buying a carton of dill pickle ice cream as well. And then he'd ordered Mandy to wait in his office.

Kiah hoped she wouldn't get into trouble for helping him. He'd tried to explain the situation to the owner but was only given a grunt and a blank stare in acknowledgment. He wasn't sure what either meant exactly, but they seemed to indicate that his input was not welcome. So he'd shut his mouth. Still, he didn't want to be responsible for Mandy losing her job.

There was no sign of the woodpecker as Kiah climbed the back porch stairs and stepped into the kitchen. He not so proudly placed the bag beside the bishop.

"So, you returned. Any success?" Bishop Nathan peeked into the bag. His eyes bugged for a moment before he burst out laughing.

Daed's look clearly asked, *What did you do now?*

Kiah remained silent. He had nothing to say. Even a flimsy excuse seemed a waste of time. This mission had clearly been doomed from the start.

Joy glanced over her shoulder from where she stood at the sink. "Oh. Ice cream. I'll get a scoop and bowls. You got chocolate for Hallie, right?"

"Fudge mint."

Joy frowned.

"Zooks'," the bishop said.

"Okay." Joy accepted that. "It's not great, but it's edible. Sorry, Kiah. You're lucky they didn't try to sell you dill pickle ice cream. I heard they got a semitruck load, last year I think."

"I heard the same. I thought it was an exaggeration." Bishop Nathan held up a carton. "But no. They raised prices and then gave away complimentary boxes. Did they give this to you?"

"Seventy-five percent off. But they wouldn't let me buy the other two flavors without it," Kiah said.

"I'll have a talk with Jeremiah Zook tomorrow after services." Bishop Nathan set the carton down on the table. He looked at Kiah. "He's the owner of Zooks'."

"I'll try the dill pickle ice cream," Aaron said. "I've heard good things about it."

"I'll try it, too. Though I haven't heard good things." Kiah shuffled his feet and changed the subject. "Are you allowed to ride horses here?" He really wanted Hallie to take him to Hidden Springs. And if she couldn't hike . . .

"On trails. Roads have too much traffic," Aaron answered.

George rose to his feet, snagged the carton of eggnog ice cream, then returned to his seat, but didn't sit. "Vanilla. My favorite," he shouted. "Want some, Mildew? Herbert?" He turned to the old man beside him—assumedly his brother—who had yet to say a word.

"May I borrow a horse?" Kiah turned to Ted. "I promise not to race it. Hallie wanted to show me something."

"I trust Hallie," Ted said, his tone clearly indicating that between Kiah and his daughter, she was the only one he trusted. "But since she hurt her ankle, I'm not sure she can ride."

George gripped the carton of ice cream and plopped down on the chair again. It cracked again, louder, then collapsed under his weight.

Kiah sucked in a breath, hurried around the table, and started to bend over George, who let out an ear-piercing wail. "It's the murderer come to finish the job! Get him away from me!" He burst into tears. He threw the carton of ice cream at Kiah, then attempted to grab his cane.

The bishop moved it out of reach.

"Go. Just go," *Daed* hissed. "You've done enough damage."

Kiah frowned. Was *Daed* seriously blaming him for break-ing George's chair? Or worse, did he believe Kiah truly was a cold-blooded killer? George was responsible for most of the trouble Kiah had gotten into today. But then again, *Daed* didn't have the foggiest idea what had truly happened. He just saw Kiah in the middle of it all.

"Go sit with Hallie. I'll bring your ice cream." Joy appeared behind him. "Go heal her broken heart."

Kiah didn't turn, but he almost imagined the bishop's gaze pinned on him, silently saying the same thing. *Heal her broken heart.*

As if he could. Even if he could prove Anna wasn't the scribe—and it didn't seem possible she could be—*Daed* still might make him leave early Monday morning, and honestly, Kiah wanted to spend all the time he could with Hallie. She was the one who claimed his thoughts and heart.

But there was still *Daed* and the Molly issue.

Kiah sighed.

The way things were going, he'd shatter her heart more.

* * *

Hallie hated being alone in the other room, especially with company there. She was a waitress, trained to serve, and it seemed wrong to sit on the bed in the living room and let her sister and *Mammi* act as hostesses. Not to mention, doing the cleanup as well.

Though from what she heard, it did seem Joy was holding her own.

Except for the loud, unexplained crash, and George's screams, followed by wails.

Hallie tossed the mostly thawed ice pack aside, scrambled to her feet, and promptly fell back—half on the bed and half off—when her ankle threatened to give out.

This was not good.

Kiah appeared at Hallie's side, apparently from nowhere. "Are you okay? I saw you fall. Why were you trying to get up, anyway? Do you need help getting back into bed?" His hands settled on her upper arms, sending delicious sparks through her. He half lifted her, settling her back on the bed.

"I need to be in the kitchen. I heard a crash. What'd you do? Give George a shove?" She was joking.

He frowned and released her, backing away. "Of course not. A chair broke when he plopped down after grabbing the eggnog ice cream. I just happened to be the first person he saw from the floor."

Hallie's eyes widened. "Was he hurt?"

He sat in the chair on the other side of the end table that was still between them. "I don't know. I was sent away when George started worrying that I'd kill him. I wouldn't, you know. I'm not dangerous."

"Except to ants." And hearts.

Kiah sighed and twisted his hands in his lap. "There is that, I guess." He sighed again. "I asked if you were allowed to ride horseback. Aaron said you could, on trails. Are there trails leading to Hidden Springs?"

"*Jah.* That is the only way to get there. Don't worry, Anna knows the way."

"I want to go with *you.* Tonight."

Hallie stared down at her throbbing, worthless ankle. "I can't walk. Or get on a horse."

"You could wrap it. And I could carry you and lift you on the horse. I'd ride with you. You could sit in front or back."

What a choice. In the front, she'd be cocooned in his arms, in the back, he'd be in hers.

"And after dark we could stargaze," he said.

She glanced out the window at the dimming light. The setting sun painted the sky with shades of lavender, pink, and orange. She'd love to, but…"You should take Anna. Not me." Her voice broke, because oh, that hurt to say. "You'll cause serious problems with your relationship with her."

"I have no relationship with her." He looked away. "But after all the trouble that managed to find me today, my parents probably won't let me stay, so I'll be courting the scribe by mail instead—as I had been. And this way I'll at least have seen the springs."

"Courting by mail. Proposing by mail. Marrying by mail." *Jah,* she probably was more than a little snarky. "What if it's to the wrong sister?" She winced and bit her lip to stop the words and emotions from flowing out.

His eyes swung back and snagged hers, holding them captive. "If it's not you, I'm very afraid it will be. Please, go with me."

Her stomach clenched as she gazed into his minty green eyes. She'd regret this, for sure and certain, but..."*Jah. Jah*, I'll go."

* * *

Kiah readied the horse Ted said he could use while George—still clutching the unopened carton of eggnog ice cream—and his wife and guests got into George's buggy. If appearances were to be trusted, he seemed to have survived the broken chair uninjured, but Kiah suspected that Ted was more than a little glad to see them go.

In fact, he was probably passing out the celebratory headache pills to everyone remaining in the kitchen.

Which was probably also why he hadn't given Kiah the evil eye when granting him permission to go horseback riding. In fact, all he'd done was tell him which horse to take and warn him about racing. Kiah had assured him he wouldn't, especially since he was taking Hallie. And that had earned him a raised brow, heavy with warning.

Kiah didn't know what he had to be worried about.

Or maybe he did.

Because Hallie was *hot*. Honey-blond hair, blue eyes, full, plump, kissable lips, a slender, but curvy body...and something about her personality that snagged his heart and wouldn't let go. There was sort of a quiet gentleness about her. She was peaceful and calm.

Kiah would just have to ignore that minor problem of how much he wanted Hallie. It should be easy enough. She was injured, so her well-being would be first and foremost, and then the springs would take center stage. Easy breezy. Ted had absolutely nothing to worry about.

He returned inside to carry Hallie out, but found her in the kitchen, hobbling across the floor with the help of some crutches someone had found. Probably Joy, since she bounced along beside her, a big grin on her face. The exact opposite of Hallie's concentrating frown.

"This is so exciting!" Joy gushed. "Your first date with Kiah. So romantic. You be sure to steal a kiss or two now."

That earned him scowls from the adults in the room and a gasp from a red-faced Hallie, who stumbled to a halt.

Joy shoved a backpack at him. "I packed cookies, water bottles, and a blanket for stargazing."

He took the backpack, not sure what else to do. His face burned like fire. "This isn't a date," he mumbled.

"Of course it is, sugar." Hallie's *mammi* patted his arm. "I already told you you're the one who's going to marry our Hallie."

Mamm gasped and *Daed* muttered something under his breath. Kiah's face burned hotter.

"Maybe this isn't such a good idea." Hallie moved both crutches backward a step.

Kiah agreed. Sneaking out under the cover of darkness while the rest of the family slept was a much better idea.

"No! You go." The *mammi* grabbed Hallie's hand, then Kiah's, and placed them together with a squeeze. "Have fun." She propelled them toward the door. Slowly, because Hallie limped. And resisted. Somewhat. Not real convincingly. Although it probably was hard to hold hands and use crutches at the same time. But he didn't want to let go.

"But not too much fun," Ted growled.

"Don't stay out too late," *Mamm* said. "Church tomorrow."

Kiah didn't answer because he was too busy enjoying the feel of Hallie's hand in his. And thinking about boosting her up on the horse, his hands on inappropriate places out of necessity. Then her arms wrapping around his waist, the crutches accidentally-on-purpose left behind...

Of course, in real life, her good ankle was on the leg she lifted into the stirrup to swing herself over, so she only needed minimal help. Though that was good because they still had an audience. Her crutches were handed to Joy, the backpack slung on Hallie's back, then Kiah climbed on and settled into Hallie's rather stiff and very loose embrace. She held herself away from him, her hands splayed at his waist.

That was still enough to fry his brain cells. "Which way?" he croaked.

She pointed. "Behind the barn. There's a trail—"

Whatever else she might've said got lost when his brain went on auto-repeat.

Behind the barn. Where couples went to kiss and chaperones turned their backs.

Behind the barn. What went on there, stayed there...

Behind. The. Barn.

CHAPTER 15

The movements of Licorice walking down the rough and rutted trail jarred Hallie's ankle even though she'd wrapped it. Tears burned her eyes, and she wanted to pull her leg up close to her, curl into the fetal position, and howl. That wasn't possible on the rump of a horse. But the spring water was cold, and maybe sticking her foot into it would help to numb the pain. Not to mention, getting off this horse and to the water with the crutches left back at home with Joy meant Kiah would have to carry her. And that just might make the pain worth it.

She just had to survive long enough to get there.

Although it might be a wasted trip, because clouds now covered the moon and not a star was in sight.

She must've whimpered or something because Kiah glanced over his shoulder. "Everything okay back there?" His voice was tight.

"Fine, *jah*. Just great." She forced the words past the wail that hovered in her throat ready to burst free at the slightest provocation.

He either didn't hear the pain in her voice or chose to ignore it.

He shifted, settling back against her chest. Of their own accord, her arms slipped around his waist and held on. He expelled a soft breath of contentment.

Licorice seemed to take it as an invitation to go faster. Hallie tightened her legs on the horse and her grip on Kiah's waist. He snuggled closer.

Warmth filled her, waking every nerve ending in her body. The pain in her ankle faded to almost nothing. This, this was wonderful. And unlike anything she'd ever felt before with Toby. Maybe the sun truly was coming up inside while it was starting to set outside. She started to wish...but no, Anna called dibs. But Hallie saw him first. Hallie had written to him for eighteen months. And Hallie loved him.

Too soon, they arrived at the springs. The sound of running water filled the air. Darkness had mostly fallen; a singing group of frogs practiced their vocals with crickets providing backup music. No other humans were there to disrupt the concert.

Without a word, Kiah slid down. "Stay put a minute." He tethered the horse, then took the backpack Hallie shrugged off her shoulders, opened it, and removed the blanket. He set the bag on the ground. "Let me find some place to put this," he said, his voice taking on a huskiness that made her shiver.

She pointed a shaky finger. "By the springs. It's flat and not so rocky."

"I'll be right back." He walked several yards forward, then stopped. "Here?"

"*Jah*. I guess." It was kind of hard to tell from where she sat and with the almost nonexistent light.

Kiah shook out the blanket, laid it smooth, then returned to where Hallie waited on the horse. He reached up. "Slide down into my arms. I'll catch you."

That would be dangerous. But unless Hallie wanted to stay on the horse, she really had no other option.

She drew in a shaky breath, leaned over, looped her arms around his neck, and slid off Licorice.

Kiah's hands grasped Hallie's waist and he lifted her down. His hands trembled against her. For a long second, she hovered there, gazing into his eyes. He glanced at her lips, then up, a question forming with the raising of his brows.

Her lips tingled.

If he were Toby, she would've snuggled near and let the kissing commence.

He wasn't Toby.

He was very nearly a stranger. Her best friend via mail these days, but still a stranger. And not only that, but she wasn't looking for a relationship. Well, maybe truthfully she was. With Kiah.

She released her choke hold on him, placed her hands on his shoulders, and pushed.

Disappointment clouded his gaze.

But he gently set her feet on the ground and stepped away.

It took all her strength not to pull him back. Especially when she was about to collapse with the new pain shooting up her leg and she couldn't walk...and the distance between them wasn't masking the pain unlike the snuggling during the ride.

* * *

Kiah probably should've brought the crutches along instead of deliberately leaving them behind, because without them Hallie wouldn't be able to walk. She balanced on one foot now, the injured one slightly raised, as if she planned to hop around.

She'd risk injuring herself worse.

He dared to step closer. "Do you want...I mean, should I...um...It might be easier if you put your arm around my waist. I can support you." Although he was a bit worried about getting too close to her after that ride together. He needed some distance to shore up his internal defenses, but she needed help and he couldn't bear to cause her more pain.

"I'm not looking for romance, Kiah." Her voice lacked conviction.

His brow furrowed. The correct answer was that he wasn't, either. That he was courting the scribe. But he *wanted* Hallie. She was the one who didn't want him. Well, maybe she did, but her words and actions were conflicting. However, a little evidence suggested her sister was the scribe, and he owed it to Anna to give their relationship an honest try even if he wasn't attracted to her. Wait. No. He owed it to Anna to be truthful. He chose Hallie.

"I said I wanted to be your friend." He *had* said that, hadn't he? Closer than friends would be more accurate. "I'm just offering to help you walk, not asking you to go skinny-dipping. The bishop and our parents would all frown on that." He was trying to be funny.

Anger flashed across her face, but he didn't know why. Women were so confusing.

She stared at him a long minute, her gaze narrowing; then she lunged toward him. Whether on purpose or by accident, he didn't know. She fell against him, and he released a quiet *oof* as her nearness forced air from his lungs. The scent of lavender filled the air. Her softness pressed against him as she wrapped her arm around his waist and slid—slid!—to his side. His nerve endings incinerated. "Glory! Have mercy." It was a prayer, a plea for divine help, and definitely a lot louder than he intended.

She froze, her body pressed against his side, then burst into tears.

* * *

It was unintentional. It was all unintentional.

Hallie hadn't intended to fall against him, just to hop closer. But she'd lost her balance on the uneven ground and put her injured foot down to keep from falling. It gave out under her weight, and she collapsed against Kiah. Then she was afraid to let go, so she slid to his side, not even considering what he must think and feel. And he cried out her given name. *Glory!* But he didn't know it. It was like they had some supernatural connection. And oh, that hurt! Because he planned on courting Anna, not putting the effort into wooing Hallie and trying to change her mind. Not that he could—it was already changed—but it would be oh so wonderful if he at least tried.

"Hallie," he said, his voice strangled. "Is it your ankle?"

Without waiting for an answer, he scooped her into his arms and carried her to the blanket.

She clung. Unashamedly. Tears dripping off her chin because the pain in her heart rivaled that in her leg. But if she was going to feel the pain of a life without Kiah in it, she might as well know exactly what she would be missing.

He lowered her to a sitting position on the blanket and knelt beside her. "Please, don't cry." He brushed at her tears with his thumbs. "I shouldn't have asked you to come with me. I'm sorry I was so selfish. I should've thought about how much pain you'd be in." He leaned in and gently kissed her forehead. "Tell me how I can make this better."

Was she forever doomed to forehead kisses and brief lip brushes with this man? She was so over this.

Besides, he was about to be used by Anna. He'd slink home, like a dog with his tail between his legs, never to return to Hidden Springs again. This was her one chance.

"Should I carry you closer to the water so you can soak your foot?" He started to push up.

"No. Not yet." She rested the palms of both hands against his cheeks.

His eyes widened. "Hallie—" Her name ended on a groan. "Are you sure?"

She nodded. "*Jah*. Very sure." She'd figure it out later. She only knew that if this moment slipped by, she'd regret it forever.

And then his lips were on hers and all thoughts evaporated.

CHAPTER 16

In his wildest dreams, Kiah might've imagined this, but reality was so much better. She—his beloved Hallie—clung to him, exchanging kiss for kiss, and raising the temperatures from the tepid just-trying-this-out beginning to the current boiling hot, can't-get-enough fever pitch. Somehow they maneuvered from the sitting up, clumsy sort of kisses, to lying on their sides on the blanket, bodies pressed against each other. Her fingers feathered through his hair, and his itched to touch hers the same way.

She made some sort of whimpering sound that triggered his answering groan. He tugged at her *kapp*, but it caught, giving him a much-needed pause. He broke the kiss to try and figure it out, but they lay there, breathing heavily. Her fingers toyed with the buttons on his shirt, smoothed her hands over the rough material. They closed around his suspenders and clutched them.

"Kiah. Oh, Kiah." Her voice was filled with desire. Maybe he imagined the need, the want. Maybe not. The world was spinning, and he was fairly positive he wouldn't make intelligent sense if he tried to talk.

It was time to stop. Or to cross the point of no return.

They'd regret that, and it was his responsibility to put on the brakes if she wouldn't.

"*Ich liebe dich,*" he whispered in her ear, even though it was way too early for words of love. Even though they were true. But there was still the issue of telling Anna he wasn't interested, and a man's word should mean something. He'd have to break his word in the letters and what he told people in town, as well as her family, about courting the scribe…or he'd have to deny his feelings for Hallie. Either way he'd be a liar.

Unless his dearest wish came true and Hallie and the scribe were the same person after all.

If only it were true. What he should've said was he came to meet the scribe. Mission accomplished. Carry on with courting Hallie.

His heart ached. But then again, she got all his questions right. And they bonded.

Hallie simply had to be the scribe.

She was. He was convinced of it. "I love you." He pressed a kiss against her neck.

She stiffened and shoved against him, rolling away. "Guys will say anything to get what they want."

True, but wait. "No. No, it's not like that."

She snorted.

"And how do you know?" Fear coursed through him. "Did some guy…or what was his name. Toby. The furniture maker's son. Did he…?" *Oh, dear* Gott. *No. Please, no.*

"*Daed* told me and Anna. Joy, too. Warned us about guys like you."

Ouch. But her *daed*. That was good.

"I'm not that guy." There might've been a shade too much desperation in his voice.

"But you are." She sat up. "You said you're here for Anna."

"Not Anna, the scribe. But I—"

"You'll tell her the same thing. You only kissed me because I asked you to. And then you thought I was easy." Her voice cracked.

What? "No!" He was the one who stopped it, for pity's sake.

She slashed the air with her hand. "I'm going to soak my foot."

At least she wasn't demanding to be taken home yet. That meant he had a chance to redeem himself. Right?

Except he didn't have a clue how.

* * *

With a strength born of anger, Hallie hoisted herself to her feet, ignoring Kiah's feeble offer of help, and hobbled to the springs. She sank down on the edge of the rock where the water bubbled up from underground, forming a small pool that broke into a brook and, if followed far enough, joined with a river. She wouldn't be doing any hiking tonight, obviously. Not even to show Kiah her favorite place. That might give Kiah too much power over her heart and she couldn't risk that.

After unwrapping her foot, she eased it down into the cold water. Then gasped at the shock of it. The water was seriously cold and after that heated kissing, she almost expected to see steam rising. She forced herself to keep her foot submerged.

Kiah paced behind her, muttering under his breath. Probably arguing, correctly, that she was the one who initiated it. He was the one who broke it off. She was overreacting to his declaration of love. Also true. But...love? Really?

Okay. Love.

But she was still upset. At herself if she was honest.

Okay, she might've fallen in love with her pen pal, too. But back when he was only a name, he was safe. While she'd had a name, she didn't have a face to go with it. She never connected the name Kiah with the man she met at Toby's funeral.

It should've been an easy enough thing to avoid Kiah Esh when she heard he was in town. But no. He arrived at her house under the cover of darkness and with his parents, who were simply referred to as the visiting preacher and his wife.

But he'd imagined *her* at the other end of his letters. *Her!* A woman wandering in a fog of grief the day they'd met over a year ago. He'd remembered her name.

He'd. Remembered. Her. Name.

That was enough to make her cry. Enough to feel oh-so-loved. That she was important to someone. Maybe even to *Gott*. Although maybe that was pushing it. She prayed but was fairly positive *Gott* had stopped listening to her a long time ago.

Bishop Nathan's words replayed. *Don't accuse* Gott *of ignoring your questions if you've been avoiding His answers.*

How did the bishop know these things?

But that wasn't the point.

She shook her head, trying to get her thoughts back on track.

It was commendable that Kiah wanted to honor his imagined commitment to the scribe even though what he believed was false. He didn't know.

Hallie couldn't tell. But she wanted to. She yearned to have his full pursuit and attention.

His strength of character was amazing.

She attempted a sigh, but it sounded more like a whimper.

Kiah immediately appeared next to her. He reached, as if he intended to touch her, but yanked his arm back to his side. "Hallie, I'm so very sorry. I know, I'm a mess—"

"A hot mess," she whispered.

He gave a sharp intake of air, but otherwise remained silent.

She leaned over and bumped his shoulder with hers. "Just kidding. I'm sorry, too. I might have overreacted."

Another long stretch of silence, but this time she didn't attempt to break it. She didn't know what to say.

Finally, he said, "I should've let your no be no."

"I said I was sure." She glanced at him.

He said nothing, but she imagined him thinking, *You clearly weren't.*

The clouds parted and the moon shone. Stars popped out in abundance.

Kiah looked around at the night lights and their reflections in the water. "This is amazing." He caught his breath. "And you'll show me a whippersnapper? Even though I know what it is now." He chuckled.

"Look and see." She pulled her foot from the water, leaving ripples.

He stood and looked down at the springs. From where she sat, she noticed a somewhat distorted reflection of him appear. But then she'd disturbed the water when she pulled her foot out.

"Wow. I'd like to see this in the daylight."

"I don't know why, but it's not as magical during the day." She refrained from suggesting that Anna might bring him. Instead, Hallie held out her hand. "Can you help me back to the blanket?"

"It'd be an honor." He crouched and scooped her into his arms.

She sucked in a gasp and resisted the urge to snuggle in his arms.

Seconds later, he deposited her gently on the blanket. But this time he didn't kiss her on the forehead.

Hallie missed it. But he was probably wise. She grasped the long flesh-colored bandage and leaned forward to rewrap her foot, but hesitated. Maybe it'd be better to wait until her foot was dry to rewrap it. She lay back on the soft blanket. "You want to stargaze?"

He stared down at her, his pale green eyes glittering in the dim light, hesitated a moment, then sat beside her. "Sure.

For a little while." But even though he laid down, he kept his distance. More than enough space for someone to lie between them.

She hated that it was her fault that he was being so cautious. Her fault he was so quiet. Her fault. All her fault.

What had the bishop said? Something about leaving the shadows and stepping into the light of the campfire? She couldn't remember his exact words. Maybe she should've listened better. Or asked for pen and paper to write it down. But that would've drawn out the uncomfortable conversation, and she'd wanted it to end. He'd still given her plenty to think about.

She rolled over to face him. "I'm sorry. For so many things."

He didn't look at her, instead keeping his sight fixed on the stars above. "Bishop Nathan told me to choose between you and Anna. Now."

And with Hallie's immature behavior, he was picking Anna. He didn't need to spell it out.

Pick me. Please, pick me.

She fought the burn in her eyes as she rolled away. The heavens were blurry through the moisture beading on her lashes.

"If she's the scribe, she's the one I imagined that I fell in love with. But if that's the case, why does my heart recognize you?" There was something husky in his tone. Maybe even heartbreak. "But…I choose you." The words were whispered.

Why did her heart long for him when she'd sworn off love? There were no words.

And since she wanted to roll into his arms and resume their earlier activities, there were no actions, either.

* * *

It was Kiah's first time stargazing with a girl. Well, the first time the stars actually factored in. Because he had stopped the horse and buggy in Shipshewana with his ex-girlfriend-slash-brief-fiancée under the guise of admiring the night sky, but really it was for other extracurricular activities. Not that they'd ever anticipated their wedding vows, but they had gone further than they should have.

Whereas, he and Hallie lay flat on their backs, staring up at the night sky, not touching and no longer talking. And it was nice. Although, if given his druthers, Hallie would be back in his arms, their breathing heavy as they communicated horizontally.

And he was a preacher's son. There was something shameful in even admitting his thoughts to himself. He needed to ask *Gott*'s forgiveness, probably. Both for his thoughts and actions.

Gott, forgive me for my thoughts and actions. But regarding Hallie, give me a sign. Give me peace…

He must've dozed off, because he awoke to Hallie shaking his arm and pointing at a kaleidoscope of colors shooting across the sky. The bright lights danced and played, a beautiful display of *Gott*'s handiwork.

"What's happening?" Fear filled her voice.

He sat and held out his arm, reaching for her. She burrowed against his side. "The northern lights," he said. "We see them occasionally in northern Indiana. Aren't they beautiful?"

"Northern lights," she said with a puff that might've been a disguised sigh of relief. "I'm not going to say what I thought was happening."

He chuckled. "The world was coming to an end? Or maybe that Jesus was coming again in a blaze of glory? That's what I thought the first time I saw them."

She bobbed her head. "They're safe?"

He hesitated. "*Jah*, as far as I know." He started to shift away from her. "We should get back to your house. It's late." Probably, but he didn't know what time it was. Whatever the case, he didn't want her to get into trouble.

"I need to wrap my foot, and since I've never seen these before, I'd like to wait a bit. Do you mind?"

"That's fine." He lay back and held out his arm. "Enjoy the show."

She snuggled against him.

Kiah smiled, glad she was back to normal. His mind was made up. He wanted Hallie. Not Anna. Not some unknown scribe. Hallie. He brushed a kiss against her cheek.

And he closed his eyes to simply enjoy the moment and dream of their future.

He was still smiling when a bright light shocked him awake and blinded him.

CHAPTER 17

"Turn off the flashlight, Anna." Hallie flung her arm across her eyes as she squeezed them shut and rolled to bury her face in the pillow. A softness she couldn't find. Instead, her cheek rested against one very hard chest. *What?* Where was she? She smoothed her hand over the plains of solid hardness. The scent of pines filled her senses. *Pines?*

"Hallie, wake up." A rough, sleep-husky male voice filled with urgency.

Not Anna. *Male?*

Mercifully, one of the flashlights flicked off. The other two aimed away from her.

Wait. *Two?*

And she was wide awake. And lost. Confused. Why was she in the woods? Who was she with…? *Kiah.* His name burst into her thoughts like sunshine after the rain. She rolled away from the suddenly sexy chest and sat. "Oops. We've been bad."

Kiah coughed. Choked, really. Followed by a trio of shocked gasps.

And then it registered that the men standing over them were their fathers and her brother.

And she'd just accidentally implied that she and Kiah had done a lot more than heavy kissing. Her face burned.

"We were stargazing," Kiah said quietly, although he sounded rather strangled. He stood, separating them more. As if he was ashamed to be associated with her.

She was ashamed to be associated with herself. She wrapped her arms around her middle, wishing she could pull the blanket over her head and disappear.

"And fell asleep." *Daed* nodded as if it was a perfectly normal thing to do. As if his mind hadn't automatically gone where hers had. Or maybe he was trying to deflect the direction this scene might go. "Of course. I did that when I was courting my wife. I'm sure you did, too." He turned to Kiah's *daed*.

"Is that the Amish equivalent of the car refusing to start or getting stuck in the mud that the *Englisch* use as an excuse?" Kiah's *daed* almost sounded like he was joking, but he admitted to nothing. He didn't need to. His mouth was set in a deep scowl—but also a truth-telling mottled red blush.

Aaron's stiff stance indicated he didn't believe Kiah for a second. Though come to think of it, he might've snuck out to chaperone them. But if he had, he would've interrupted their passionate kisses instead of waiting until they fell asleep. So maybe not.

"So are you still looking for the scribe or are you courting Ted's Hallie?" Kiah's *daed* tilted his head and looked between Kiah and Hallie. There was a hint of something in his voice. A knowing sound that confused Hallie. There might've been a hint of condemnation mixed in.

If only the last part of his statement were true. "No," Hallie said. She untangled her arms from her knees, reached for the bandage, and started to rewrap her still-throbbing ankle.

"*Jah*," Kiah said at the same time.

Hallie looked up at him, confused. "*Jah*?"

Kiah sighed. "No."

"And that clears things up nicely," Kiah's *daed* quipped.

Hallie's *daed* chuckled.

"I'm praying about it," Kiah said a bit defensively. He crossed his muscular arms. "But what I want—need—to say is I love Hallie and—"

"A bit premature, don't you think? Considering you've just met?" Aaron snorted. "But assuming it's true, what is there to pray about?"

They didn't just meet. They'd been corresponding for over a year. But she couldn't say that.

"There's all kinds of things to pray about, but specifically, I meant praying about what to do about talking to the real scribe, if she's not Hallie, and if I accidentally find her since I'm no longer looking," Kiah said. "If the scribe is Anna, she knows I'm here and why. I'm not real sure how to handle telling her the truth yet. I don't want to cause problems. If she's Hallie's *mammi*, it doesn't matter since she's convinced I'm here to marry Hallie anyway, and if it's someone else, I can simply tell her I fell in love with another girl. But that needs to be wrapped up." He looked at Hallie and his expression softened. "And then I need to win Hallie's heart."

Oh. That was sweet. A rush of emotion flooded over Hallie, and in that moment, she loved Kiah, too. But, "Anna called dibs." The words exploded from her. "And love hurts."

She winced at the reminder of the past pain, the days spent crying, the oh-so-dark-depression that she'd barely climbed out of.

The three men holding flashlights exchanged glances.

"Somewhere down the road, a man will always break a woman's heart." Her throat was raw. The words ripped from deep inside.

Kiah startled. Stiffened. Stared. He opened his mouth, probably to deny it.

"No. No, I can't do it again. I can't. I won't. Kiah is too risky." She hadn't intended to say it—any of it—out loud, but it all burst forth, uncensored. She wanted to curl up into the fetal position, arms wrapped tight around a big, fluffy pillow for protection for her fragile heart.

"Is this what your bishop means?" Kiah's *daed* pointed at her with his flashlight. She squeezed her eyelids tight against the brightness, then opened them when the light faded.

"Bishop Nathan talked about me?" Maybe Hallie wasn't supposed to hear that. It hurt. Hurt! Her eyes stung. She dropped the tangled cloth she'd been trying to wrap around her ankle and fisted her hands to try to keep the tears at bay.

"He shared a few things," *Daed* admitted. "Like about how losing your boyfriend affected you. Of course, I already knew all that."

Oh. Was that all? No big secret there.

"Me too," Aaron said.

"He shared how concerned he was," *Daed* went on as if Aaron hadn't spoken. "And"—*Daed* looked deep into her eyes—"about your extracurricular activities."

Oh. *Oh.* So now Aaron and Kiah's *daed* knew she was the scribe. His *daed* knew how wounded she was . . . and he knew that Kiah's heart recognizing her was spot-on. Would he tell Kiah? Had Bishop Nathan sworn him to secrecy? Or was she so broken that Kiah's *daed* knew beyond a shadow of a doubt she'd destroy his son, and he'd just quietly take him away, praying he'd forget that girl in Hidden Springs? He'd be better off without her.

Truth.

And, oh, that ripped a hole in her heart, leaving it shredded and bleeding.

She was wrong, wrong, wrong to kiss him. To encourage him.

Now she had that memory to keep her awake, remembering things that weren't to be. Like her and Toby. Her and Kiah.

Her original plan was best. It was too terrible to even consider. But necessary, even if she didn't dare voice it to herself.

"Hmm. I see what he meant." The visiting preacher continued to observe her.

What had the bishop said? But she knew better than to ask.

Hallie dipped her head to belatedly hide her expression, and her emotions, from the visiting preacher. From Kiah. From her *daed* and brother. The last two men worried enough about her emotional stability. They didn't need to know that Kiah Esh could push her over the brink.

* * *

Even with the dim light from the moon and the spotlighted edges from the flashlights, Kiah could see—maybe even feel— the fear rising in waves from Hallie. He somehow was more afraid for her and wanted her to be restored. He wished he knew more of what was going on inside her heart so he could help her heal. The concern in his father's expression—like that for a straying church member—smacked of the knowledge he was privy to something about Hallie that bothered him. As if maybe she was still on the rebound despite her hot kisses. Or maybe the extracurricular activities were worrisome.

But would he share those fears with Kiah? Or would he spend his time on bent knees beside his bed praying that *Gott* would intervene and break them up, as he'd initially done with Molly? That was when Molly stepped out on him. Was no girl good enough for Kiah in his parents' opinion? Sometimes it seemed not.

But then again, Molly had recently done something to win *Daed*'s approval, since he was now firmly in the give-up-your-foolishness-and-marry-Molly court.

At least whatever was shared back in the kitchen seemed to be enough to take the attention off the fact that he and Hallie had been asleep in each other's arms. And that their fathers had no idea how far their making out might have gone. Except for Hallie's comment, which implied an untruth. Kiah was grateful the focus was off of him and Hallie in that way. His face heated, but still part of him was willing to face the logical consequences of sleeping together—being forced to marry Hallie—in order to get Hallie as his wife... except that might erect even more walls between them.

However, Kiah *knew* Hallie touched his heart in a way Molly never had. No girl ever had reached him that way. He needed to have a talk with his *daed*...

Hold on a minute. What did Hallie say?

"Wait." Kiah turned back to Hallie. "Love hurts? And sooner or later a man will always break a woman's heart? I'm *too risky*?" There might have been more than a twinge of pain in the last statement. He didn't want to be too risky. Nor did he want to break her heart.

Hallie stared at him.

Kiah wasn't a preacher's son for nothing. "First John four-eighteen says, 'There is no fear in love; but perfect love casteth out fear.'"

What it boiled down to was that Hallie wasn't in love with him. Yet.

Either that or he was taking scripture out of context, but he'd rather not go there at this hour of the night. Whatever hour it was.

As if on cue, Hallie's *daed* yawned. "Anna was the one who sounded the alarm when you weren't home in bed. She woke everyone, which made us realize that Kiah hadn't returned, either."

And that brought everyone's attention back to Kiah and Hallie sleeping together under the stars.

"I imagine she wasn't happy." Hallie dipped her head and resumed rewrapping her ankle.

"That would be an understatement. She's rather furious at you for stealing her man," Aaron said. Then his eyes widened and he clamped his mouth shut.

Kiah frowned.

"I didn't steal her man. I merely acted as hostess and tour guide during her absence." Hallie sounded angry. "And he will be returned none the worse for wear."

The fathers exchanged looks again.

"None the worse for wear? Wait. Merely *acted*?" Kiah fought an overwhelming urge to sweep Hallie back into his arms and remind her of what they'd shared a few hours earlier. It hadn't felt like acting. Not from where he stood.

Hallie didn't answer or look at him. Instead, she struggled to her feet.

"And furthermore, I'm *not* Anna's man. Even if she did call dibs and even if she is the scribe, that doesn't mean she owns me." He was beginning to lose his temper.

"No, but Molly does," *Daed* muttered.

Kiah growled deep in the back of his throat. "No, she doesn—"

Hallie took a step, wobbled, and started to fall.

Kiah stepped nearer and wrapped an arm around her. She clung.

He hesitated a moment, glanced toward *Daed*, then swooped her up into his arms. He carried her to the horse, kissed her cheek, then boosted her up. His hands might have grazed an inappropriate place or two—he noticed softness—but he didn't stop to consider where. Then he turned to collect the blanket and the backpack.

Aaron was silently folding the blanket, a half-smile on his face.

"You take Hallie on home," Ted said. "Put her on the recliner in the living room so her *mamm* can look at the ankle. Hallie can sleep there for the rest of the night if her *mamm* decides she doesn't need to go to the hospital. You and Anna can discuss your relationship on Monday."

"Before you go to visit George," his *daed* added.

Kiah nodded, even though he didn't want to visit George. Of course, he didn't want to talk to Anna, either. No avoiding that, though. They had to break up even though they never dated.

"You also need to address the Molly issue," *Daed* said.

"There is no Molly issue," Kiah replied. He'd settle that with him later. He swung up on the horse, settled behind Hallie, wrapped his arms around her, and pulled her close.

"Just so you know, Anna will expect you to take her to the singing tomorrow evening," Aaron said, handing him the backpack.

"You should," Hallie said, her voice tight. "Considering you think she's the scribe."

The three men on the ground exchanged looks. Again.

Kiah didn't want to. He wanted to focus on Hallie. But he did need to talk to Anna if only to tell her what the bishop said: Dibs smibs. And that they were through. Period.

But if Anna was the scribe, that was rude, too.

He'd figure out a nice way to break up with Anna later.

He breathed in Hallie's lavender scent. Inhaled it, really.

For right now, Hallie was in his arms.

And he intended to enjoy every minute of it.

* * *

Hallie was battling tears by the time they rode up to the house. They hadn't fallen yet, but they burned her eyes, making it hard to see despite the brightness of the moon.

She sensed Anna's presence outside the house rather than

saw her; anger radiated off her sister in waves. But at least she wouldn't act like a shrew in front of Kiah.

"Where were you? I was *so worried*." Sure enough, Anna approached the horse.

"Hallie's hurt. I need to get her inside. Your *daed* said to put—"

"Oh, you poor baby," Anna cooed in a sugary-sweet voice.

Baby. It figured. Hallie turned her head toward the barn. Away from Anna. A tear escaped. Dropped. She blinked, hoping to keep the rest from following. That would only prove she was a baby.

Kiah shifted behind her. "She's hardly acting like an infant. Your *daed* told me to carry her in and put her on the recliner so your *mamm* can look at her ankle."

Hallie wasn't sure whether *Daed* actually told Kiah to carry her or not, but if he didn't, he probably meant to. There was a thump as Kiah jumped off the horse.

"She can walk." Anna sounded a tab upset. "What'd she do? Pretend to step in a hole and fall against you, claiming she couldn't walk? Call her bluff, Kiah."

Kiah moved up beside Hallie and gave her a quizzical look as if he wasn't sure how to answer.

Hallie supposed it might have appeared as if she had, but she hadn't. She scowled. That was Anna's trick. She'd even tried it with Toby. It seemed as if Anna and Hallie were always competing for the same guy. As soon as Anna found out Hallie and the guy were interested in each other, the competition began.

Hallie gathered her courage, slid off the horse, and promptly sat on her bottom in the dirt when her ankle gave out. She might have whimpered.

"Oh, so dramatic." Anna huffed a tiny bit. But then she reached out and patted Hallie on the top of her *kapp* as if she decided she needed to show a little sympathy. "You poor thing. Do you need Kiah's help up?"

"No. I've got it. I'm not helpless, Anna," Hallie snapped. But she felt helpless. And hopeless. The little glimmer of light from that morning had long since faded. All that remained was the suffocating darkness. She wished Anna and Kiah would leave so she could bury her face in her arms and howl.

But no. Instead of leaving, Kiah crouched beside her, a hand warm on her shoulder, the other on her lower back. "Hallie, *liebling*, I know you don't need my help, but I'm going to lift you anyway. Your *daed* said to carry you in, I think, and since I'm trying to get on his good side...It's kind of an uphill battle, you know, seeing as I'm an illiterate, murdering, young whippersnapper."

"What?" Anna jerked back, as if unsure whether to make a run for safety or not. "Murderer?"

"He killed George's ants." And despite herself, Hallie giggled at both the ant misunderstanding and the woodpecker and the whippersnapper confusion. A foreign sound to her own ears.

Kiah's hand on her back slid downward, killing the giggles. Then it jerked up as if he realized what he'd done.

"Illiterate? Then someone else writes the letters to the scribe for you? Reads them to you?" Anna sounded properly horrified.

Kiah frowned, but instead of answering her, he scooped Hallie into his arms and rose. "Don't worry, sugar. I won't drop you."

Hallie snuggled against him, looping an arm around his neck, as he carried her toward the house. She tried not to look at her sister.

"And what's with all the endearments? You know that's not our way," Anna said, following them.

"Maybe it should be." Kiah stopped and turned slightly. "Besides, the scribe used some endearments when she responded to my letters." There was a challenge in his voice.

Hallie couldn't remember using any. If she did, it was accidental. Unintentional. Wait. She had said that she loved him, but she hadn't meant it in the romantic sense. Maybe she had, but that was her secret. And she'd signed a letter or two with *Yours*, meaning "your friend." Did that count?

Anna made some unidentifiable sound. "Or *you* did?"

Jah, he had. The words had been a healing balm. And Hallie— um, the scribe—had told him so.

Hallie sighed and relaxed against him.

"You mean you don't know?" A teasing note appeared in his voice.

"Maybe I do and maybe I don't." She gave him a flirty smile.

Kiah sucked in a breath. "You mean you're admitting that you're not the scribe?" There was a measure of something, underlined with relief, in his voice.

Hallie felt a mixture of relief knowing that Kiah wouldn't pursue Anna for *that* reason . . . and a bit of fear that his attention would be back on her as the most likely suspect. But would she still get into trouble if the bishop told Kiah's dad and Aaron, and was she still supposed to keep it a secret from Kiah?

"I heard *Mammi* is." Anna stated it as fact. "And if she is, you can't take her seriously. She's married, you know. And a bit off in the *kapp*."

That was untrue. Well, mostly untrue. *Mammi* could be wacky. And dense sometimes. Not to mention, once she set her mind on something, she couldn't be convinced otherwise. But that aside, it was also unkind.

"I came here to court the scribe." Kiah continued toward the house, his arms tightening around Hallie. "Told her so, in my last letter."

Except, he'd told their fathers that had changed. Would he tell Anna the same? Was he letting Anna down gently? Subtly? Except her sister had never been one to pick up on hints.

Hallie forgot to breathe when Kiah opened his mouth.

"Well, *grossdaadi* might have issues with you courting his

wife. Besides, I'm pretty sure it's against the rules." Anna laughed. "Of course, it *could* be me, sworn to secrecy. The scribe is top secret here, you know. But that doesn't matter. What does matter is, how would you know any of this if you can't read or write?" She followed them.

Kiah made some sort of growling sound that did strange things to Hallie's middle.

"Illiterate or not, I insist you take me to the singing tomorrow night." A flirty sound still filled Anna's voice. "I told all my friends that you would."

Hallie winced. It took all her strength to remain silent. But she couldn't blurt out the truth. She had to protect her sole source of sanity—the scribe's column. Because Anna was right in that it was top secret and if she told anyone, the bishop would take the job away. But the rules obviously didn't apply to him.

"I'm not illiterate," Kiah said firmly. "And if I take anyone— Be a dear and open the door for us, please."

Anna did, holding it wide while giving Kiah a sweet smile. "You're not illiterate? But you said you were."

Kiah sighed. "George thinks I am, because I was looking for the scribe." He carried Hallie through the kitchen and into the living room, and gently deposited her on the recliner as her *daed* directed. For a brief moment, he gazed into Hallie's eyes.

"*Danki* for your help." She attempted a smile. It wobbled. The effort brought a fresh round of tears to her eyes.

Kiah raised his hand as if he intended to brush them away.

"You can't take George seriously," Anna said, interrupting his sweet move. "But that aside, who would you take to singing?"

Kiah hesitated. He pulled his hand away and slowly straightened.

Hallie forgot to breathe.

"I'd take Hallie," he said. He hesitated for a beat or two as if trying to come up with a good reason. Then, "I feel sorry for her. She needs to have fun."

Because he felt sorry for her? What? They made out because he *pitied* her?

Never again. Her emotions spiraled, she slumped, and her eyes burned more. She brushed at them to keep the tears at bay.

Had her calling him "too risky" and his reaction changed his mind? Had she lost her chance?

She looked away.

"Hallie?" Anna snorted. "She'd kill the fun for everyone else."

And that was fact.

CHAPTER 18

Kiah was shooed upstairs to bed by both his *mamm* and Hallie's *mamm*—who were waiting in the living room—as if he'd be overcome with lust at the sight of Hallie's bare swollen ankle. The ludicrousness was astounding, but he did understand the need to protect her virtue.

Still, he was glad he hadn't taken advantage of her surprising welcome of his embrace. The hunger as if she were half starved for love and affection. The unexpected flare of passion. If she was the scribe, he'd know why. Or at least he thought he would. Hallie struggled with low self-worth. Abandonment. A desire to be loved and accepted for herself. And the scribe alluded to those emotions in her letters.

Physical passion had been the wrong approach. And now that he wasn't with her, he saw it with surprising clarity.

Which also meant that, even if he hadn't figured it out, this made it more than clear there was no way Anna was the scribe. The scribe's letters had revealed someone with a peaceful, calm, and gentle temperament and insecurities more like Hallie's than Anna's brash flirtations. And the scribe's identity was to be kept secret? Really? No wonder no one in town was able to help him find her and kept suggesting other possible candidates. That also explained all the details the scribe had shared and those she hadn't. He knew her favorite pizza toppings and favorite dessert on her birthday, but not her birth date nor how many siblings she had.

He stared out the second-floor gable window in Aaron's bedroom, hoping vehicle lights would turn into the circle drive. He wasn't Hallie's husband and had no voice in the medical decisions made, but he'd like a professional diagnosis. Not Anna's snide-sounding "she stepped in a hole, pretended to twist her ankle, and fell against..."

At least part of that was true. Doubt set in. Had Hallie accidentally stepped in a hole? But he'd seen her fall in the kitchen. Plus he'd seen the swelling. No. He believed Hallie got hurt by accident. Hopefully her *mamm* did, too, even though she hadn't seen Hallie fall.

Vehicle lights flashed in the driveway, highlighting the three men just now coming out of the woods. The men who'd found him and Hallie sleeping in each other's arms. Ted broke into a jog, flashlight bobbing.

Kiah wanted to do the same—race downstairs to Hallie. She was going to the hospital, good, but he would be forced to stay home. Here. Not home.

He wanted to be with her. Hold her hand. Pray with her.

He could still pray.

Aaron came into the room. "They're taking her to the hospital." He tossed his blue flashlight on the rumpled black and white pieced quilt covering his bed, then glanced at the undisturbed matching quilt on Kiah's borrowed bed. "You might want to get some sleep. They aren't excusing us from attending church in the morning."

Too bad, but understandable, since Kiah's *daed* was the visiting preacher. But despite Aaron's wise warning, Kiah lingered in front of the window. Watching. Waiting.

Across the hall, Hallie's bedroom door clicked shut. Good. Anna wasn't going to spew her poison. But that was unkind. Anna had been mostly nice. Concerned. It was just her comment about it being deliberate.

But Hallie had said, "Oops, we've been bad," implying that he and she had done more than fall asleep…

It couldn't be true that this was deliberately set up. Couldn't. Simply couldn't.

He sagged.

But it was. Or at least it seemed to be.

It was truer than true.

Maybe.

Outside, Hallie hobbled to the vehicle on crutches. Guilt filled Kiah. He really should've found a way to carry the crutches on horseback. It would've been so much easier on Hallie. And she wouldn't have injured herself worse and fallen against him.

It. Was. An. Accident.

Truthfully, he would've missed that. He'd wanted to kiss Hallie. But then again, it had started them down a very slippery slope. Hopefully, no one would mention them falling asleep in each other's arms to the bishop. Kiah would be in serious trouble and *Daed* would be shamed.

He glanced at Aaron's reflection in the windowpane and met the teenager's gaze.

"Don't worry. Your secret is safe with me. Unless she's in the family way…" The last word trailed off, but was underscored heavily with an implied threat.

Kiah's face heated. Burned. He turned his attention back to Hallie as she carefully maneuvered into the back seat of the vehicle. The driver took the crutches and put them in the trunk. "She won't be."

Aaron sat on his bed and pulled his socks off. The mattress squeaked. Thankfully he let the topic drop.

Hallie's *mamm* climbed into the vehicle next to Hallie. Her *daed* stood alone, shoulders slumped, as the driver left. It was too bad Ted couldn't go, but he needed to be here since the family had guests. He worried about Hallie and probably would be a comfort to her. Ted turned and trudged inside.

There'd be two sleepless men in this house tonight. Three, if Kiah's *daed* stayed up all night to tweak his sermon. He'd been known to do that…like every single time he was scheduled to preach.

Kiah pulled down the window shade and, keeping his back toward Aaron, prepared for bed. He might not get any more sleep, but he knew better than to roam around someone else's house all night. At home, he'd head out to the barn and pretend he was checking on the horses. Here, Anna might join him. He might as well put the enforced quiet time to good use and pray.

He and *Gott* were overdue for a serious conversation anyway.

* * *

Hallie managed to keep from crying, but barely. The medical professionals refused to consider *Mamm*'s "unprofessional" diagnosis of a badly sprained ankle—and just prescribe her a boot that would immobilize the ankle until it healed—until what seemed like every doctor and nurse on duty came by to poke, prod, and rotate. And, of course, everyone had to comment.

Finally, someone came and took her away for X-rays.

Then, and only then, did she get a professional diagnosis that agreed with *Mamm*'s.

Prescription and follow-up orders in hand, and *Mamm*'s temper barely under control, they were finally discharged in time to get home and slide the cinnamon rolls they'd made in advance into the oven to warm for breakfast. Well, *Mamm* did. Hallie was sentenced to the recliner and covered with a blanket until her prescription for a walking boot was filled. In the meantime, her elevated foot was wrapped and well packed in ice.

The rooster crowed and noises came from the bedrooms above as well as the one on the first floor where Kiah's parents were staying.

Hallie snuggled deeper under the covers and shut her eyes. It might be an unspoken lie, but if she pretended to be asleep, she wouldn't have to see the judgment or false sympathy from anyone. She hadn't sprained her ankle, or made the injury worse at the springs, on purpose, but Anna believed she had just to get Kiah's attention. Even Kiah's *mamm* had a faint judgmental look in her eyes last night. But that might have more to do with their not coming home until they were fetched.

Hallie and Anna used to be so close, sharing all their deepest secrets. But Toby had chosen Hallie despite Anna's plays for him. And *Mamm* had tried to recruit Hallie as a midwife apprentice when Anna had to beg. Then the sibling rivalry had begun and Anna started her smear campaign, accusing Hallie of all sorts of falsehoods that only became worse with Toby's death. It hurt. *Daed* said Anna was jealous, but Hallie wasn't sure of what. She was fairly positive Anna wouldn't want her life.

Especially the ever-present dark clouds of sadness.

* * *

Kiah hadn't expected to fall asleep while praying, but he must've because something jarred him awake. He lay there, staring into the darkness at the unfamiliar shadowy shapes, listening to the soft snores coming from the other bed, and wondered where he was and what had woken him. Then it came to him. He was at Hallie's house. And it was Sunday. Except, he'd been having the most pleasant dreams about kissing Hallie at Hidden Springs while the northern lights played overhead. He yawned and wanted to roll over and go back to sleep and replay those dreams. But then the rooster crowed. Kiah stumbled out of bed, got dressed in his work clothes, and went downstairs to help with the necessary Sunday morning chores.

Hallie lay on the faded blue recliner, eyes closed and a log cabin quilt in shades of blues and greens pulled up to her chin.

Why was she sleeping here?

And then his memory flashed. It hadn't been a dream.

She'd sprained her ankle. And her *mamm* had taken her to the emergency room. But before that…

They had done some kissing—make that a lot of kissing—at the springs.

His body warmed. Heated. Burned.

The thickness of the fabric effectively hid any hint of curves, but not the fact that she feigned sleep. Her breathing was too fast and he was pretty sure she peeked out at him through thin slits in her lashes. Besides, a telltale blush colored her cheeks.

He was tempted to somehow call her bluff, but a slight shuffling noise alerted him he wasn't alone with Hallie. He turned away, meeting Joy's twinkling eyes. Her sleep certainly hadn't been disturbed by the previous night's drama.

"You certainly keep life interesting," Joy whispered with a glance at Hallie. "Dill pickle ice cream, murdering George's ants, kidnapping some of his cats—"

"Unintentionally. I think they stowed away." He forgot to whisper.

"*Daed*'s not happy. He said we had enough cats without stealing them from George."

So what else was new? It seemed Kiah was forever doomed to be on Ted's bad side. He sighed. "I'm certainly not going to offer to catch cats here to 'return' to George. I'd probably catch the wrong cats, and that would be a cat-astrophe!"

Hallie snorted.

"Aha!" Kiah swung around. "I knew you were awake."

Joy giggled.

Hallie belatedly snapped her eyes and mouth shut, then seemed to realize it'd do no good. Especially since her mouth still twitched. She blushed and opened her eyes.

"Pretend to be asleep, why don't you?" Kiah teased. He was so tempted to bend over her and kiss her good morning, but that would be frowned upon.

What they'd done last night was definitely discouraged before marriage. And they hadn't even—

"I didn't twist my ankle on purpose," Hallie blurted.

Kiah blinked. "Of course you didn't. I saw it happen."

"So did I." Joy nodded.

But then the doubt swirled back in about when she'd tripped and fell against him at the springs. Had that been on purpose as Anna claimed? The fact that she knew about it when she hadn't been there made it suspect. Had it been preplanned and discussed in detail before he'd even arrived? Or was it something Anna herself had done? That seemed more likely.

But how could he ask such a thing?

Hallie sighed. "I'm supposed to stay off of it until I get the boot. Which means I'll miss work Monday."

"Huh?" Kiah stared at her.

She looked at him, then rolled her eyes. "My foot."

Oh. He nodded. "Well, good then. Because I need to talk to you." He'd figure out some way to ask that burning question.

Hallie grimaced. "Is it time for the talk, part three?"

He frowned. Women were so confusing.

Joy stepped forward, stopping next to Kiah. "The talk, part three?" She tilted her head.

"The one where he reminds me that he's here to court the scribe and there can be nothing between us," Hallie explained, glancing at her sister.

"But *Mammi* is the scribe," Joy protested, "and she's married."

"And I no longer care who it is. I want Hallie."

A man harrumphed.

Kiah turned as *Daed* stepped up next to them. He glanced from Kiah to Hallie and back to Kiah. "Kiah *will* be marrying Molly this fall."

CHAPTER 19

Long after everyone else left for church, Hallie stared into the stillness of the living room, mulling over Kiah's father's stern words.

Kiah will marry Molly in the fall.

Other than a look of irritation, Kiah hadn't denied it. Of course, that would involve talking back to his *daed*, and that would've been frowned upon.

Or it could've been the plain and simple truth, and he was doing what he accused Molly of doing: cheating.

And he accused her—the scribe—of keeping secrets. And she was, by order of the bishop. But his...

That was huge. Ginormous.

And even if he had to keep the engagement secret until two weeks before the wedding, as some Amish communities decreed, he was still taken and should've honored that prior commitment instead of kissing Hallie.

Instead of coming here to find and court the scribe.

He should've stated point-blank that he was in a relationship in his very first letter. Or at least by the second when he'd told her about his ex-girlfriend.

He'd definitely used *Molly* and *ex* in the same sentence in his letters.

Jah, they needed to talk.

He needed to know exactly what she thought of him. The two-timing jerk.

He and Anna were two peas in a pod.

And Hallie's heart had begun to thaw under Kiah's considerable charm.

No more. Men couldn't be trusted.

The silence stretched endlessly, and despite Joy having left a notebook, a purple pen, a word-search puzzle, and a romance book for Hallie to read, she was bored. Who wanted to read a love story when real-life relationships were doomed? Like she'd blurted at the springs, love hurts. And sooner or later a man would always break a woman's heart. *Jah*, she'd known Kiah was *too risky*. She'd known, and yet allowed him to start making inroads into her heart anyway.

She mentally rewrote part of an old nursery rhyme.

Kiah, Kiah, filled with sweet caramel apple pie, kissed a girl and made her cry…

She was alone now. Who would know?

And cry she did.

She must've cried herself to sleep, because she woke up to *Mammi* checking her forehead for a fever, while muttering about Hallie's flushed complexion. Joy set a bowlful of fudge-mint ice cream beside her while Kiah arranged a checkerboard on a tray.

Voices came from the kitchen. Anna came into the room, handed a mug of something to Kiah, and whispered something; then she ran upstairs, humming.

Humming! Anna never hummed unless she was cheerful, which meant Kiah had succumbed to her considerable charms, the jerk.

The cheater, cheating on the cheater with an innocent scribe and her sister. Unless he lied about Molly's unfaithfulness... or his *daed* pushed a different agenda by believing cheating Molly's story...

Hallie's throat closed and her eyes burned. She blinked rapidly. She'd cried enough if *Mammi* had noticed Hallie's blotchy skin.

"No fever," *Mammi* said. "Maybe the quilt is too heavy, and it's making you hot."

She was hot, but it wasn't because of the blanket. It was more due to her temper, which had reached the boiling point. She glared at Kiah, the cheater, who according to his *daed* must've been engaged the whole time they were kissing last night and now had obviously made plans with her older sister. They'd likely do some kissing, too.

And even if the blanket did contribute to the heat, it didn't matter, because there were men present who weren't members of the family and she was reclining. The poor souls might be overcome with lust at the sight of her bare toes. She rolled her eyes. Then she sighed.

"Eat your ice cream," Joy said. "It'll cool you off. Plus it's chocolate and that makes everything better."

That was debatable. She opened her mouth to argue the point, but then shut it. They wouldn't care anyway.

"It's fudge mint," Kiah corrected.

"Fudge, chocolate, whatever." Joy waved a hand in dismissal and nudged the bowl closer to Hallie before turning and trotting off. *Mammi* followed her.

"Wouldn't the mint negate the chocolate part of the fudge?" Kiah asked. He turned to Hallie and frowned. "Are you angry at me?"

Had he noticed the glare, the clenched fists, or was he picking up on some other signal?

She pursed her lips. "Furious. *Jah*. I am. Full disclosure, Esh," Hallie bit out.

He stared, his frown deepening.

"You're engaged? And what's up with Anna and her whispering and humming?" Hallie elaborated.

For a moment or two, his mouth gaped. Then he shook his head. "Oh. No, I'm *not* engaged. I'm not even dating anyone, and I don't know why *Daed* said that. I'll discuss it with him later. Privately. You should know better, Hallie." He lowered his voice. "After last night…" He sighed. "I hope you do anyway."

She had thought she did, but his *daed* had sounded pretty certain. And it seemed as if he'd know.

"And Anna…" Another sigh, this one heavier. "She's not the scribe. At least I don't think she is. It doesn't seem as if she could be, anyway. But even if she is, it doesn't matter. You're the one I love. So since she told me that you didn't want to go to the singing, and that you wouldn't go even if you could, and somehow I got roped into taking her I figured I *would* take her to the singing as you suggested and tell her that I've fallen in love with you, and if you'll have me, I plan to court you."

Hallie's heart clenched. So Anna tricked him into taking her to the singing anyway… and Hallie already knew what sorts of tricks Anna would use. Kiah would likely forget all his grand plans. Once again her sister was trying to steal and ruin something precious to her. Like she tried with Toby. Tricking him into meeting her places, telling him lies about Hallie that he needed to know…

She shook off the negativity.

Kiah drummed his fist on his knee. "She already reminded me that your *mammi* is the scribe, and she's married. Everyone tells me so. I haven't quite figured out what to say to that, though. Because they are right. Your *mammi* is married. Not to mention, several decades too old for me. If she even is the scribe. Not that it matters because I choose you."

Hallie stared at him, barely keeping her mouth from gaping. He took full disclosure seriously. And maybe she should have asked for full disclosure much sooner. Hopefully, he wouldn't demand the same from her.

"I really wish I hadn't written that my intentions were to court the scribe, but I was so convinced in my thoughts and dreams the whole time we were writing that she was you, I didn't think past that." He quit drumming his knee and reached for her hand. Their fingers brushed, sending a sizzle straight up her arm to her heart. Then he pulled back and gave a quick glance around. "Why couldn't you have made things simple and actually been the scribe? Not that it matters. I still believe you're really her."

She checked to make sure they were alone. If Bishop Nathan could tell Kiah's *daed*, she could be honest with Kiah.

But then again Bishop Nathan was the bishop. He made some of the rules. Including the one about the scribe being secret. He could break his own rule without repercussion. If she did, she would lose her creative outlet.

On the other hand, they were alone. And if she cautioned Kiah to silence, who would know?

She held her finger to her lips, saying, "Shhh," then motioned him closer.

He stood and bent over her, and she felt his warm breath on her face. The scent of something cinnamon . . .

Close enough to kiss . . . if she wanted to.

And, oh, she wanted to.

She puffed out a breath.

Secrets first, kisses later . . . If the issue of his engagement to Molly was cleared up.

"Don't say anything. Top secret. But I *am* the scribe," she whispered.

He pulled away enough to gaze into her eyes. She tried to make them open and honest.

He leaned back farther, then sat with a loud, "Ha. Nice try. But I wish you were. It would save so much hassle if the scribe were truly the woman I fell in love with at first sight so long ago."

What? He no longer believed she was? Why not? But still…Aww. That was sweet. But apparently, her attempt at being open and honest appeared to be dishonest and shifty.

His lips formed a smile that flickered and quickly died. "I honestly wish you were."

He didn't believe the truth when it stared him in the face. Turnabout was fair play, right?

"Love at first sight is a myth."

He leaned closer again and winked. "Just kidding. I know you're really the scribe."

She narrowed her eyes. "And I honestly wish you weren't engaged."

* * *

Kiah didn't know why *Daed* would say such a thing. He *knew* that Kiah had broken up with Molly because she stepped out on him, but unfortunately, *Daed* also knew that Molly had been begging Kiah to take her back.

As if it didn't matter that she cheated on him.

It did matter to him. She didn't even have a good reason. Just that it was his fault. How was it his fault? He didn't make her agree to date any of the guys who asked her out. He didn't ask anyone to take her to that party she attended. He didn't even go to those sorts of parties. He was a preacher's son, for pity's sake. *Daed* would tan his hide.

Reputation mattered. And *Daed* came down hard on Kiah when he messed up. The scolding for falling asleep in Hallie's arms might be delayed, but it would eventually come, and it promised to be harsh. But why couldn't it end up with him being forced to marry the woman of his dreams even if his reputation suffered?

But that aside, Molly still insisted that her stepping out was Kiah's fault. He'd never figure women out.

But with Hallie he'd like to try.

There was no point in pursuing that, though, until he cleared up the scribe confusion he'd accidentally created with Anna. For that matter, why had Hallie felt the need to lie to him and pretend she wasn't the scribe? Didn't she feel the same connection toward him that he felt toward her? The worst part was, he despised liars. He tried to always tell the truth. Was it too much to expect the same?

Apparently so.

He pushed the tray holding the checker game closer to her. "You start."

"I don't remember saying I wanted to play." Hallie picked up the bowl of rapidly melting ice cream and took a bite.

"Your *daed* said…" He inhaled deeply. "I'm sorry, Hallie. Your *daed* told me to get the checkerboard out and play a few games with you. I should've waited until you woke up and asked if you wanted to play instead of assuming."

She took another spoonful of ice cream. "I'm just upset that you're engaged and we…um…kissed more than we should have." She whispered the last six words.

They shouldn't have kissed at all. His fault, but at least he'd have the memory of kissing his dream girl to warm him during the harsh punishment that was sure to come.

He glanced around. Both of their fathers were coming into the room armed with steaming cups of coffee and two cookies each.

"*Jah*, me too. And *jah*, we did," he said, then grimaced. That probably made little sense, but it was all he would say with their chaperones listening in.

He searched for a change of topic, something that would be safe to discuss with an audience, but she returned her spoon to the bowl and moved a checker. "You're going down, Esh."

Kiah chuckled, resisting the urge to check the expression on his *daed*'s face. He wasn't used to trash talk from women. Of course, Kiah wasn't used to it, either. But with Hallie he liked it. The trouble was that the shock of it drove any and all rebuttals from his mind.

In its place was an overwhelming desire to kiss her senseless.

Not only was that forbidden, but he would also probably destroy his brain cells in the process. And considering his thought process was faulty yesterday due to the massive headache and pain pills, he didn't want to give Ted any more reason to believe Kiah was an idiot.

Though maybe he was, since he firmly believed this would work out in the end, with *Daed* giving up the Molly foolishness, and Kiah getting his happily-ever-after with Hallie.

Too bad real life was messier.

Without putting any thought into it, he picked a random checker on the front lines and moved it, but unfortunately that proved to be a foolish move since within a couple more moves Hallie was able to jump three of his game pieces. Three of them!

She did a shimmy or something under the covers that he couldn't see well enough to enjoy with the heavy quilt covering her.

That probably was a good thing, considering both of their fathers were in the room.

But the shimmy or whatever it was likely hurt since she winced.

Joy chose that moment to reappear with an ice pack. She also had a bowlful of green-tinged ice cream that she handed to Kiah.

He frowned at it. Dill pickle ice cream. Now that it was in his hands, he wasn't sure he was brave enough to try it. He swirled the spoon around in it, trying to work up the courage. Aaron had said he'd heard good things about it, but he wasn't there to ask if he liked it. No, he'd gone fishing with some friends until the afternoon singing. He'd invited Kiah, but Kiah had wanted to spend a few quiet hours with Hallie before he took Anna to the singing. She was excited about their date. He considered it a means to an end. If it went as he planned.

"Your turn, Esh," Hallie said, drawing his attention back to the board.

He stared. More than half of his game pieces were stacked up in a neat pile next to her elbow. How had that happened? He hesitated to accuse her of cheating, but, well…

He cleared his throat. "Cheater."

She giggled. "You gotta get your head in the game, Esh."

He blinked, looking from the board to her. "So you admit it?"

"I admit to nothing, Esh. You snooze, you lose."

"I wasn't exactly sleeping. I was sort of remembering what you said about being the scribe and wondering why *it's such a big secret*?"

Hallie looked down at her quilt-covered lap. The men who had been conversing quietly with coffee and cookies silenced.

No one answered. Kiah wondered if Hallie even dared to breathe.

Someone—in addition to Hallie—had told him it had to be kept secret. He couldn't remember who.

It was rather an unfair rule in his opinion.

Oh! And she'd told him to be quiet and he'd just blurted it out. Hopefully he wouldn't get her into trouble.

And hopefully the Molly issue would work out.

His future happiness depended on being with Hallie.

* * *

Hallie watched as, without another word, Kiah started picking up the pieces of the unfinished checker game and putting them away.

She quirked a brow at him. "We weren't finished, yet."

Kiah sighed. "I clearly need to have all my wits in place to interact with you."

"And that's a lost cause," Kiah's father muttered.

Kiah slumped, folded the game board, and returned it to the well-worn box. He quietly closed the container, stood, and turned to face his *daed*.

His *daed* stared back.

A muscle jumped in Kiah's jaw.

No words were spoken.

Hallie didn't know what the point of the nonverbal communication was, but his *daed* looked away first, returning his attention to his mug of coffee.

Mr. Esh might be a preacher, and Kiah might speak highly of him, but the man was a bully, and for some reason, he didn't like Hallie. Whatever the bishop had said about her hadn't done her any favors.

Not that she needed any. She might want Kiah's devotion and crave his love, but she didn't want to go through the pain of loving and losing ever again. However, she did want to take a chance with Kiah. Even she knew she was too wounded and would be a very bad addition to any relationship. Kiah would be much better off finding love with another girl. Even Anna, if she ever decided to stop playing the field.

But it would break Hallie's heart completely to witness Kiah and Anna fall in love and start a family.

The best-case scenario would be for Kiah to return to Molly in Shipshewana. She was obviously sorry or she wouldn't be trying to win his heart again. And that way, Hallie wouldn't have to see him and his new love. Or old love. Whatever.

Hallie tugged the quilt higher and tucked it under her chin.

Kiah quietly returned to his seat near Hallie and picked up his bowl of dill pickle ice cream and scooped out a spoonful. He took a deep breath and shoveled it into his mouth. His face turned an odd shade of greenish white, and his lips puckered, but to his credit, he ate it and didn't gag. However, he did put the bowl and spoon back on the tray. "Wow. Remind me not to get that again." He hesitated, then glanced toward his *daed*. "I will eat it, though."

It somehow reminded her of a proverb *Mammi* used to say: *Waste not, want not.*

But surely that wouldn't apply to green-tinged dill pickle ice cream.

She opened her mouth to protest because she really didn't want Kiah getting sick but caught the slightest movement of *Daed*'s head in her peripheral. She glanced at him and he tilted his head toward Kiah's *daed*. *Jah*, and the visiting preacher certainly didn't need any more ammunition against her.

Would *Daed* tell her what Bishop Nathan said about her to turn Preacher Esh so firmly against her?

Probably not, if it was hurtful.

But maybe, if they were on the same team.

Even though she'd been tempted enough by him to reveal her secret, now she was determined that Kiah simply couldn't court her. Because with her wounds, it seemed as if his parents would never accept her as a partner for their son…and that would doom their future happiness.

She picked up her bowl of ice cream.

Maybe the mint did negate the chocolate in the fudge because it didn't make anything better.

CHAPTER 20

Kiah took another heaping spoonful of the nasty-tasting dill pickle ice cream. Hopefully he wouldn't make himself sick in the effort not to make his *daed* look bad, but the faster it disappeared, the sooner he wouldn't have to eat it.

Daed said something in a low tone that Kiah didn't catch, but Ted chuckled. Whatever *Daed* said, though, was accompanied by a baleful glare toward Hallie, which Kiah just couldn't comprehend.

No matter how hard he tried, he didn't understand *Daed*'s attitude. Sure, he'd never been all that excited about Kiah looking for the scribe he so "foolishly pursued," but *Daed* had joked about it, teased and poked fun. Kiah could go on this "fool's adventure," then come home and get serious about a "local girl"—though *Daed* hadn't actually mentioned Molly by name until recently.

He'd never been so negative and downright hateful until they arrived here and met...

Kiah sucked in a breath.

Hallie.

What did *Daed* see—or think—was wrong with Hallie?

She was beautiful, hardworking, smart, funny, and sure, maybe a little sad, but that was understandable given the circumstances. Even *Daed* said that grief had no timetable.

And hadn't *Mamm* said that a girl never truly forgets her first love?

It made Kiah more than a little sad to realize that a portion of her heart would forever belong to that other guy.

And that might be why Molly had started pursuing him so aggressively. He had been her first love...

Although she really hadn't been his.

The thought made his stomach hurt. He'd used Molly every bit as much as she'd used him.

Even though he'd been flattered by Molly's attention, he'd always imagined himself in love with some shadowy female he saw only in his dreams, and then in misty form. He wouldn't be able to describe her to his best friend, but he figured he'd know her when he finally met her.

And he had.

Hallie.

Except, she'd been at her boyfriend's funeral, and even he knew better than to start pursuing her then.

And then the scribe wrote her way into his heart. Of course, he'd imagined her to be Hallie and never for an instant considered she might not be. Until *Mamm* and *Daed* started planting doubts in his mind. And even then the "knowing" continued. Hallie was the scribe. She had to be.

And then *Daed* started pushing Molly on him.

The weird part was *Daed* was never all that fond of Molly to start with.

Never.

He'd heartily disliked her.

At least until...

There was that mission trip *Daed* went on to...

Hold on a minute...

Kiah twisted to better see *Daed* and maybe suggest they take a long walk together and talk this situation out.

But then he caught movement out of the corner of his eye. He glanced that way and saw Hallie finish her bowl of ice cream and set the empty dish aside. She stared at him, her blue eyes wide.

Kiah tried to smother a sigh. Now was not the time to confront *Daed* about the Molly issue. They were guests here, and involving this family in the Esh drama wouldn't be a good idea.

He met Hallie's eyes. For a long moment, he gazed into the warm blue depths. He wished he could lose himself and stay there forever.

Sadly, it'd probably be considered rude to just sit there and stare into her eyes. Especially since her *daed* had told him to entertain her until time for singing. He might as well use the time to talk. "Tell me what to expect at the singing tonight. Or maybe what to talk to Anna about."

Just like that, the warmth in her eyes chilled.

Thunder cracked outside, loud enough that the house shook. The noise reverberated, as if *Gott* Himself agreed with whatever emotions worked through Hallie.

She pursed her lips. "Ask Anna if she heard rumors about a boy kissing a random girl after a buggy race."

That wasn't fair. She had to know that. He'd be forced to confess to kissing Hallie.

If the Amish grapevine worked as well here in Hidden Springs as it did in Shipshewana, everybody and their cousins three districts away had heard about it. Shoot, the news might've reached his hometown by now.

He gulped. "I think I'll ask about the notes she needed to take regarding the home birth yesterday. How they would be used in *The Budget*." He hesitated. "Although that topic is taboo among mixed company. So maybe not." Not only that, but they'd already determined Hallie was the scribe.

Hallie smirked. Another loud crack of thunder. And the answering throb of pain in his head.

Not another headache...

Then the clouds burst. From the window behind the recliner Hallie sat in, Kiah watched the rain come down in sheets.

And Kiah's stomach dropped. He'd really hoped to get this settled tonight. "Break up" with Anna and ask Hallie to consider letting him court her...

Were his plans about to do the same? Dissipate like so many droplets of water?

* * *

Hallie didn't want to get involved in Kiah's quest to break up with Anna. She wanted to discuss his pending marriage to Molly.

Even though he'd mentioned her in person, she mentally reviewed his letters for references to the other woman. The letters were all bundled together in a large white plastic mailing envelope and tucked away in her hope chest underneath the shades of violet Lone Star quilt she'd made for her eventual marriage bed back when she still had dreams.

Dreams Toby had destroyed when he announced he wouldn't be caught in a purple bed. His favorite color was tan. And even though she hated shades of brown, she'd made a replacement quilt in those colors just to make Toby happy.

She'd planned to sell the lovely lavender quilt, but with Toby's death, she'd sold the tan one instead.

But that didn't matter. What did matter were the new dreams that had sprung to life with Kiah's visit and the crushing despair that he might marry his ex-girlfriend Molly after all.

Though she was fairly positive that he'd been adamant that he and Molly were history.

So why...

She'd review the letters just to confirm Kiah's words when she could get up to her room and be alone again, but it made zero sense that his *daed* would be announcing Kiah's pending wedding to Molly if they were in fact no longer a couple.

Kiah somehow managed to scrape out the last bit of the highly questionable dill pickle ice cream, and he set the bowl down on the tray beside hers. He inhaled deeply. "You have questions and I have no answers." His words were whispered, since both of their fathers still sat across the room drinking coffee and eating cookies. "But I will talk to *Daed* when I get a chance and try to get to the bottom of this."

He'd better, if he planned to court and marry her.

And if she decided he was worth the risk. *He was.*

Her emotions were a messy jumbled glob of disorganized confusion where Kiah Esh was concerned.

And no matter which choice she made, she was probably going to get hurt.

Wasn't there a verse about guarding her heart? It probably was written as a warning to women if there was one.

Kiah's face was still slightly green, and his gaze was fixed on the window behind her. He was a preacher's son; he'd know if such a verse existed. And if he didn't, his *daed* would, because he *was* a preacher.

She cleared her throat. Kiah's attention snapped back to her. "Is there a Bible verse about guarding your heart?" She asked loud enough to get their fathers' attention, just in case Kiah didn't know.

And maybe to earn a few positive points with his *daed* to counteract all the negative ones racked up against her.

Kiah blinked at her and frowned. Then glanced at his *daed*.

There was complete silence; then her *daed* reached for his Bible. "Proverbs, I think," he murmured.

Figured that her *daed* would know. A burst of pride shot through her. Shameful of her, but he wasn't even a preacher.

The two men leaned over the Bible together, skimming the pages.

"Aha!" Kiah's *daed* found it first. He jabbed the page with his thumb. "Proverbs four twenty-three says, 'Keep thy heart with all diligence; for out of it are the issues of life.'"

Maybe not exactly what she remembered, but the first part was close enough. She didn't have the foggiest of ideas what the second portion meant. She opened her mouth to ask, but Kiah's focus was on the window behind her. Again.

She tried to twist enough to see, but couldn't. It was getting dark inside the house, though.

He glanced at her. "The sky is getting black from the storm clouds. I was wondering about your brother, fishing. Is he near shelter?"

"He's at a friend's house, fishing at their pond. He'll be fine," *Daed* answered.

"He knows to take shelter," Hallie added as an *Englisch* vehicle drove by on the road, blaring its horn.

She looked at *Daed*.

He stared back at her, his face grim.

A terrible sense of *been there, done that* filled her.

Except this time, Toby's life wasn't in the balance.

But it might be an omen that she'd eventually lose Kiah, too.

* * *

There was a third eardrum-shattering crash of thunder. And then hail pelted the buildings. Kiah stood and moved closer to the window.

"Is that hail?" Hallie asked, a touch of fear in her voice. She dropped the footrest on the recliner with a thud. And groaned.

"Table tennis–ball size." Kiah was impressed. He thought he heard the distant wail of tornado sirens but wasn't sure. The vehicle's horn was still blaring while getting farther away. The sky didn't appear to have a greenish tint. Still, with what this district had been through...He opened his mouth. "Do you have a tornado shelter?"

"Interior room," Ted responded. "The pantry." There was a hint of apology in his voice. "Unless you want to use the crawl space under the house. And in Hallie's condition..."

Kiah glanced at her, lying on the recliner, and remembered the swollen redness of her ankle from the glimpse at the springs. *Jah*, dragging her through the dirt in the crawl space might injure her worse.

"But there's not enough room for everyone in there," Hallie said.

Ted sighed softly and stood with a slight frown as if worried to leave her upstairs and partially vulnerable. "You and your grandparents. The rest of us can go to the crawl space."

"Except *Mammi*, *Daadi*, and I will need help getting down on the floor and up again." Hallie folded back the edge of the blanket, revealing more of her lavender-dress-covered curves. His new favorite color.

"Kiah can stay with you to assist," Ted said.

Ted was going to trust Kiah to stay with Hallie during the storm with only the grandparents to chaperone? It could get awkward since her *mammi* seemed to have matchmaking on her mind...

Ted stood and walked to the stairs and called up for Anna and Joy. Then he went into the kitchen. "Oh, Joy, I didn't know you were in here with the other women."

Joy laughed and said something Kiah didn't catch as he

scooped Hallie and her blanket into his arms and trailed after Ted into the other room. Kiah's *daed* followed him.

The *daadi* came out of the pantry and picked up a dining room chair, then followed Hallie's *mammi* as she grabbed her wheelless walker and hobbled toward the pantry.

Kiah stopped to wait.

The other women headed for the outside door—presumably to the crawl space.

Except Anna. She bounded into the kitchen and skidded to a stop as her gaze met Hallie's. Anna glared and Hallie snuggled a little closer into Kiah's chest.

As much as Kiah enjoyed the feel of Hallie pressed against him, along with the spine-tingling sensations—sensations he already always felt around her—he hated to be the cause of strife between the sisters.

Bishop Nathan had warned Kiah. But how could he have avoided it?

Ted apparently noticed the tension in the room, because he stopped, turned, and retreated to stand next to Kiah. "Get to the crawl space, Anna." His tone didn't leave any room for argument.

Without a word, Anna strode over to the hooks by the door and grabbed her black bonnet and sweater and followed the other women out the door. Kiah's *daed* followed behind her.

Ted rested his hand briefly on Kiah's shoulder, giving it a gentle squeeze and making Kiah feel as if he'd somehow managed to gain a positive opinion from Hallie's *daed*. And with any luck at all, maybe he'd manage to keep it.

Then Ted turned and followed the others from the house, shutting the door firmly behind him. Kiah carried Hallie to the pantry door.

While Kiah's attention had been distracted by Anna and Ted, the *daadi* had arranged four dining room chairs around the small room serving as a pantry. Except, Hallie was supposed to keep her foot elevated and there wasn't enough room to lay a pallet on the floor, unless she—and the blanket—were woven under and around the legs of chairs.

So much for the help with the up and down from the floor. They didn't need assistance, but Ted had still told him to stay and "assist," so he would.

Kiah frowned and gently placed Hallie on a chair and awkwardly draped the blanket over her. That was the best he could do, short of lifting her injured leg up and letting it recline on his lap. It would solve the problem, but he wasn't sure about the rules in this district. He'd already managed to get them both in enough trouble without deliberately looking for more.

The bothersome *mammi* cackled. "Go ahead and elevate her ankle, boy. You know you want to. I won't tell."

He wouldn't try to figure out how the *mammi* knew his thoughts. She probably held a forbidden advanced degree in mind reading. And the fact that she wouldn't tell? That probably meant it *was* against the rules.

Hallie's *daadi* chuckled. "Now, Gloria, you shouldn't tease the poor boy." He glanced at Kiah. "Go ahead and elevate it. Just keep it well covered with the blanket and keep your hands off."

Kiah shifted his chair closer to Hallie and gently lifted her blanket-covered leg onto his lap. Judging by the pained expression that crossed her face, she got no pleasure from the movement. He found none by hurting her.

Hallie's *mammi* shifted. "She likely needs a fresh ice pack." She reached for her walker.

The *daadi* shook his head. "I'll get it." He looked at Hallie. "Hand me the warm one, Glory."

Kiah jerked.

Hallie whimpered. Probably because he jostled her foot.

Kiah glanced from the *daadi* to Hallie and back again. Then Kiah shook his head. The old man must have referred to his wife by a pet name. Gloria and Glory were similar enough to be substituted for each other. Though why would he ask Gloria to reach across him to grab Hallie's ice pack?

"I dropped the ice pack when Kiah picked me up," Hallie said. Her cheeks flamed an interesting shade of pink. She also avoided Kiah's gaze.

Interesting. And telling.

Very telling.

So...Her name was Glory Henrietta. No. That still didn't work. Glory Hallie...Glory Hal...The answer lit up like a neon light. "Glory Hallelujah. GHB." He might've shouted it.

The three others in the room blinked as if the light was blinding.

The *daadi* paused half out of his chair. He gripped the cane a bit tighter—his knuckles whitened—but he very slowly continued to straighten into a stand. "Let me fetch the ice pack, boy; then you can explain yourself."

Hallie's face pinkened enough to rival the imaginary neon light. No explanations were needed. Hallie really *was* GHB. She'd told the truth. Kiah sat there and grinned at her even though she stared at the blanket as if it were the most fascinating thing ever.

Hallie cleared her throat. Twice. She still didn't look at Kiah. "To change the subject...I have a question about the verse Preacher Esh read. You know. Proverbs four twenty-three, where it says, 'Keep thy heart with all diligence; for out of it are the issues of life.' What do you think the second part of the verse means?"

Silence.

Her *mammi* blinked owlishly behind her bifocals or trifocals, whatever they were, her gaze fixed on Kiah as if he alone knew the answer.

He was still struggling with the exciting discovery of his own...Hallie was GHB. For sure and for certain. His heart had truly known her from the beginning. To play theologian now? Impossible.

Her *daadi* hobbled back into the room, cane tapping. He handed the ice pack to Kiah.

Kiah awkwardly tried to slide the freezing bag into place without looking since Hallie's *mammi* was still looking at him and her *daadi* was frowning and Kiah wasn't supposed to look or touch.

Hallie winced, leaned forward, and adjusted it herself.

Her *daadi* reclaimed his seat. "I think it means that many of the issues people face are directly a result of the problems in their hearts. The commands of *Gott* are a gift to those who will diligently keep them alive in their hearts."

Hallie bit her lower lip. "Something to mull over later."

Her *mammi* shifted, then pushed her glasses up. "Or as the *Englisch* say, garbage in, garbage out. Or maybe you are what you eat. Or birds of a feather flock together. Or—"

"So it doesn't mean not to let love in?" Kiah asked, mainly to interrupt the *mammi* because she was on a roll. And because he was guessing at Hallie's problem, and her fixation with this verse's idea, while also recalling her "love hurts" and "too risky" protests last night.

Hallie's *mammi* cackled and reached to pat Kiah's knee near Hallie's ankle. "You'd better let love in, boy. You're the one who's going to marry our Hallie."

Hallie coughed.

But Kiah wouldn't object at all.

CHAPTER 21

Hallie covered her burning face in her hands while trying not to wiggle her foot that was still on Kiah's lap. Even though the pantry door was open, the room was only dimly lit, and that was by *Daadi*'s flashlight, which urgently needed fresh batteries.

Hallie was going to die. That was the plain and simple truth. Either the undiluted pain from her badly sprained ankle would kill her, or she would die from embarrassment, and maybe from acute longing mixed with a liberal helping of fear and trepidation. It was hard to say which would deliver the fatal blow.

Sheesh, she didn't even know which one hurt the worst. When was the last dose of pain medication she'd taken, anyway? Before everyone left for church to be sure. Maybe at the emergency room. She couldn't remember taking any since she left the hospital. That would probably relieve the pain from all three sources. Especially since it made her drowsy and she could pretend this was all a very vivid bad dream.

Someone down below in the crawl space pounded the floor hard. Hallie jerked, moving her foot, and bit back a moan. They apparently thought they were having too much fun in the pantry. But why would they think that? Fun? No one was laughing. No one was tap dancing with a cane, walker, or crutches...Maybe they were checking to see if they were still alive. But why?

Mammi, who shared Joy's exceedingly happy personality, stomped the floor with her walker in response and then started giggling so hard she caught the hiccups, which made *Daadi* chuckle. Kiah sat as still as a stump but grinned at the older couple as if they made his day.

Hallie envied them. Once upon a time, she'd enjoyed being happy and carefree and she could have fun with the best of them.

But with the loss of Toby, what might've been depression...Or maybe it had hit before Toby passed.

She'd loved Toby. She had. But he'd started to get very demanding, insisting she submit to his likes and dislikes as a good Amish wife would. She also had to clear every purchase with him before she made it. So even the dishes she'd use in their eventual kitchen reflected his rather drab taste.

She'd gotten rid of the dishes, too.

As if there was something wrong with color! *Gott* Himself used colors—lots of colors—other than shades of brown.

She glanced at the rows of home-canned food on the shelves. Yellow, orange, red, and green. That was just the vegetables.

Kiah shifted, his hand atop the quilt sliding her throbbing ankle to a different spot on his strong leg.

He winked at her and blew a kiss.

That made her tingle with anticipation. She smiled.

Toby's kisses? They weren't anything to whisper about with her friends. In fact, they weren't anything exciting at all. Wet and sloppy...She could happily live without them. But her best friends, Gracie and Elsie, were convinced she'd grow to like them.

She never did.

But Kiah's kisses...oh my word. He was a master at the fine art of kissing.

With that in mind, why did she have to focus on Toby in the hereafter when there was a possibility of finding her happily-ever-after in the here and now with Kiah?

Because Toby had sworn that death wouldn't separate them? But weren't the wedding vows "until death do us part"? She kept waiting for *Gott* to reach down and grab her, but perhaps *Gott* instead was giving her permission to live.

What sounded like shattering glass and hard pounding from small boulders penetrated the previously pleasant atmosphere.

"What the..." Kiah jolted to his feet, somehow transferring her blanket-covered legs to *Mammi's* lap, but not without considerable after-the-fact pain.

Hallie barely kept from yowling.

Kiah scooted out the pantry door.

Shattering glass? Wait. Maybe he shouldn't be out there. Should she call him back? It surely wasn't safe—

"Whoa! These hailstones are as big as softballs," he called from the kitchen.

Softballs? Did hail come in that size?

Hallie straightened, tempted to go see the supersize hail for herself, but even that slight movement caused a tidal wave of misery. Never mind yowling. She was fairly certain she howled. She fought a wave of nausea.

Daadi gave her a strange look and muttered something about roof damage as he slowly stood and followed Kiah into the other room.

Softball-sized hail. Hallie had never seen such a thing. But that aside, wasn't it dangerous to leave the safety of an interior, windowless pantry for a kitchen filled with windows during a possible tornado with softball-sized hail?

She glanced at *Mammi* who was craning her neck, apparently trying to see for herself.

Another sound like glass shattering, followed by a moment of silence before a softer, gentler sound of probably much smaller, gentler hail—maybe pebble-sized—started tapping on the porch roof.

Daadi and Kiah returned to the pantry wide-eyed and grinning now that most of the danger was over.

Men.

Daadi glanced at *Mammi* and winked. "Do you want to go out courting this evening and view the storm damage?"

Mammi fluttered her lashes. "I can't think of anything more romantic."

Hallie could.

But Kiah's green eyes collided with hers. A spark heated them. And suddenly it seemed like the most romantic idea in the world.

Until her heart crashed in sharp, cutting shards around her feet.

He'd already planned a date with Anna.

And a pending marriage to Molly.

* * *

As soon as the storm passed, Kiah carried Hallie back out to the recliner and left her to straighten the blanket and situate the melting ice pack. The living room windows had survived.

Kiah went to try to help with the broken window cleanup, but the *daadi* looked at him. "I need you to hitch a horse up to a buggy. And park it near the house for Gloria. Do it now so we won't be here when we're needed." He chuckled.

He was just kidding, right?

But Kiah nodded and headed for the barn.

Kiah was leading one of the horses out of the barn as the

other family members emerged dusty and cobwebby from the crawl space.

Daed stopped and stared. "What are you doing, son?"

"I'm getting one of the buggies ready for the grandparents to go on a romantic date to view storm damage," Kiah explained. Hopefully, the "date" to the singing with Anna would be canceled.

Anna crawled out, stood, and brushed herself off. "Is that for us? I need to shower before we go." She turned away. "I get first dibs on the shower," she called.

Daed looked after her and shook his head. Then he glanced at Kiah. "You need to get another one ready for you to take Anna to the singing."

"I figured I'd be needed here—"

"Best to get Anna out of the way," Ted said as he approached. He gave Kiah a pointed look.

Huh? Oh. Oh!

Kiah would rather go on a romantic date with Hallie even if it was just to see the damage. It sounded ever so much more pleasant than trying to tell Anna that he was interested in her sister. That had the potential of going so badly. In fact, it probably would.

He sighed. But it needed to be done and it was good to know that somehow he'd ended up on Ted's good side.

Ted half smiled and winked; then he and Kiah's *daed* stood out in the middle of the circular drive, staring up at the roof with matching glum expressions. It would need to be replaced. *Daed* probably planned to stay an extra day or two so he and Kiah could help reroof the house.

He was glad for the extra time here despite the cause.

The plains of Illinois got more tornadoes than Kiah was used to. But other than roof damage and broken windows from the softball-sized hail, the Brunstetters' home appeared to have escaped any serious damage. At least it was still standing. That was a major plus.

The grandparents hobbled from the house and Kiah went to assist the *mammi* into the buggy while the *daadi* folded the walker and put it in the back. It appeared as if they might also plan to visit a few friends and family members. Or they at least were being prepared in case they needed to get out of the buggy for any reason…like Kiah should have been last night by hauling along Hallie's crutches.

The older couple drove away and Anna rushed from the house. She wore a pretty light green dress and carried a white plastic dish full of deviled eggs to serve at the singing. She paused beside Kiah, gave him the dish of eggs, and waited, hand poised like a fancy lady, while he put the container of eggs on the floorboard, then turned to assist her. Molly used to do the same thing. It turned Kiah's stomach.

She didn't smell like lavender. Well, maybe a hint of it, but it was mixed with a sort of overpowering floral scent that tickled his nose and made him want to sneeze. Thankfully, he held it in.

But even though he knew the truth, that was more proof that Anna wasn't the scribe. One of the letters had mentioned that she—the scribe—had an aversion to strong scents. Anna's perfume was definitely strong.

"I need to run in and, um, do something," Kiah mumbled once Anna was settled.

Anna acknowledged him with a regal nod.

Kiah dashed inside. Hallie stared glumly at a word search puzzle, marker in hand.

He bent and brushed a kiss across her forehead. "I'm telling her that it's you I love. Don't worry. This will all work out somehow."

Joy buzzed into the room before Hallie could respond. "Here's your pain medicine."

With a sigh, Kiah trudged back out to where Anna waited. He climbed in beside her, clucked his tongue, and drove the horse and buggy toward the road. His thoughts whirled as he tried to formulate exactly what he needed to say when he brought up the dreaded discussion of the scribe. He needed to be totally honest about the one he loved being Hallie from the beginning.

As he made the turn onto the road as if he were going to Zooks' discount grocery, he inhaled deeply and almost choked on the odor of flowers. *Lord, please help this conversation go well.*

They approached an intersection and Anna leaned over Kiah, her arm brushing his and giving him another full, overpowering lungful of her perfume as she pointed left. This time the sneeze burst forth before he had a chance to prepare. He didn't even get his mouth covered and he likely gave Anna an unplanned shower. His face burned.

Anna jerked back, out of his personal space. "Eww! How rude! I was just pointing out the way you should go. Didn't your *mamm* ever teach you to cover your mouth when you sneeze? Now we're going to be late because I need to clean up. Again. I'd just taken a shower, you know."

No, he didn't know, but he'd assumed she had. Especially since she emerged from the crawl space announcing to everyone within hearing that she had first dibs on the shower—and then she'd run for the stairs.

"I'm sorry. It was an accident," Kiah muttered. His hands had been full of the reins and she'd invaded his personal space in the first place...not to mention his allergy. He refrained from asking if her *mamm* had ever told her not to take a bath in strong perfume. His district in Indiana had rules against wearing perfume because so many people were allergic, including Kiah to certain scents, which obviously included whatever Anna wore.

But Hallie's gentle lavender scent didn't bother him. He loved it. It was restful and calming, just like Hallie.

Anna and her perfume stressed him out.

Why hadn't Hallie warned Anna? Didn't he tell the scribe about his allergies in a letter? He was sure he had. Almost sure.

Well, he might have forgotten to.

He sighed. "I'm sorry," he said again. "I meant to tell the scribe about my allergies in a letter. But I might have forgotten." But even if he had remembered, Anna wouldn't know.

"I have no idea what you're talking about." Anna grabbed a hanky from somewhere in the deep, dark recesses of her purse and a small bottle of hand sanitizer. "But I'll be fine. I can finish cleaning up there. Like I said, I was trying to show you which way to go."

Kiah nodded. "I do understand verbal directions."

"Turn left. I wasn't sure, since you said something about needing a scribe."

Kiah made the turn, then scratched at a mosquito bite on his neck and said nothing. She'd thought he was illiterate, too. So what did she even see in him, other than a means to hurt Hallie?

He obviously should have planned the trip to Hidden Springs better. Maybe arranged a certain date, time, and place to meet, instead of a spur-of-the-moment decision to join his parents when he discovered *Daed* would be a guest preacher at Hallie's church.

He probably should've asked the scribe if she even wanted to meet instead of just assuming that, of course, she did.

But then again, the scribe was Hallie, who'd been working hard to keep his attention off of herself from the beginning.

He sighed again and drove the horse around a downed limb.

She would've said no, and he would've had to honor that.

But… Kiah brightened… Somehow in his spur-of-the-moment plans, *Gott* put him literally across the hall from the woman he loved. And gave Kiah the opportunity to meet and fall in love with Hallie without the "scribe" label coloring his judgment. After all, hadn't he declared to witnesses—the *daed*s and brother—that he was picking Hallie instead of the scribe?

If only he could plan to spend more time with Hallie tomorrow so he could convince her that her being the scribe was only confirmation for the feelings that had sprung up.

Wouldn't it be nice if he could pick up the ants tonight? It'd be more time to spend with Hallie...

Perhaps, if *Gott* smiled on him, Kiah could eliminate both Anna's interest and the need to meet with the schoolteacher on Monday, because if the teacher were as desperate as Bishop Nathan implied to find a home for the ants, she might be willing to fetch them from the school tonight. That would save him a side trip on Monday and disruption of her classes. And a bunch of uncomfortable chitchat with the scholars who would be curious why he wanted their ant farm.

He didn't. But the ants would be well loved by George.

The horse plodded through a mud puddle.

"Turn right at the intersection," Anna said.

Kiah nodded, following directions. They passed a small building with a vestibule. He nodded toward it. "Is that the school?" *Gott, are you smiling?*

There didn't seem to be any hail damage here.

"*Jah*, the singing is at the next house." Anna pointed ahead and to the right.

Kiah got another strong sniff of her perfume with her movement. This time he was prepared and covered his mouth before he sneezed.

"Are you allergic to something?" Anna asked.

Hadn't he just said he was? More proof positive that Anna didn't care two hoots about him. Despite calling dibs, she'd insulted him and didn't seem to know anything about him—except for his interest in Hallie. And even being sneezed on, she didn't care enough to remember.

Kiah hesitated a long minute, not wanting to hurt Anna's feelings. Odd, because he wouldn't hesitate to be honest with Hallie. He turned his head away and inhaled a fresher breath. Exhaled. "I'm allergic to some perfumes."

"You should've said something earlier," she said.

He had. Though he hadn't specified perfume. Would it have done any good?

He nodded again. "I didn't notice until we got into the buggy." Which was sort of untrue. He noticed when she'd handed him the deviled eggs. But they were standing outside and it didn't bother him as much as it did in the enclosed confines of the buggy. That seemed like too much trouble to explain. "Just open all the windows on your side so the air circulates."

Anna quickly obeyed. He held the reins in one hand and opened his own windows. Too bad the grandparents had taken the open buggy...except as chilly as it was, it might have encouraged Anna to snuggle.

The rain-scented fresh air helped. Kiah inhaled deeply.

Anna flapped her hand toward a farmhouse on the right side of the road. "The schoolteacher lives at the house we're going to for the singing. Convenient, don't you think?"

Almost like God was orchestrating this.

Kiah drove around a huge puddle.

All he had to do was find the teacher in the crowd, talk to her, put the ants in the buggy—and pray the farm didn't break and infest Ted's buggy in the process—and save himself that trip tomorrow so he'd have more time to spend with Hallie...

Oh, Anna was still talking?

"I think this was the first teacher they hired who literally lives next door to the school. She's a great teacher, too. The one before her was the sweetest girl ever. Everyone loved her, but she was so tiny and nice, the scholars wouldn't listen to her. She only lasted a week or two. Sad, really, that she got fired for being too nice. She was one of Hallie's friends, too."

"Was?"

"They're still friends, it's just that the dynamics changed. She got married. Both of her friends are married now."

As if Hallie only had two friends, total?

But that aside, this was the most talkative Anna had been since Kiah's arrival—except for a few minutes they'd talked yesterday when she came home to get the notes. That still confused him. Since Hallie was the scribe, why did Anna need the scribe's notes? Or did she refer to a different sort of notes, maybe directly related to midwifery?

Kiah drove the buggy into the muddy field and parked between two other buggies. He cleared his throat. Hunted for courage to ask about a taboo subject. "Why did you need notes when you were hurrying to a home birth yesterday?" His face heated.

Anna sort of giggled and her face turned pink. "*Mamm* is training me and there is ever so much to remember. It comes naturally for some people like Hallie, but I have to work at it. Unfair, really, especially since she is so selfish to waste a gift *Gott* gave her by doing nothing except working at a restaurant."

"Maybe *Gott* gave you other gifts," Kiah suggested gently. But at least the notes made sense now. They were midwife notes and not scribe notes.

Anna shrugged. "Such as? And why? I want the midwifery job."

"I don't know." His turn to shrug.

Anna giggled again and made a motion at the side window. "We'd best go in. A chaperone is coming this way."

Kiah belatedly set the brakes and opened the door to climb out. He'd have to finish the conversation later. "Can you introduce me to the schoolteacher?"

"Sure, but about that, remember, I've got dibs." Anna flashed him a flirty smile.

"It's about the ant farm." But dread churned in Kiah's stomach. He somehow needed to make her understand that he was here for Hallie without straining the relationship between the sisters even more.

* * *

Hallie mentally paced the floors all evening. After her grandparents left, followed by Kiah and Anna, Joy went with a girlfriend to the singing. Although technically she was too young to date, she was old enough to start mingling and getting to know the other youth, some of whom came from other districts. Sometimes even other states. Like Kiah.

As cute as Kiah was, the girls would flock around him.

But of course, Anna had dibs. And that bothered her. Big-time.

And even though Hallie wouldn't have gone even if she could—the emergency room doctor and *Mamm* had grounded her to the recliner until she got her walking boot—being left home with the two sets of parents was really uncomfortable, especially being around his parents.

Though, truthfully, no one paid the slightest bit of attention to her. Both fathers worked on boarding up the broken windows while the mothers cleaned the glass and rain and melted hail water from the floor. Both jobs would be considered necessary, even for the Lord's day, when one was expected to rest.

But considering the way both of Kiah's parents eyed her, sooner or later one or both of them would attempt to talk to the broken girl their son had decided he was in love with.

Sight unseen.

Okay, well, they *had* met, not even five minutes spent together and she in a cloud of grief. And yet they both remembered the other.

Amazing.

It reminded her of the Bible story of Hagar and how she called *Gott* the *Gott* who sees.

Did *Gott* see Hallie? Did He hear her? Did He remember her?

The flash of light yesterday morning when she was writing seemed to indicate that He did see her. And He heard....

Tears burned her eyes.

She wasn't worthy.

"Who am I?" she whispered. *Lord, help me to believe that You do see me and hear me. Help me to trust. Help my unbelief. Help me to truly begin to live again.*

Somehow, something that she could only call peace flowed through her.

And Hallie knew that *Gott* did see her. He did hear her. And more importantly, He cared.

And she cried, but this time they were tears of healing.

CHAPTER 22

Kiah stuck out like a sore thumb. At least it seemed he did. He and Anna had no sooner joined the youth when a flock of energetic girls came over, batting their eyes and chattering about whatever they could think of. Not that Kiah understood a word of it since they were all talking at the same time.

And while Anna didn't hang all over him, she did stay close enough to stake her claim...even though none of the other girls paid attention. It was flattering—but very uncomfortable.

With all the girls circling Kiah, all the boys came over and surrounded the girls—which made Kiah think of the eye of a storm, or maybe the very center of a cell...what was that called? The nucleus? Maybe. And that made him think of identifying the schoolteacher.

He studied the group of women, but none of them resembled any teacher he'd ever had.

Of course, none of his teachers were giggly and batty-eyed around the scholars. And all these girls definitely had the giggles and fluttery lashes. That confused him.

He leaned close to Anna. "Which one is the teacher?"

Anna pointed off to her right. When Kiah frowned and shrugged, she clarified, "Maroon dress. Dark hair."

That didn't help a whole lot either, but at least it narrowed it down to ten.

"Glasses. Big glasses."

Oh. *Jah*, they stood out. Especially since they were a dark gray shade. And huge. "What is her name?" It started with a *G*. He remembered that from Hallie's earlier game to evade detection.

If Anna heard, she ignored him. One of the guys started calling names for his team of volleyball. At least it worked to thin the crowd around Kiah. Finally he could breathe and move without accidentally bumping into something feminine and starting a scandal.

Anna and Kiah ended up on different teams, but thankfully Kiah was on the teacher's team.

These Amish took volleyball seriously. Like it was a trophy-worthy competition sport. When Kiah and the teacher rotated near to each other in the game, Kiah leaned close. "I'm Kiah Esh."

"I know who you are." She smiled coyly. "And I'm the teacher. I heard that you were looking for me."

Discomfort worked through Kiah. *What?* Though it was true. He was. Just not for the reasons implied in her smile. Kiah hesitated, gawking at her, just long enough to miss the ball when it was hit in his direction. His face burned.

Someone muttered something about a weak link.

Someone else shouted to get his head in the game.

The teacher laughed. "Bishop Nathan. Ant farm. And just to save time and frustration, no, I'm not the scribe. But I wish I were." She added an eye flutter. It looked forced and awkward.

Kiah nodded. Since the scribe was secret, he couldn't very well say that he'd found the one he was looking for.

"*Jah*, you can have the ant farm. George is the one who provided it to the school anyway. It seems fitting that he'd get it back." The teacher now sounded more common sense, straightforward, and no-nonsense. Normal, Kiah guessed.

It did actually seem fitting for George to get the ant farm since he bought it for the school. Hopefully, George would leave the ants in the glass farm container, whatever it was called.

"May I pick it up tonight? The ant farm? Well, actually right now?" If he could, he'd have more time with Hallie tonight—especially if he came up with a logical reason for leaving the youth gathering early. Though Anna might not appreciate that.

He glanced toward the other team just in time to catch Anna give some guy a flirty look. The guy winked. *Hmm.* It reminded him of Molly and turned his stomach.

However, if the other guy offered to take Anna home, this might all work out.

On the other hand, why was Anna so jealous of Hallie if she could attract male attention on her own? He thought back to the sisters' interactions. This behavior fed Hallie's insecurities, kept her home, and put Anna in the spotlight.

But her secret was out. And Kiah wouldn't hesitate to remind Anna about it if she pitched a fit about him and Hallie.

A shrill whistle jarred his attention from Anna and her crush back to the schoolteacher, who had two fingers in her mouth and was getting everyone's attention. At least it wasn't fingernails dragged across a chalkboard. He cringed at the thought.

Everyone stopped talking and stared at the teacher.

"Kiah and I are going to walk to the school. Who wants to come with us?" The teacher didn't even yell.

Immediately ten hands went up.

All female. Excluding Anna's.

A beat or two passed and approximately the same amount—give or take one or two—of male hands rose. Of course. Because the girls were going.

The teacher smiled at Kiah. "I'll go tag a chaperone to go with us," she said, much quieter, then walked away.

Kiah nodded and caught the volleyball when someone tossed it at him. A couple more youth rotated into the game, and Kiah moved to the back row to serve.

They played about half a game before the teacher reappeared with a middle-aged couple. She made that shrill whistle again. "Let's go get that ant farm," she added.

Almost all the volleyball players—excluding Anna—joined together in a huddle behind Kiah and the teacher and they started across the wet and muddy cornfield to the schoolhouse.

* * *

Soon after Anna and Kiah left, *Mamm* came into the living room with a small green pill bottle and a glass of water. She shook a pill out into her hand and handed it to Hallie. "I'm so sorry I forgot to give you a pain pill earlier. I hope you weren't too uncomfortable."

Hallie forced a smile. "It was manageable. Joy gave me a pill about thirty minutes ago." At least as long as she didn't move, it didn't hurt too much. The jostling due to the hailstorm and all the shifting and changes in position had left her cranky and emotional...even if there had been happy moments in Kiah's arms and her ankle on his knee, at least before Anna swept through in a cloud of flowery scent for their singing date.

That on top of the sleeplessness of most of the night before—except for the time spent sleeping in Kiah's arms—it was amazing she wasn't a weepy mess.

She took the pill, set it aside for later, and gulped the cold water, then shifted—and winced as *Mamm* moved the quilt off her ankle and removed the mostly melted ice pack.

"I'll be right back with a fresh one," *Mamm* promised as she hustled back into the kitchen.

Daed said something to *Mamm*, his voice a low rumble Hallie couldn't understand in her exhausted, pain-filled state, and *Mamm* answered.

Hallie closed her eyes. She'd try to pray about Anna and Kiah instead of stressing over them. If *Gott* saw fit to answer her prayers yesterday morning by sending a flash of predawn light and Kiah, then surely He could answer prayers about her relationship with her older sister and Anna's unfounded jealousy of Hallie.

She closed her eyes. *Lord Gott* . . . and there she must've dozed off or something, because she woke up to Kiah's *mamm* easing an ice pack onto Hallie's ankle.

"I didn't mean to disturb you." Mrs. Esh sat in the chair next to her. "We haven't had a chance to talk. I'm sorry you were injured, but I'm glad you're here so we can get acquainted. I'm Ruth." She shifted her chair closer and lowered her voice. "My husband tells me you're the scribe. Tell me how you met Kiah."

Hallie blinked in surprise. Was the woman an ally or was she looking for more ammunition against Hallie? "Um, briefly, at the furniture shop the day of my boyfriend's funeral. We didn't exchange more than ten words, but we remembered each other. Then we only corresponded by mail, he as himself and me as the scribe."

"And how is that identity different than the real you?" Mrs. Esh asked, tilting her head.

"I couldn't include anything that would identify me as the scribe either in the letters or in real life. Which really confuses me because Bishop Nathan made the rules and he broke them the first time someone came looking for me."

Mrs. Esh's mouth twisted as if she tasted a lemon.

Hallie grimaced, remembering Kiah's *daed*'s equally pinched expression. Maybe she shouldn't have criticized the bishop. She inhaled deeply. "I'm sorry, Mrs. Esh. I shouldn't have said that." She might have just accidentally burned a bridge while "under the influence" of pain medication.

"Call me Ruth. Bishop Nathan told my husband because Kiah made an impression on him. He wanted us to know that you're a fine girl and Kiah would be blessed indeed if he married you."

Then why did Mr. Esh seem to disapprove of her? She couldn't ask. That would be rude. But she could ask about something else… "Why did Kiah come to court me…uh, the scribe…if he's promised to marry Molly this fall?"

"It probably will be earlier than fall." Mrs. Esh's mouth twisted again. "That's complicated."

"Complicated."

"I can't tell you. But let's just say that it's, um, difficult."

"Can Kiah tell me?" *Jah*, she was pushing. But if it was a pushed-up wedding, then Molly must be pregnant. Hallie gulped.

Mrs. Esh sighed. "I doubt that he even knows yet. He's going to balk, but he has no choice."

What? How? Why?

"But let's talk about more pleasant things. Tell me about you. You work at a restaurant in town…as a waitress?"

Why was Ruth acting like she was getting to know her as a future daughter-in-law?

"*Jah*, but I also make their pies." She wouldn't brag that she'd won blue ribbons at the fair. Of course, that was secret, too, due to the pride issue.

"And your *mamm* hopes that you'll become a midwife."

Hallie nodded.

"But you don't want to because…?"

Mamm and the bishop were telling all her secrets. Hallie swallowed. "Fear mostly. What if I make a mistake and someone dies?"

But admitting to fear reminded her of Bishop Nathan's advice to stop lurking in the shadows and step into the light of the campfire. That was something to ponder, especially since *Gott* kept bringing it to mind. What exactly did it mean? To stop hiding from life, maybe?

She did hide from life… *Oh, Lord, help me to be brave and to embrace life the way you intended instead of hiding in the shadows, terrified of getting hurt. And if You want me to become a midwife, shove me through that wide-open door because I won't go willingly.*

How was that for brutally honest?

Now *Gott* already knew she didn't want to be a midwife and He wouldn't make her…

Actually, He probably would. He was probably rolling on the floor laughing right now.

Mrs. Esh grasped Hallie's hand. "Are you okay, dear? You look a bit pale. Are you going to get sick?" She looked around as if there was an immediate need for a pail.

"I'm fine. I was thinking about being a midwife. It's not as amazing as some people"—like Anna—"think. There's a lot of responsibility and so much potential for things to go wrong." *Mamm* had told her once that a woman was never so close to death as when they were giving birth. Anna treated it as a lark, like she was just there for a frolic and not the serious, life-altering event it was.

"Your *mamm* says you are a natural. And that she won't let Anna into the birthing room yet."

Really?

"She says she uses her for errands, housekeeping, and crowd-control," Mrs. Esh continued.

Then what did Anna take notes on? One hundred and one ways to amuse small children and calm a stressed husband while the wife was giving birth?

Okay, that was a bit snarky.

"What do you want to do with your life, Hallie?" And the tone of her voice suggested strongly that *Mamm* had told her that Hallie didn't want to marry. That she wouldn't go to frolics so she could be courted. That she was a virtual hermit...

Oh, Lord... she was.

And then Kiah stepped into her life and she threw herself into his arms like a desperate woman. Though, admittedly, he responded to her the same way.

A heated rush. Time was of the essence. They must act now or forever hold their peace.

"I do want to marry and have children. I do. I'm done grieving and I want...I want Kiah." Then her face flamed and she dipped her head so she didn't have to see his *mamm*.

So his *mamm* couldn't see her.

And he was engaged...

Hallie's stomach roiled.

She tugged at a loose thread on the quilt. "Mrs. Esh—"

"Ruth, please." There was something Hallie couldn't identify in her voice.

"I shouldn't have said that. He's engaged and I don't want to come between them..."

"*Jah*, you do."

Hallie glanced up.

"And I want you to." Ruth gave her a sad sort of smile. "But you can't. It's complicated. And if you do, my husband will be ruined—" She sucked in a breath, stood, and stumbled from the room, shutting the bedroom door firmly behind her.

"What?"

* * *

The ant farm was much larger than Kiah expected, but as crazy as the elderly man was over ants, he supposed it would make sense for George to order the deluxe model instead of the standard size. If Kiah had known it was so big, he would've driven the buggy over to get it. Another man had to help him carry the large glass case across the field to the borrowed buggy.

"I'm so happy to be rid of that," the teacher said as Kiah slid the ant farm into the back seat and wrapped the ragged old buggy quilt around it. After all, he didn't want Ted's buggy infested with ants.

"I imagine George will be glad to have it back." As fond as the man was of ants and cats, he would be over-the-moon excited.

However, Anna wouldn't be as happy when she discovered that Kiah was ready to go. The singing hadn't even started yet. Youth were still arriving, mingling, and playing either volleyball or basketball. He hadn't seen either Aaron or Joy yet.

But Hallie waited, and he had some serious courting to do.

Time was of the essence, unless by some miracle *Daed* let Kiah stay for an undetermined amount of time. And he doubted that would happen since *Daed* was in a mood unlike any Kiah had seen. It was as if the stress had exploded the moment he met Hallie.

But Kiah didn't understand why, nor did he know what Molly had to do with it. And where did *Daed* get the idea he would be marrying Molly when he hadn't courted her—or anyone—for a year and a half? He most definitely would not marry Molly.

He needed to discuss that with *Daed*, but it'd be in bad form to talk about it now. That would have to wait until they got home.

And hopefully, Hallie would wait until he got this mess fixed and could return for her.

The other youth rejoined the volleyball game as Kiah finished securing the ant farm; then he plodded across the muddy pasture to try to find Anna. Hopefully she would be understanding and cooperate fully with him.

In fact, he probably should pray about it.

He stopped in his tracks and bowed his head. *Lord, please help things to go smoothly and work this out according to Your will. I'd really like to spend time courting Hallie, if at all possible.*

That probably made the prayer a bit selfish, but surely *Gott* understood.

He opened his eyes and looked up to see Anna and another girl approaching.

Kiah sucked in air. "Anna, what's your favorite pizza topping—other than cheese?"

Anna's brow hitched. "Pepperoni, of course. Why?"

The scribe—Hallie—liked pineapple and Canadian bacon.

Kiah smiled. And opened his mouth to tell her what she and he already knew. She wasn't the scribe.

Anna held up a hand. "David asked if he could give me a ride home tonight. I've been wanting him to notice me forever. I think he got jealous when he saw me with you. If you don't mind, I'm going to ride with him. You and I can go out for pizza tomorrow."

Kiah smiled. "Perfect. Except not for tomorrow night. I found the scribe and I'd like to spend time talking with her."

"It's *Mammi*," Anna stated confidently.

And Kiah's smile widened. If Hallie couldn't tell, then he wouldn't, either. "Maybe David might like to go out for pizza tomorrow night. Invite a few other friends so it appears less likely that you're chasing him." Because if David was a good Amish boy, it might make him a bit uncomfortable to be openly pursued.

Kind of like how Kiah felt about *Daed*'s declaration that Kiah would marry Molly in the fall. He wanted to run the opposite direction as fast and as far as he could.

Anna's friend nodded. "We can get a group together. Super fun. You can invite Anna's *mammi*, since you want to talk to her." She looked at Kiah.

"I'll keep that in mind," Kiah said, but he wanted to be alone with Hallie—not on a group date with her *mammi*. "But since you found another ride home, if it's okay, I'm going to leave. I have George's ants, and I'd like to get them delivered tonight." Maybe that'd save even more time tomorrow. Especially if he could show George that he didn't need—or want—reading and writing lessons.

"Have fun talking with *Mammi*." Anna smirked. "You might want to make sure *Daadi* is close by." She and her friend turned and walked away. Snickering.

Whatever. Kiah knew the truth. He swung around and headed back toward the buggy. He'd make a stop at George's, deliver the ant farm, and read a short chapter of the Bible out loud, then be on his way to court Hallie. Even if it was a game of checkers where he'd have to keep an eye on her to make sure she didn't cheat.

"Kiah." A female's voice called to him.

He turned.

A not-so-joyful Joy ran toward him, tears streaming down her face.

CHAPTER 23

Hallie reached for her crutches to follow Mrs. Esh—Ruth—to the bedroom just so she could get to the bottom of such a strange comment. How could Kiah's refusal to marry an ex-girlfriend—one he hadn't courted for over a year, if he'd been truthful—possibly ruin his father? And if Kiah hadn't been with her, why would they have a rushed wedding? That didn't make a lick of sense. Yet apparently, whatever claims Molly had made had quite the hold on the parents. Kiah didn't seem to be too bothered, because he didn't know about it, or he didn't care, or he was playing Hallie for a fool. No. Kiah, with his full-disclosure mindset, didn't seem the type to play dishonest games. Nor did he seem the type to not care about his responsibilities.

And if he didn't know about it...

Well, how could that be?

But soon he would...and then what would he do? If it was possible to truly ruin his *daed*...? Her stomach churned.

How would—could—it ruin his *daed*?

His *mamm* was right. Kiah loved his *daed*—his parents—and would make sure he—they—were not ruined, if he could do anything about it.

He was a good son. A good man.

Hallie's eyes burned. And she'd admitted to Mrs. Esh—Ruth—that she wanted Kiah. Like a loose woman. Although she didn't mean it that way. Ruth had inferred her approval of Hallie except that Hallie's joy would be Ruth's pain once her husband was ruined. Someone was going to have a broken heart, and Hallie had a sinking, nauseating feeling it would be her.

Hallie let the crutch drop and buried her face in her hands mostly to hide her emotions from anyone who might walk into the room. But *Mamm* was in the kitchen doing something, maybe making herbal tea since water was running. *Mamm* had a theory that any sort of caffeine in the afternoon was bad for people. She couldn't prove it, though. Hallie wasn't sure she agreed, but that was why it was called a theory. It was unproven.

And that was a lovely rabbit trail. And now she needed caffeine.

She rubbed her fingers across her eyes to wipe away any tears that might be trying to escape, and looked up…at Preacher Esh.

Something that might be sympathy glittered in his green eyes so much like Kiah's. For a moment, he actually looked as if he cared. As if he might have overheard her conversation with Ruth. As if he was sorry. As if he loved with a love that the Bible said that *Gott* has for His children.

As if he wasn't the grumpy, judgmental ogre he'd appeared to be thus far, but instead the loving, caring man of *Gott* that Kiah claimed he was.

Hallie tried to find a smile, but it flickered and died, because truthfully, she was more than a little scared of the preacher. He'd not been the friendliest man during this visit, and Hallie felt she'd been found wanting.

The preacher pulled in a breath, exhaled, and reached out a shaky hand to lightly touch her *kapp*-covered head. He didn't linger, but pulled away quickly. Another deep breath. His green eyes filled with tears and he murmured something about collateral damage and caught in the cross fire that made absolutely zero sense. A third inhale. "They say that the road to hell is paved with good intentions. They are right." Then the preacher turned and walked away, heading toward the room that his wife had disappeared into.

That was all very confusing.

But somehow, Hallie picked up on deep sorrow as if he regretted doing whatever he'd done that was labeled as good intentions. And that maybe he was paying a high price, too.

But who was caught in the cross fire and who was collateral damage? Her? Kiah?

Or both?

* * *

A chill wind blew as Kiah stopped midway back to the singing and watched Joy rush toward him. Tears streamed down her cheeks and dripped off her chin.

"What's wrong?" he asked.

She opened her mouth and emitted a high-pitched wail that seemed to last forever and was mixed with half and quarter words that didn't seem to make any sense. In fact, the only word that Kiah understood was *Aaron*.

Aaron, who had gone fishing with friends and may not have found shelter when the hailstorm hit.

"Is he all right?" Worry caught Kiah in the chest and whisked the oxygen from his lungs.

Joy let loose another stream of broken syllables that ended with the clearly understood word *killed*.

Considering that the hail Kiah had seen was softball-sized, it was conceivable that Aaron had been killed.

Though this farm showed no storm damage. Just heavy rain.

Kiah slumped and pulled in a fortifying breath. More loss. How much would Hallie and the rest of this community be expected to bear? "The buggy is this way." He motioned with a tilt of the head. "Take me to him." *Give me strength, Lord.*

Joy followed him to the buggy and climbed in while Kiah untied the horse from the rock he'd used to hold the reins. Then he climbed in next to her, released the brakes, and backed out.

His throat threatened to close up as he drove to the road. "Which way?" His voice sounded husky, even to himself.

Joy sniffled and wiped her face with her sleeve. "Back toward home. At Lapp's pond."

Kiah nodded, though he didn't have the foggiest idea where Lapp's pond was. "Do you have your cell phone? Mine died." He turned onto the road.

"I don't have one. What do we need a cell phone for?"

At least she seemed much calmer.

"To call nine-one-one."

Joy's eyes widened. "They'd help? I knew you'd know what to do."

Kiah wasn't all that anxious to deal with the police. He forced a half-smile. Not that Joy noticed. "Is it much farther?"

"Turn left at the intersection and about a quarter mile on the right. I hope they're not all dead."

Kiah hoped none of them were, but he clearly heard the word *killed.* And Aaron. But maybe he misunderstood and Aaron hadn't been killed. "How many were there?" He glanced at her. "And your brother is...?"

"Aaron." Joy frowned. "I thought you knew that."

"He's still alive?" He turned at the intersection, slowing to dodge downed branches.

"Oh. He was when my friend and I left. But they might not be. I hope we're not too late."

Jah. Kiah hoped not, too. But Aaron was alive. That was good.

Joy was silent for a few minutes. "They were drowning them."

"Who?" He'd be dealing with bullies?

"Stop!" Joy leaned forward. "There. We'll walk from here. Maybe we'll have the element of surprise." She jumped from the buggy and took off running before Kiah could tell her to stay.

Kiah took a leap and ran after her. His gut churned. What was he getting into?

* * *

Hallie waved at *Daed* to get his attention when he wandered into the room with his cell phone in one hand, an index card in his other, and a purple pen, cap off, stuck behind his right ear.

He glanced up at her. "I need to make a couple phone calls, as soon as I find the numbers."

He didn't have a smartphone. Basic phones were allowed, but not smart ones unless one had a business and special permission from the bishop. He had neither.

"Okay. I was just wondering if the Eshes confided in you about what is going on between Kiah and his ex-girlfriend."

Daed frowned. "No, but it worries me, especially seeing your attraction to the Esh boy. I'm excited to see your interest flaring to life, but I am worried about the aftermath. I don't want to see you hurt worse."

She didn't want that, either.

"I haven't asked, though, because these people are mostly strangers and it's none of our business at this point," *Daed* continued, lowering the phone.

At this point, implying that if she and Kiah got more serious, it would be their business. Except, she was about as serious as she could get. Thanks to over a year of pen pal status, coupled with getting to know him in person, she was dangerously close to being in love with the man. A little serious courtship and it'd be in the bag.

Daed's serious expression seemed to indicate that he was aware of it, too.

"They're staying over a day or two to help with repairs," *Daed* said. "I'll try to bring the matter up. If he doesn't."

Hallie nodded. "*Danki.*"

Daed sighed, offered a sad sort of smile, then continued across the room toward his collection of business cards in a wicker basket on the end table beside his chair. "I'm going to order what we need for repairs and see how quickly they can deliver. If they can't deliver tomorrow, then I'll arrange a ride to pick up the supplies."

Jah, it'd be wise to get the job done while they had assistance. Two extra men who were willing to stay over and help. Plus Aaron, if he had time off work assisting the area's farrier. He was an apprentice there to see if he liked it and wanted to do that.

The sound of raised voices came from the master bedroom. Loud enough to know Preacher and Mrs. Esh were arguing, quiet enough to not understand what they were saying.

Daed sighed again and sat in his chair and shuffled through his stack of business cards.

"This is awkward," Hallie said.

Daed nodded. "Your *mamm* made tea and went to rest in the *dawdihaus*. She thinks there's a possibility she might be called out for another birth in the next day or two."

Hallie smiled. One of her best friends, Gracie, was due with her first child any day now. A couple days ago, *Mamm* had told Hallie the baby had dropped. The one birth Hallie would willingly attend. If she could. She scowled at her throbbing and swollen ankle, buried under mounds of melting ice and blankets.

The bedroom door opened and the Eshes stepped out. Ruth's face was red and blotchy as if she'd been crying. Preacher Esh appeared frustrated. "We're going for a walk," he said.

"I suggest behind the barn. More privacy." *Daed* rolled his eyes at Hallie, then keyed something into his phone. "Levi, this is Ted Brunstetter. Do you replace window glass? Give me a call."

CHAPTER 24

Kiah hurried behind Joy, who almost ran to the pond. Her shoulders were shaking, but whether from anger or tears, he didn't know. He would've guessed tears, but her run was more furious than upset. Besides, Aaron and his friends appeared to be fine. No bullies were harassing them. In fact, they stood waist deep in the water that had to be cold, laughing and poking sticks at something. Just boys having fun. Maybe he should've gotten all the facts before rushing to the rescue.

Joy stopped right on the bank and planted her fists on her hips, then started shouting at them in a random mix of Pennsylvania Dutch and *Englisch*, clearly furious. The boys mostly ignored her, at least until she kicked her tennis shoes off and stomped into the water.

Would Hallie be similar if riled? He'd seen a spark of this "life" in Hallie's eyes and would be looking forward—God-willing—to future scoldings as long as he had the right to be in her life.

Kiah, who still didn't have an inkling what the problem was, followed her, with his shoes on, simply because he felt he should.

Of course, he also should have listened to her rant so he'd know what the problem was, but it was just too spellbinding watching joyful Joy throwing a temper tantrum. But clearly, no human's life was in danger.

If Hallie was anything like this when not weighed down with grief, then his heart was truly hers. Of course, it was anyway, but he looked forward to calming her someday and making it all better.

And he wasn't the only one who thought so. At least one of the boys—not Aaron—had stopped poking the water with his stick, and stood still, gaping at Joy with something akin to admiration. And shame. Definitely shame.

And that boy made a shrill whistle that would have put the schoolteacher to shame. "Guys, stop." And he reached down into the pond and pulled up...

Kiah blinked and looked again. A white trash bag with something wriggly and jiggly inside it. Kittens, he guessed, judging by the size of the wriggly-ness. Joy wanted Kiah to help her rescue the kittens. And while he'd love to make her smile again, being her coconspirator in this wouldn't really endear him to Ted, who complained about him accidentally kidnapping George's cats. Bringing him newborn kittens who likely needed to be bottle-fed would be even worse.

On the positive side, they already had a gigantic ant farm in the buggy to be delivered to a man who loved ants... and cats.

Problem solved, if Joy—and George—agreed.

Joy snagged the bag from the boy who rescued the creatures. "*Danki*, Menno."

Menno blushed, but looked at her with admiration while a much-happier Joy turned to Kiah with a semisweet smile. "Let's get these poor babies to the buggy and make sure they are okay. I knew you'd fix this, Kiah."

Menno slumped.

Kiah gawked. He'd done nothing—except show up. Her temper and a seventeen-year-old boy—give or take a year—with a crush were the ones who made a difference.

Except Aaron turned away, head bowed, as if he was ashamed, too.

Kiah climbed up the sloped edge of the pond, realizing too late that the only pair of shoes he'd brought with him this trip was wet. His socks were wet. And he hated wet feet.

He had to deal with it. Or go barefoot.

Joy sloshed through the water behind him, and as he turned to look at her, she shoved the bag into his hands. He glanced at the dripping bag, filled with rips from the sticks—those poor kittens—then looked at Joy again.

She'd dropped to the muddy ground and was putting her dry shoes on over wet socks while ignoring Menno's repeated, "Sorry, Joy."

Menno apologized and Aaron looked ashamed. Kiah wasn't sure about the other boys or what they thought. One of them made a noise of protest like he wanted the bag back. Kiah could either fight Joy's battle or get the kittens out of the bag…With her brother and possible future potential beau there as backup if she resumed her rant, he picked the task in his hand and sloshed to the buggy. He needed to get those wet, miserable kittens out of the bag and make sure they were all right.

Once at the buggy, Kiah opened the bag. There was movement, so some of the kittens were alive, but he didn't hear any meowing. That wasn't a good sign. Unless the kittens were still very young.

Kiah cautiously reached in and pulled out a very wet, very tiny newborn kitten. Its eyes weren't even open yet. It was still alive, but barely. Had the mother been killed in the storm and the boys found the kittens and were showing them "mercy" despite their laughing and poking? George and Mildred probably wouldn't be excited to nurse kittens, but Kiah couldn't see Ted welcoming them. *Jah*, he'd start with George.

Kiah laid the kitten on the buggy floorboard and reached in again.

There were five kittens total, all in about the same shape. He crumpled the bag as Joy arrived, tears flowing again.

He sighed. "What now?"

"One of the boys, Peter, said they're just going to be drowned anyway because they have too many cats," Joy sniffled.

"I have to take the ant farm to George—" Kiah began.

"You're brilliant!" Joy was all smiles again.

And hopefully George wouldn't refuse the ants and baby cats. Kiah's stomach cramped.

But thirty minutes later, George cuddled five kittens while Mildred searched for a medicine dropper and Kiah and Joy struggled to carry in the ant farm while George's brother directed every step.

Twenty minutes later, George and his brother fed newborn kittens and exclaimed—with tears—over how quickly Kiah "learned" to read and write.

Joy's tears must have been contagious since George cried... and then after Mildred pulled him aside to whisper that George had recently been diagnosed with a benign brain tumor and would be having a risky surgery. They found the message from the doctor on their seldom checked cell phone that afternoon. Kiah blinked back tears of his own. It explained so much...and made him glad to have brought a smile to the man's face.

Once back in the buggy with Joy beside him, Kiah's tears turned to a grin. He was on his way back to see Hallie.

He couldn't wait to spend the evening with her.

But she was asleep.

And Ted wouldn't let Kiah wake her.

Instead, he helped his *daed* and Hallie's *daed* finish covering the roof with tarps.

* * *

Hallie was roused out of strong-pain-pill-induced sleep in the wee hours of the morning by *Mamm*, who seemed to be under the impression that even though Hallie's appointment was scheduled for eleven, if they were there before the staff arrived, they'd be seen early.

And so they were sitting in the driver's van in the parking lot at six.

Mamm might have been way too optimistic, because while the office staff handed Hallie a clipboard with what seemed like a ream of paper to fill out when they opened at eight, they stubbornly insisted on seeing patients at their scheduled time. They didn't do walk-in appointments, thank you very much.

But by noon they were back on the road, heading toward home. *Mamm* fumed at the *Englisch* medical professionals, but she did the same thing, scheduling appointments to visit the pregnant Amish women. It was just that home health care was more flexible, and of course, babies came when babies wanted. Not by appointment.

When the van driver pulled into the driveway, a pickup was parked next to the house, and behind that a buggy. Aaron and Kiah were helping the *Englisch* driver unload packages of shingles and carrying them up the ladder to the roof where both *daeds* waited.

Hallie exited the vehicle and, unfamiliar with the walking cast, plodded slowly toward the house, watching the flexing of Kiah's muscles as he climbed the ladder with the bundle of shingles. She probably enjoyed it way too much, especially considering Kiah had stripped his shirt off.

Sadly, Kiah's *daed* must've noticed her gawking because he said something to him, and Kiah quickly grabbed his shirt from where it lay on the roof and covered himself.

Levi Wyse, who was married to Hallie's friend Elsie, worked on repairing window glass. He smiled at Hallie as she hobbled up on the porch, then glanced at *Mamm*. "Elsie's inside, helping Gloria get dinner on the table. She brought a meal over to help out since Hallie was injured and the visiting preacher is staying longer."

"That's a blessing. *Danki*, Levi." *Mamm* bustled past Hallie and went inside.

"She has something to tell you, too." Levi's gaze shifted from Hallie to the window, his face turning red.

Hallie could guess what Elsie would whisper.

Both of her best friends would be mamas this year.

Leaving Hallie behind once again.

And Hallie's wedding—to Toby—was supposed to have been second.

But, honestly, she was thankful to have been spared.

Whistling caught her attention and she glanced over her shoulder. Kiah hefted another bundle of shingles from the bed of the truck, flexing his arm muscles way more than necessary. He winked, then headed for the ladder.

"I think someone likes you," Levi said quietly.

It was Hallie's turn to blush.

She turned away from Levi's low chuckle and hurried inside.

But, *jah*, she was fascinated with Kiah, too.

A bad thing, considering he was promised to marry Molly and he would honor his parents' wishes.

* * *

Kiah might've been a little too obvious and maybe flexed his muscles a few too many times when Hallie was outside, because both fathers—his and hers—were eyeing him as if he were trouble waiting to happen. Now that Hallie had her walking cast, he wanted to take her out somewhere. Maybe for that malted milkshake the one man gave him money for. Okay, really, the money had been for helping muck out stalls, but a malted milkshake had been mentioned. And he was sweating enough in this muggy heat that a milkshake sounded especially good...especially since he had to put his shirt back on.

He should've been smart and asked for directions where to go for said date, but he hadn't. If there was such a place around here, Hallie would know.

He also needed to explain to her that he—and Joy—left the singing way early, before the singing even started actually, and went to visit George. That Anna had dumped him in favor of another guy, and...

Wait. If the other guy brought her home, it had been very late, because Kiah hadn't seen Anna since he left the singing. Not last night, and not this morning.

He glanced over at Ted. The man used his sleeve to wipe sweat from his brow. Adjusted his hat. And didn't seem concerned at all that he might have a missing daughter. Although, there was a possibility that Anna had come home late and was sleeping in. Or maybe even was in the kitchen, cooking something that smelled so amazing his stomach was on constant rumble.

However, the woman who'd arrived with the man introduced as Levi had brought casserole dishes full of food, so maybe she was the amazing cook. It didn't matter who so much as when, because he was starving. Both for real food and for time spent with Hallie.

Mostly for time spent with Hallie.

CHAPTER 25

Hallie glanced around the kitchen. *Mammi* and Joy set the table, while Ruth sliced the creamy cheesecakes that Elsie must've brought since they had sprigs of peppermint on top. Elsie added peppermint to everything she could. Something warmed in the oven. She didn't see *Mamm*, Anna, or Elsie.

Joy set a big homemade vegetable tray on the table near the condiments already there, then grinned at Hallie. "Elsie brought over grilled hot dogs, brats, and hamburgers, buns, potato salad, and dessert. Isn't it wonderful? We had the vegetables, and *Mammi* made her apple salad to go with it."

Ruth used her finger to wipe off the knife after she finished cutting the cheesecakes. "I just love cheesecake. I never had peppermint flavored before." She stuck her finger in her mouth and smiled.

"Elsie loves peppermint," Hallie said with a smile. "Where is she?"

"She's in the *dawdihaus* with your *mamm*," *Mammi* answered. "I think she's adding to her family." She smiled and winked. "But you didn't hear that from me."

Joy giggled.

"Is Anna in there with them?" Hallie asked, stopping her progress into the room. If she was, she'd wait until later to see her friend.

The three other women in the room looked around. "I haven't seen her since she left for the singing with your future husband," *Mammi* said.

Ruth coughed. Choked, really.

Hallie's face burned. She tried to avoid looking at Ruth.

"And that was early in the afternoon, when my honeybun and I left," *Mammi* continued.

"She and Kiah must've stayed out really late." Hallie ignored *Mammi*. Hopefully she didn't sound as jealous as she felt. But her voice shook. She forced herself to resume movement and walked to the table.

Joy frowned. "Anna caught a ride home with another guy. I don't know who. Kiah and I left early, before the singing even started, to rescue some newborn kittens and deliver them and the ant farm to George. You were asleep when we got home, so Kiah went to help secure the tarp to the roof." She hesitated and gave Hallie a worried look. "You slept on the recliner all night, but you didn't see Anna come in? I'll check if she's still sleeping." She hurried from the room.

"Kiah has never been unfaithful to you." Ruth placed the knife beside the sink and turned to face Hallie. "Never. From the moment he returned home after meeting you eighteen months ago and breaking up with Molly, he's been faithful to the scribe. Never even left the house for frolics or youth events. Just for church and work. I know nothing makes sense right now, but you needed to know that much." She pulled in a shaky breath. "And that is all I can say."

Hallie stood where she'd stopped, midway between the table and the door, and stared. She wasn't sure what to say, if anything. Except, "Why... what..."

Ruth swiped at her eyes and crossed the room. She tugged

Hallie into her arms and kissed her cheek. "I'm rooting for you, dear Hallie. Don't give up hope." She squeezed and released before Hallie had time to react.

Rooting for...? *What?* Don't give up hope? Wasn't it fairly obvious that at least where Kiah Esh was concerned, there was no hope for her? Maybe someday, with someone. And maybe, if *Gott* smiled, she'd feel a portion of the passion, the excitement, the tingles she felt with Kiah.

Although, her parents and grandparents would argue that love is a decision. Not an emotion. As the Amish ministers loved to point out during wedding sermons, marriage is for keeps. For better. For worse. For richer and poorer. During sickness and in health. Until death parted...

Death parted.

That meant Toby had it wrong. Relief rushed through her. She was *not* obligated to join Toby in the hereafter. She could live. She could love. If she was brave enough...

And with Kiah...

Lord, let it be so.

Hallie rearranged the condiments on the table as Joy came back into the room. "Anna was sleeping. Sleeping! At noon! And wow, is she hard to wake up. I had to whomp her with a pillow! Several times." She sighed heavily as if she was put out, but she grinned.

Hallie guessed it could be acceptable, especially considering Anna had been up all day Saturday, most of that night with a laboring *mamm*, all day Sunday, who knew how late Sunday night. Sleep was not overrated.

But, wow, it was great to learn that all Kiah had done was take Anna to the singing and some other guy had given her a ride home. And it was also wonderful to know that he'd been faithful to her—the scribe—for the past eighteen months. He truly was devoted to her.

And it was beyond amazing that Hallie had somehow won Ruth's favor. Though she imagined that the bishop and her parents talking her up probably had a lot to do with it.

"Hallie," *Mammi* said. "Go to your friend."

It took a moment before Hallie remembered that Elsie was in the *dawdihaus* with *Mamm*.

Hallie nodded and moved to tap on the doorway of the entrance to the *dawdihaus* from the kitchen. There wasn't any answer, so she opened the door. "*Mamm*? It's Hallie."

"We're in the bedroom," *Mamm* called.

Hallie walked through the super-tiny kitchen, into the small living room, and pushed open the bedroom door. Elsie lay on the bed, dress unpinned, while *Mamm* ran a stethoscope over Elsie's belly.

"It's a little early yet, but sometimes we can hear heartbeats at three months. Not this time, though."

Hallie smiled at her friend. "I'm so excited for you and Levi. You are so blessed."

Elsie kind of half giggled. "I'll feel more blessed when the miserable morning sickness ends."

"That's supposed to be a sign of a healthy baby," Hallie said.

Mamm wiped off the stethoscope and handed Elsie a tissue to get the gel off her belly. "You can repin your dress; then Hallie can talk to you about a healthy diet."

Elsie groaned. "I can see baked sweets going away."

Mamm laughed. "They aren't good for you anyway." She gathered her supplies and put them in her black midwife bag. "I'll be in the main house kitchen, if you have any questions, and I'll come visit you in a month." She winked at Hallie, grabbed her bag, and left the room.

Elsie scrambled to her feet and quickly repinned her dress. She pulled Hallie into a hug and squealed. "I'm so excited! Levi is, too, but he's more panicky about it. He's babying me and questioning everything I do. 'Is it safe for the baby?' I'm not suddenly helpless."

Hallie returned her hug, then released her and they sat on the edge of the bed. "Men usually are like that with their first." *Mamm* had told her when Hallie's friend Gracie whined about Zeke being overprotective. "But there are some things you need to avoid and some you need moderation..." She went on to talk about them.

Elsie stared, jaw gaped. "I thought you didn't want to be a midwife."

Hallie grimaced. There was a time she wanted to be one. Until she caught *Mamm* crying over a stillborn baby. "I have a midwife for a *mamm*. I know this stuff. I don't want the responsibility if things go wrong." They rarely did, but still. There was always the chance. Maybe she should talk to *Mamm* about how she handled those fears and possibilities. Maybe she could learn to trust and rely on God to give her wisdom to do her best.

A door creaked. "Girls. Dinner is ready," *Mamm* called.

Hallie leaned in to give Elsie another hug. "You'll do fine. *Mamm* is the best midwife in town—"

"The only one." Elsie gave her a pointed look.

"You need to trust *Gott*. He's got you and Levi and that precious baby in His hands."

"Listen to yourself. Don't you think He has you, too? Maybe with a man other than Toby?" Elsie stood and straightened her dress.

"Such as?" Hallie looked away to hide her burning face. What had Elsie heard? Had Kiah seen his best friend Zeke and told him everything? Had Zeke told Gracie who then told Elsie?

But Elsie shrugged. "I don't know. Just someone. Toby was dark-mooded and he would've dragged you down, too. You deserve someone better. I might not know who he is, but *Gott* does."

And Elsie would, too, as soon as Kiah joined them for dinner. Except, Hallie still didn't understand that situation.

"And I want you to deliver my baby."

Hallie scoffed. "If *Gott* wants me to be a midwife, He's going to have to drop a laboring woman in my path and no other options."

* * *

Kiah helped *Daed* secure a shingle that didn't seem to want to be wedged into the tight spot *Daed* placed it, then started to follow Ted and Aaron down the ladder.

"Son." *Daed* caught his arm when Kiah was near the edge. "We need to talk."

Kiah stopped and turned to face him. He raised his eyebrows. They did need to talk, but now, with the Brunstetter family waiting on them for dinner, seemed bad timing.

Daed half smiled. "I know what you're thinking and you're right. I did mean later. Tomorrow sometime. Bishop Nathan will be joining us and possibly a few others…"

Okay. That sounded ominous.

Kiah frowned and clenched his jaw. A muscle might have jumped. Whatever he or Hallie or both of them had done must've been very bad. Either that or the church leaders were going to come down on him hard for pursuing the scribe when *Daed* insisted he'd marry Molly.

Which was another reason he and *Daed* needed to talk.

"So we'll be here tonight and tomorrow?" Kiah asked. He tried not to act excited. But, hello, more time with Hallie.

Daed shrugged. "We might be here a little longer. We might leave following the meeting. It all depends on what the ministers decide."

So many questions sprang to the tip of Kiah's tongue, but he bit them back. Now it was time to eat. Unfortunately, *Daed*'s words had stolen Kiah's appetite. But since *Daed* tightened his lips and expression, he wouldn't say more now anyway.

Kiah gave a brusque nod, turned on his heel, and descended the ladder. Irritation ate at him. Molly tied into this somehow, but how and why? *Jah*, she wanted him back—she made no secret of that—but he'd also made it plain that he was not interested. He was done. Finished.

And he had been extremely confident that he could out-stubborn her.

Apparently, he'd been wrong.

He hadn't expected her to run to *Daed* with some tall tale that *Daed* had bought into, hook, line, and sinker.

And worse, he couldn't for the life of him figure out what she'd claimed. *Daed* knew, he *knew*, Kiah had quit going to youth events and focused completely on the scribe. His true love. The one he'd hoped and believed would be Hallie. So any of the obvious reasons Molly had concocted to trap him into marriage had to be bogus.

He stomped up the steps to the porch and opened the door. The men were lined up at the kitchen sink, taking turns washing up. He stopped at the door to remove his still-soggy sneakers, then got into line behind the rest of the men.

Aaron was directly in front of him. He glanced over his shoulder and lowered his voice. "Peter's *daed* said to get rid of them."

Huh? Kiah frowned at the back of Aaron's head for a few moments. Then he realized, the kittens. "In the future, I suggest George."

Aaron snorted. "*Jah*."

Of course, that might be how George ended up with so many cats. All animals needed a good home.

A side door opened and Hallie came into the room, followed

by a redhead. Both women were smiling. And then a shuffling sound followed. Kiah glanced over his shoulder. A bleary-eyed Anna scuffed into the room. She staggered over to the table and plopped down in a chair.

How late had she stayed out last night? She reminded him a lot of his ex-girlfriend. She probably wanted to take the long way home... Well, he shouldn't judge her for that. His gaze shot to Hallie, who whispered something behind a cupped hand to her friend. Both of them looked at him. His face heated, but he deliberately winked. *Jah*, he'd want to take the long way home with Hallie. With a side stop or two for "stargazing."

Her face flamed red and she glanced away.

A hand landed heavy on Kiah's opposite shoulder and squeezed.

Kiah turned his head.

"No flirting in the kitchen, boy," *Daed* whispered.

At least he didn't say ever.

Kiah gave *Daed* a cheeky grin. "What better place to heat things up?"

* * *

Hallie's ankle still throbbed despite the walking cast. She headed for the bathroom after dinner and stared into the medicine cabinet. She wanted to ease off the strong pain pills and return to her normal life—minus the depression—at least while Kiah was still visiting.

She swallowed an over-the-counter pain pill.

She wasn't sure how long the Eshes were staying, but *Daed* whispered to *Mamm* at the table. Hallie had overheard something about a conference call—whatever that was—between the ministers here in Hidden Springs and the ministers in the district where Preacher Esh served in Shipshewana. Kiah would be included in the chat, as would *Daed*.

It both scared and excited Hallie at the same time because the call must have something to do with her and Kiah and maybe his promised marriage to Molly. *Daed* glanced at her, then Kiah, so she must be right.

Hallie wanted to be included, but she was a woman and couldn't be worried about men's business. As if not being invited would keep her from being concerned.

Since the meal was over and Levi had finished replacing the broken windows, he and Elsie left.

Mamm shooed Anna back to bed for a rest since there were three women due to deliver any time—including Hallie's friend Gracie.

Hallie and Joy were tasked with dishes while the men returned to work on the roof. Except *Daadi*. He went to putter—his words—in the barn.

Mammi, *Mamm*, and Ruth went to sew or crochet or darn socks in the living room. Joy and Hallie were supposed to join them when they finished dishes and cleaning the kitchen.

Hallie had just dried the last dish and put it away while daydreaming about doing this in her future home with Kiah, when the clip-clop of horse hooves caught her attention.

Bishop Nathan parked near the porch and emerged from the buggy.

Hallie went to the door to invite him in.

Bishop Nathan waved her away. "Preconference call talk, so I know the whole story. I'll join the men on the roof."

He left, going up the ladder.

Hallie watched him go. *What was the whole story?*

CHAPTER 26

Kiah caught movement in his peripheral vision and glanced that way as Bishop Nathan climbed onto the roof. He motioned for Kiah to follow him, then crossed the roof to where *Daed* was fitting another shingle into a different tight place.

Ted and Aaron were working on the opposite side of the roof, over the front of the house.

Bishop Nathan lowered himself beside *Daed* as *Daed* sucked in a noisy breath and all the color seeped from his face. His eyes widened and darted from the bishop to Kiah and back.

"I told Ted I'd stop by for a preconference call talk," Bishop Nathan said. "I do hate going into these things blind. So fill me in. What is going on?"

"I, uh, haven't had a chance to talk with Kiah yet." *Daed* frowned.

"So, tell us both together. Sit down, Kiah. Go ahead, Clem."

It'd been years since Kiah had heard *Daed*'s given name. Everyone just called him Preacher.

"I, uh, haven't had a chance to prepare." *Daed* tried again.

"That's fine. Just lay it all out there." The bishop looked up at Kiah, who still stood. "Sit down, Kiah," he said again.

Kiah sat, bracing his feet against a shingle. Bile clogged his throat. Whatever this was about, it wasn't good.

Pounding from hammers came from the other side of the roof where Ted and Aaron worked.

Daed sighed. "My brother's oldest daughter left the Amish and embraced a very evil culture. Drugs were involved. Unable to keep a job, she moved to what is called 'the Red Light District' in Chicago. My brother didn't want anyone to know. It's a great shame." His voice cracked. Broke.

Kiah remembered Uncle Bud's tears when he came to talk to *Daed* about Caroline six months ago. He hadn't known the details, but what he did know turned his stomach. His cousin made bad choices.

Daed swallowed. "Bud asked me to go talk to her, to try and get her to come home, to offer help. Rehab, or something. I agreed." He pulled in a shaky breath and wiped the sweat from his brow. "So, I called a driver and asked him to drop me near that area. A block or two away. It was daylight, and safe then, or so I was told. I walked down there and found Caroline's room. A dingy, stinky place. She goes by some other name now. Something unusual. I guess she thinks it's sexy." He shuddered as he spat out the word.

The bishop winced.

Kiah's stomach cramped.

Daed cleared his throat. "Anyway, I talked to her. Offered help. To my shock, she refused, but she walked me out. Gave me a hug. I was her favorite uncle."

He was. All Kiah's cousins loved Uncle Clem. But what did this have to do with him?

Daed pulled in another shaky breath. Tears rolled down his cheeks. He gulped. "I failed my mission, but went home, determined to keep Caroline in my prayers. Then Kiah started getting serious with the scribe and talking about meeting and marrying her. I wasn't thrilled. I didn't want him to move away. I need him. So I encouraged him to court a local girl."

That was true. He had. The last two weeks that seemed like the only topic *Daed* brought up when they were alone. But it was good to know *Daed* needed him.

"Then right before we came here, Molly showed up. She claimed she was pregnant. Claimed Kiah was the father—"

Kiah sucked in air. Shot to his feet. Steadied himself.

Bishop Nathan raised his hand. "Sit down, Kiah."

"But—"

"Sit!" the bishop bellowed. "Let your *daed* finish."

The hammering on the other side of the roof stopped.

Kiah pressed his lips together. Sat.

"I knew it wasn't Kiah's child," *Daed* continued. "And I told her so. But then she pulled out pictures of me in the Red Light District and hugging my niece, who didn't look even remotely like the sweet Amish girl our community knew. No one would ever believe that she was my niece and that I was there for a good cause. And Molly blackmailed me. She marries Kiah and names him as the father or she goes to the bishop and other ministers with the photos. As well as a few well-known gossips. A preacher could never be seen hugging a woman like that and still hold his calling. And I could never hurt my brother by revealing publicly what his daughter has become."

Daed was crying openly now. Kiah struggled for air. This *would* ruin *Daed*, but why did Kiah have to sacrifice everything?

Bishop Nathan tugged at his beard. "You realize she'll use that tactic to control you and get her way for the rest of your life. You'll never be free from her lies and you would have trapped your son as well. No. Tell your ministers the whole story. Tell your brother why you told. Contact your niece, if you can, for her statement. Stand firm and do not let this girl bully you and Kiah." He handed *Daed* a handkerchief.

Daed blew his nose. Loudly.

Kiah's stomach churned. *Daed*'s situation was far worse than he could've imagined, but it seemed as if Bishop Nathan was a wise man and had a good solution.

"The truth will set you free," the bishop declared. "The ministers here and I will support your story. I know the truth when I see and hear it. Kiah is free to marry Hallie—"

Thoughts stalled. The conversation replayed. *Jah*, Hallie was his—if she agreed. Kiah stood up and cheered. *Danki, Lord.*

Ted and Aaron looked over.

Daadi appeared in the opening of the barn.

Bishop Nathan held up his hand. "After courting a reasonable amount of time."

Daed looked up with a teary smile, love in his eyes. "And I'll move my horse farm to Hidden Springs—or expand the business to include a location here, so Kiah can keep his job once he marries. And I'll still be near to my son."

Tears burned Kiah's eyes. "*Danki.*" That was directed to both of them. His voice broke. "May I take Hallie out for a buggy ride tonight?"

He glanced across the roof to the eavesdropping, also-teary Ted, who simply nodded.

*   *   *

After that loud cheer from above that could only have come from Kiah, Hallie's afternoon dragged by in even slower motion. If only she could have listened to Bishop Nathan's conversation herself, but no. She was trapped inside with the other women while time crawled and the overhead hammering continued.

The bishop left. *Daed* appeared with a watery smile and a tender look. He didn't say anything, though.

And maybe the strong pain pills were still in Hallie's system because she dozed off. She woke later, a crick in her neck, a half-darned sock in her hands, to find Joy setting a chicken salad sandwich and raw vegetables on a tray beside Hallie.

"The men are picnicking on the roof. *Mamm* and Anna just left. They got called to a birth. *Mammi* and *Daadi* are having alone time in the *dawdihaus*." Joy rolled her eyes.

Ruth carried in a glass of lemonade and set it next to the plate. She gave Hallie a tender smile. "And Kiah said to tell you he'll take you on a buggy ride later...as soon as they finish the roof—which should be soon—and tell you everything. So eat your supper, and get ready to go."

Hallie's stomach ached and she pressed her hand against it. Was she ready to hear what he had cheered about? Was she really ready to start living again if Kiah's cheer meant what she hoped?

Ruth apparently noticed. She patted Hallie's shoulder. "I think it'll turn out okay. My husband says he feels positive about it. He'll fill me in tonight. And from the little I've seen of him since noon, Kiah can't stop smiling."

Saturday morning *Gott* had given her a verse. Psalm 30:5: "Weeping may endure for a night, but joy cometh in the morning."

And it did. With Kiah.

Both Joy and Ruth returned to the kitchen, and soon brought their meals into the living room so Hallie wouldn't be alone.

Hallie forced herself to eat. If Kiah was smiling and wanted to take her on a buggy ride, it had to be good news. In fact, maybe even the answer to her prayers. But she didn't have time to dwell on it or speculate because as they ate, Ruth peppered her with a buggy-load of questions. Questions all meant to get to know Hallie as Kiah's future wife? She could only hope.

Thirty minutes later, the men came in. They smelled ripe from working all day in the sun. Kiah gave her a smile but kept his distance. "I'm going to take a shower and then would you like to go on a buggy ride?"

"Full disclosure, Esh?" She tried to hide her grin.

He chuckled. "I'll be right back."

Fifteen minutes later, he was hitching the horse to the buggy as Hallie hobbled out to get in. A cloud of dust rose as another buggy raced into the driveway.

Hallie stopped, just beside the buggy, her mouth gaped. Zeke and Gracie. Zeke had the reins, which was surprising because he was a much more cautious driver than Gracie.

"Where's the fire?" Kiah quipped.

"We need the midwife." Zeke ignored his friend and stared at Hallie. "We were grocery shopping, and well... The baby is coming."

On cue, Gracie moaned, clutching her stomach.

"*Mamm* left about an hour ago." Actually, that was a guess. Hallie didn't know exactly when they left. But an hour was probably close. "Someone went into labor, but I don't know who."

"We. Need. Her," Gracie ground out.

Hallie stepped closer and rested her hand on Gracie's arm. Her friend was prone to overreacting. "First babies usually take a while. Go home and I'll leave her a message."

Gracie groaned, arching back. "I. Need. To. Push."

Could labor really progress that fast? Or was something wrong? Hallie jerked away from the buggy. She stumbled but caught herself. She took a step toward the house. "I'll borrow a phone and call *Mamm*."

Zeke gave his wife a look, his eyes wide. "You can't push yet. We haven't found the midwife."

Gracie ground down with a moaning sound that Hallie had heard before. She really was pushing.

A choking sound from Kiah's direction. It was definitely not proper for him to be there hearing this. What would his reaction be?

Hallie gulped. There was no time for phone calls. This baby was coming in the buggy unless they could move Gracie now.

Really, Gott*? You had to dump a laboring* mamm *on me?*

At least it was Gracie. Hallie wanted to be there for her delivery anyway.

"Kiah, run inside and tell Joy to take down the shower curtain and spread it across the bed your parents are sleeping in and get the extra birthing supplies. Zeke, carefully get Gracie out of the buggy and into that bedroom. Gracie—"

"We have groceries in the buggy," Zeke said.

Kiah ran for the house, slamming the door open. "Joy! *Mamm!*"

"I'll send Joy to take care of them. In the meantime—"

Gracie ground down again.

"Right." Zeke jumped out of the buggy, pulled Gracie into his arms.

She screamed.

Zeke followed Kiah at a jog…which probably really hurt Gracie because she yelled.

Hallie took a breath. Then turned and hobbled as fast as she could toward the house and her friend.

* * *

It had been less than an hour but felt like an eternity. Joy and *Mamm* were still gone, Ted and *Daed* were drinking coffee and playing checkers. And all Kiah could do was pace alongside Zeke. A click and a shuffling sound and he turned. A very disheveled Hallie emerged from the bedroom. Zeke rushed toward her. "Any news?"

Kiah followed.

"The baby had the cord wrapped around his neck and was blue. I had Gracie rub him and he's a nice, healthy red now. Gracie is fine." Hallie offered a wobbly smile as if realizing she should've started with this information. "You can go to her. Them. I'll be back in a minute to weigh him."

Zeke took off at a run.

"*Daed*, I need your fish scales to weigh the baby."

Ted nodded, stood, and headed upstairs since his fishing gear was in the attic. Kiah remembered seeing it the day of the woodpecker attack.

Daed stood. "I'll get the new *mamm* a glass of juice." He went into the kitchen.

Kiah pulled Hallie into his arms. He was proud of this amazing woman.

She sagged against him. "What did Bishop Nathan want?"

He chuckled. Of course his girl would want to get to the important stuff before they were interrupted again. "Long story short, Molly was blackmailing *Daed*. I do not have to marry her. I'll tell you the long version later."

She nodded.

"Bottom line, I'm allowed to court you, if you'll have me. Hallie, I love you. Will you allow me to court you? Maybe marry in the fall?" He held his breath. Stroked a finger down her cheek and imagined a lifetime of this. *Please,* Gott*?*

"Marrying my pen pal was my secret wish." She raised her head for his kiss.

Mine too. He drew her near and lowered his lips to hers as she wrapped her arms around his neck.

Are you loving the Hidden Springs series?
Don't miss Zeke and Grace's story in
The Amish Wedding Promise.

Available now!

ABOUT THE AUTHOR

Laura V. Hilton is an award-winning author of more than twenty Amish, contemporary, and historical romances. When she's not writing, she reviews books for her blogs and writes devotionals for the *Seriously Write* blog.

Laura and her pastor-husband have five children and a hyper dog named Skye. They currently live in Arkansas. Laura enjoys reading and visiting lighthouses and waterfalls. Her favorite season is winter, and her favorite holiday is Christmas.

You can learn more at:
Twitter: @Laura_V_Hilton
Facebook.com/AuthorLauraVHilton

Want more charming small towns?
Fall in love with these Forever contemporary
romances!

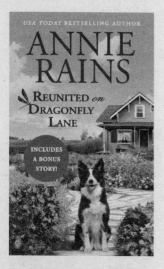

REUNITED ON DRAGONFLY LANE
by Annie Rains

Boutique owner Sophie Daniels certainly wasn't looking to adopt a rambunctious puppy with a broken leg. Yet somehow handsome veterinarian—and her high school sweetheart—Chase Lewis convinced her to take in Comet. But house calls from Chase soon force them to face the past and their unresolved feelings. Can Sophie open up her heart again to see that first love is even better the second time around? Includes the bonus story *A Wedding on Lavender Hill*!

DREAM A LITTLE DREAM
by Melinda Curtis

Darcy Jones Harper is thrilled to have finally shed her reputation as the girl from the wrong side of the tracks. The people of Sunshine Valley have to respect her now that she's the new town judge. But when the guy who broke her heart back in high school shows up in her courtroom, she realizes maybe things haven't changed so much after all…because her pulse still races at the sight of bad-boy bull rider Jason Petrie.

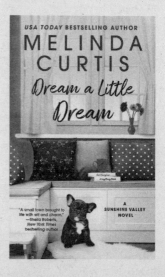

"Holiday is a consummate master of witty banter."
—*ENTERTAINMENT WEEKLY*

SANDCASTLE BEACH
by Jenny Holiday

What Maya Mehta really needs to save her beloved community theater is Matchmaker Bay's new business grant. She's got some serious competition, though: Benjamin Lawson, local bar owner, Jerk Extraordinaire, and Maya's annoyingly hot arch nemesis. Turns out there's a thin line between hate and irresistible desire, and Maya and Law are really good at crossing it. But when things heat up, will they allow their long-standing feud to get in the way of their growing feelings? Includes the bonus story *Once Upon a Bride*, for the first time in print!

A WEDDING ON LILAC LANE
by Hope Ramsay

After returning home from her country music career, Ella McMillan is shocked to find her mother is engaged. Worse, she asks Ella to plan the event with her fiancé's straitlaced son, Dr. Dylan Killough. While Ella wants to create the perfect day, Dylan is determined the two shouldn't get married at all. Somehow amid all their arguing, sparks start flying. And soon everyone in Magnolia Harbor is wondering if Dylan and Ella will be joining their parents in a trip down the aisle.

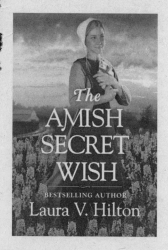

THE AMISH SECRET WISH
by Laura V. Hilton

Waitress Hallie Brunstetter has a secret: She writes a popular column for her local Amish paper under the pen name GHB. When Hallie receives a letter from a reader asking to become her pen pal, Hallie reluctantly agrees. She can't help but be drawn to the compassionate stranger, never expecting him to show up in Hidden Springs looking for GHB...nor for him to be quite so handsome in real life. But after losing her beau in a tragic accident, Hallie can't risk her heart—or her secrets—again.

HER AMISH WEDDING QUILT
by Winnie Griggs

When the man she thought she would wed chooses another woman, Greta Eicher pours her energy into crafting beautiful quilts at her shop and helping widower Noah Stoll care for his adorable young children. But when her feelings for Noah grow into something even deeper, will she be able to convince him to have enough faith to give love another chance?

ONE LUCKY DAY
(2-IN-1 EDITION)
by Jill Shalvis

Have double the fun with these two novels from the bestselling Lucky Harbor series! Can a rebel find a way to keep the peace with a straitlaced sheriff? Or will Chloe Traeger's past keep her from a love that lasts in *Head Over Heels*? When a just-for-fun fling with Ty Garrison, the mysterious new guy in town, becomes something more, will Mallory Quinn quit playing it safe—and play for keeps instead—in *Lucky in Love*?

FOREVER FRIENDS
by Sarah Mackenzie

With her daughter away at college, single mom Renee isn't sure who she is anymore. What she *is* sure of is that she shouldn't be crushing on her new boss, Dr. Dan Hanlon. But when Renee comes to the rescue of her neighbor Sadie, the two unexpectedly hatch a plan to open her dream bakery. As Renee finds friendship with Sadie and summons the courage to explore her attraction to Dr. Dan, is it possible Renee can have the life she's always imagined?

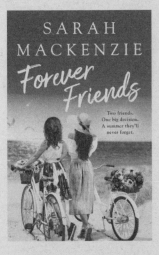